There's a Bomb in My Luggage

G.P. Huffman

For Bettrys

Zero

Note: I hastily have completed this entry and moved it to the front. Forgive the stains. The large, slightly yellow oleaginous one, a crater almost in the slick pale blue of the rear panel of the pamphlet that must serve as my slate, is whale tallow; the curiously misshapen egg is thin ink from this blasted leaky Chinese pen; and those crinkly little shots in the margins—I am trying my damnedest not to mar my handiwork, this my final work—are tears and, less poetically, nasal drip. Tanya, I see no way out of this predicament, and I see now that I may not finish this shameful account. I want you to know what happened to me, how it ended. And I want you to know that I am sorry.

* * *

I have had some hours to kill. The first I passed entering combinations, starting with 0–0–0–0, into the lock on the metal box in the trailer. I should have jotted down the numbers that were on the face when I started, as whoever thumbed the barrels might have been careless and left a clue as to the correct sequence. Alas, my mind was on other things.

The fuel is gone, spent, wasted. Much of it, too much, I used trying to back up the embankment upon which the truck is stranded. The tires spun, the chassis shuddered, the engine struggled alarmingly, but all my blind, railing effort moved me not a centimeter closer to freedom, to safety. At the end of it I beat my hands upon the steering wheel, pummeled the groaning dash. What stopped me from using even more of the petrol was the sudden realization that even if I were to dislodge the truck I would now not have enough to burn to reach the waypoint.

Last evening, as the dark-dark deepened, I poured the final canister from the trailer into the tank. Even with the heat of the engine, kept idling with the occasional jab of the accelerator to halt its sputtering, I was cold, colder than I had ever been. There is a hatch, I have discovered, between the cab and the trailer. Its navigation is awkward in my parka and the intervening space, small though it is, bitterly cold despite the rubber accordion, but I do not know that I could brave the trek around to the back, whether I could again work the great stiff latch there without removing my gloves. Thankfully there are the pamphlets. A large copper pot containing ashes was bungeed in a corner. That the ashes were someone's—those of someone with whom I was acquainted, I mean—I do not know but suspect; I have dumped them. The pot is now my brazier, the pamphlets and the boxes containing them my coal. The fumes are noxious, the blaze pitiful and weak. I must remember regularly to work the trailer's high, corroded vent. The cold on these occasions howls and whistles. Why is it that I hear shrieking laughter?

Tanya, which do you think would be less painful: freezing or asphyxiation? Which would be faster? I attempt to call to mind all the lore, hogwash likely, that I have heard about both. Dying from exposure to the cold brings a paradoxical burning feeling, followed by a pleasant drifting forgetfulness, followed by the long sleep. The eyes crack if enough moisture remains. Asphyxiation—O! for a cask, yes even of puckered nutty sherry, the dotard's drink; what I have is a third of a bottle of grass vodka, held against the need to start a fire more quickly than my fumbling fingers allow—engenders bleeding from the pores. A right mess, I imagine, and when does it begin? Before or after the final breath? I will not risk it. When the time comes, dear heart, I will go by degrees.

Night—real night, not that feeble, undulating gloaming—closes. I am in the trailer, which shudders in the gale's fury. It is colder tonight than last, or I am losing my own heat, deserted finally by even such an old, stalwart companion. I slap my limbs and rub my thick trunk, jog in place, do a silly sort of hula to keep warm and awake. Tonight I dare not sleep. The balance is too precarious. Earlier, basking in the near-warmth and tonic glow of my small fire, I almost slipped away in my tight squat, overpowered by carbon monoxide, the soothing friendly demon, consort of the dancing flame. When I roused myself it was nearly too late, as I could barely stand. Stars were bursting before my eyes as a panicked slap of my rubbery arm struck true on the vent release. I lay in a crumpled heap, unsure of whether I had succeeded. I rose only because I could feel something terrible happening to my nose, my aristocratic nose, the prominence of which I have always considered a mark of breeding, of character. It was the onset of frostbite, I am sure you have guessed. I was able to save it, I think, closing the vent and leaning right down over my fitful flame.

Do not laugh, dear. You always had a different opinion of my proboscis, I know, but I would like to save it, save all of me. I write with levity, but mine is gallows humor, I assure you. Never as a child was I as frightened as this. I really think I may not last the night.

One

The morning on which I left I woke filled with a deep sense of incongruity. Not only was our apartment not really our apartment (the first feeling was vague, as if every object in the home had been moved slightly, half a centimeter at the most), but I also was not myself. I moved groggily into the kitchen, assuming that there things would sort themselves out, that my perception would shift subtly back into place, perhaps with a smart click. Not even strong black coffee could put me right. In fact, the brew, from the dark Vietnamese beans, the chocolate-tasting ones, only deepened my sense of wrongness. The liquid was the wrong color, too light, though I had used the correct measure of beans and had ground them perfectly, and had little squashed floating orbs of oil on its limpid surface. The flavor too was off, and I poured all but a swallow down the drain. Shaking, I dropped the cup onto the tile, where you no doubt discovered it, not, I hope, with your bare or stockinged foot.

I moved to the living room, where our dear Fabriana, lying on the sofa as a prolate sausage, rose and with arched back and spiky tail hissed in my face, spat! I tried to touch her, but she fled and hid herself behind your grandfather's portmanteau. I hurried to the bathroom and, flipping on all the lights, gazed into the mirror. I looked the same, I really did. That was no doppelgänger on the glass, only my apish self. I brushed my teeth, then urinated. The water swirled out of the bowl in the right direction. Calmed slightly, I walked back to the bedroom.

In the sacred space of the boudoir I initiated my grooming ritual, building from the inside out, first selecting socks and briefs and tossing them on the rumpled covers of the bed. An undershirt comes next, as you know, and there I encountered trouble. The walk to my wardrobe takes me past your jewelry stand, where I often linger to ponder the provenance of pieces that I do not recognize. Usually I do not allow these sudden appearances to vex me but mark them out as silly things. My memory for the origins of adornments is limited; they are probably old family treasures that you rotate through the stacked drawers and onto the velvet of the prop-topped box at the pinnacle according to some secret formula and schedule (involving moon and tides, mayhap). That day something did vex me. A gaudy brooch, a mermaid with an emerald tail, had pride of place in the central crèche. This thing was like nothing you have ever worn, Tanya, like nothing you ever would wear. It was huge, for a start. It was hard to imagine the unavoidable physicality of that recumbent fish-woman riding the rise of your breast—even your ample swells seemed inadequate berth. Secondarily, it was ugly. Garish and lewd, ink on seaman's strong right arm seemed a fairer treatment. Its presence baffled me. Was it a private trifle, something that caught your eye in a crowded junk shop? Was it more intimate, a gift signifying some inside joke, a ridiculous memento? As I wondered, my eye was drawn to something else. A bit of white, the corner of an envelope, it turned out, poked from under the velvet at the back edge of the box. I gave it a tug, but it was firmly ensconced. A little prying and lifting freed it, but I did not stop there. Convinced that the supple turf concealed further bounty of untold secrets, I clawed it away, dismantled the entire stand. There was nothing more to discover (I left the drawers in disarray, so you likely thought that we had been burgled when you first found the mess), so I turned my attention to the envelope.

It was the latest phone bill, the tardiness of which I had already noted. I scanned its four pages front and back, quickly homing in on two unfamiliar telephone numbers. Where are area codes 255 and 227? Who do we know there? As I mulled the mysterious digits, something about the numbers kept drawing my eye. There were too many of them. These were not area but country codes, ones I did not know, nowhere we had traveled. I looked them up in the Handy Facts for Travelers pocket book that you chide me for keeping on the night stand: the former is Tanzania, the latter Niger. I knew that I had not called such places, and it seemed unlikely that you had dialed them from our home phone for any reason, even as part of your charity work. I did not let it bother me, though, assuming that there was a simple explanation. I would just ask you about it later. Resolved, I started to tuck the bill back into its envelope, ready to shave, shower, and get on with the day. Startled by the flash of something on the inside of the envelope as I slid the bill in, I quickly yanked the sheets free once more. A message, composed of letters cut from magazines and newspapers, was pasted in shaky sine on the back wall of the envelope:

Get out of the house, now!

My apprehension had been growing as the strangeness compounded, and this message, which even though I discovered it in your jewelry stand I knew was intended for me, did something dreadful and irreversible to my psyche. I began packing my Dopp kit and carry-on bag. I threw on clothing and ran wet fingers through my hair. I did not shower, shave, nor even sponge or splash my more troublesome areas. I did not mildly abrade my humid, stale armpits with the sorry white nub of deodorant cake that you have urged me often enough to replace. You can see the state into which I had been pushed. For some reason I pulled the bookmark out of that hack Cavanagh's latest (just released on the 16th, you will recall; I did not start reading right away because of other obligations but was rushing to eviscerate it in the next issue of *Lit*) paper turd, noting that I was on page 192 on my hand with a blue felt pen I found in your nightstand. I stuck the book and pen in the zippered compartment at the top of the bag. My plan had been to leave the abhorrent message on the floor of the bedroom, to put as much distance as possible between it and myself, but in that moment the fear that I felt, the sure sense that something terrible would happen in that place were I to ignore the emphatic instruction, coalesced into a more palpable whole, connected to its physical catalyst by threads of fate that I could now almost detect. I stuffed the envelope in next to the book. Even after these preliminaries, my flight will still seem nonsensical and self-indulgent, I am sure. For now please believe that my terror was sincere and that I was not only looking out for myself but also trying to protect you.

I shrugged on my shoulder bag and rolled the carry-on to the door, banged it open and loaded the luggage into my Audi. I got in and started the engine, resting my hands on the wheel for an indecisive moment. I backed out and was on my way. Driving down Kirkland I made a sudden, rather dangerous turn onto Irving and looped back around to the house. Leaving the engine running, I went inside and made a quick trip to the bedroom. This time I forgot to lock the door on my way out, I think, so your impression that we had been burgled probably began before you saw the chaos of our chambers. Starting out again, I made my wobbly way to Logan, the mermaid brooch stuffed between two socks in the left member of a pair of burgundy balmorals nestled in the bottom of my rolling carry-on bag.

* * *

At an airline ticket counter I was able to book a seat on the eleven o'clock flight to Hong Kong. When I sat breathlessly on one of the hard black plastic chairs at the gate, the amber digits of the clock on the wall near the muted television read 09:40.

Don't ask me why I chose Hong Kong. I vaguely recall hearing a story on National Public Radio's *Morning Edition* a few days before explaining both pitfalls awaiting and opportunities afforded the

17

populace after declaring independence and joining the Taiwan–Singapore Alliance. I felt some wispy nostalgia while half-listening to the piece. I had been to Hong Kong only once, with my father when I was fifteen. It was the summer of the handover, and we were there in what must have been late June, the pale last days before the calamitous (as we and many of those with whom we dealt viewed it, though money still had to move) event, on father's business. I remember reading novels in the sultry swaying green of Kowloon Park while father parleyed on the city isle with retreating Brits of shortsightedly nationalistic bent on behalf of the eager Chinese. Kowloon has its own Beacon Hill—did you know?—quite different from the one to which you are accustomed, of course. During those sweaty afternoons I chanced my first exposure to Kurt Vonnegut, Gabriel José de la Concordia García Márquez, and Kimitake Hiraoka, volumes taken along on the advice of retired librarian and longtime neighbor Patricia Clark.

You know that the words of these men are like comfort food to me and I surely knew it well, having reread those early books so often, having repeated the truism so frequently at home and during social events, but it did not occur to me at the time to take along those works, to revisit more honestly, more completely that formative experience, instead of sticking myself with Cavanagh's wretched bundle. Still, I had some time to kill there in the ticketing area and a deadline for the review, so I pulled the book from my bag. Even the cover was offensive, one of those hipster affairs, supposedly wry but never as knowing as Warhol, mixing advertising, comic book sketches, and lurid primary colors. The last bit gives such covers a distinctive odor, so that I can detect them even in the dark and sidestep them like dog shit on some neglected verge. But this one was Cavanagh and, thus, unavoidable. Page two hundred seven:

> We walked like long-legged birds across the dewy garden and settled just over the orchard slope beyond the field of view of the long, sad eyes of the manor. Katrina breathed like a young animal, the crushed dark velvet of her dress rising in sudden swells; even her breath carried youthful excitement, an eager, charming, cloying, puppyish vapor. I bent close to inhale.

Rip her bodice, already! Take her right there beneath the ripening fruit, your fertility and death symbolism hanging out where everybody with a seventh-grade education can see it plainly. Who cares that poor Katrina is in mourning at her mother's wake, reunited with family that she has not seen for difficult years. Popsicle Jesus. People give this stuff awards. Not *Lit*, never *Lit*. I was just working myself into an indignant frenzy when I realized that I needed to urinate. Corpus. I would take mine over his any day. I slipped the book back into my suitcase and wheeled off to the men's room.

After doing my business at the reeking splotched urinal, I washed my hands—a full minute of scrubbing and not a sacerdotal dip and trouser wipe is required for the effect that people claim to desire—and tidied up in front of the toothpaste-speckled mirror; I had a fly-away eyebrow, as you call it, on the left, which I smoothed with wetted forefinger and thumb. I was about to pronounce matters good but noticed with chagrin that my shirt, the dark gray button-up one with short sleeves, from the left side of my closet, looked as if I had slept in it. Have you given up ironing? I must rely on you since you have forbidden a maid. Rosaria was very good, and I am talking strictly about her cleaning and organizing abilities. I regret that, you know. The shirt was catastrophically rumpled. I bent to my luggage, tilted it and unzipped the main compartment, thinking to change quickly into something slightly more presentable. Half of my clothing was missing. What remained was scrunched to the sides and bottom, padding for the metal cylinder that now occupied most of the space. Four light-emitting diodes, red, blue, yellow, and green, broke the smooth surface near the top of the cylinder. All were dark. The end caps had been welded in place (skillfully, the seams were nearly undetectable). No wires were visible, no liquid crystal display shone menacing digits, but I knew that the device was a bomb. I suspected immediately and without evidence, probably from watching so many matinée thrillers at the tumbledown student theater near the office, as you know I do when confronted with particularly thorny editorial issues, that the cylinder was packed with radioactive debris. My first instinct (as you would ~~chuckle~~ cackle over even in such serious circumstances) was to flee. I had even taken a step away, poised to leave the case and its cargo there in the restroom, to exit the airport, to drive home, change clothing, and go to work as if nothing had happened.

I remembered right away (I could commit crimes if I wanted, could become a lawyer or go into banking, I have often told you) that one of my business cards was in the plastic-paned holder on the back side of the carry-on. I bent, zipped up the main compartment, acutely aware of what I might be exposing myself to with every second of proximity, and moved to whip the card from its sheath. At that moment a door banged open, and an overweight Indian emerged from a stall, trailing an unmistakable fug of processed curry. I stood, nodded, and wheeled my bag back out into the general confusion of the terminal.

I walked quickly up the concourse, looking surreptitiously for places to ditch the luggage without appearing to do so. I became acutely aware of security cameras in corners and beneath dark domes on the suspended ceiling. Every badge or uniform caught my eye and sharpened my step. I passed the screening area and entered a dimly lighted dog-leg corridor. The overhead signs revealed that this was the long walk to short-term parking. I saw only one other traveler, but members of the maintenance staff were surprisingly prevalent. They seemed to be shirking their duties in that quiet corner of the airport, meeting for wooing, texting, or, from the appearance of some of them, buying and selling narcotics. A disgustingly obese Hispanic man closed the panel of the cleverly concealed janitor's closet in which he had been rummaging and with a hunted look pushed a large gray plastic bin on wheels slowly down the hall. He wore a light blue jumpsuit with the number 62168 stenciled on the back in white, which made him look like a prisoner. The tunnel was interminable, and I was running out of time. I stopped, feigned a glance at my watch (which I was not wearing), turned around, and, muttering, hurried back the other way.

Near the café I paused to gather my wits. I was beginning to think that I should leave the airport. I leaned against a silver alcove that had once held a pay phone, part of a pod of six, only two of which still served their purpose. I rolled my shoulders slightly, like an athlete preparing to warm up, and tried to control my breathing. I think that I jumped when one of the phones started ringing. I remember looking around to see whether anyone had noticed and deciding that no one had. For some reason I could not force myself to walk through the doors, which I was facing, and into the open air. The phone kept ringing, persistently, perniciously, and people did begin looking in my direction. The ringing just went on and on, way beyond what any reasonable person would have allowed, each vibration seeming louder, more insistent than the last. People were becoming irritated. I moved to the end of the cluster and picked up the handset.

"Listen carefully to what I have to say, Tolyan, and nothing bad will happen to you or anyone close to you." The clarity of the man's speech, the clipped, correct enunciation, the lack of muffling or distortion, so that he could have been standing next to me, just the two of us beneath a great ivory dome or some place with similarly intriguing acoustics, caught me out, but what shocked me into silence was the violation of his using a familiar form of my given name, this unknown malevolent person. He continued. "Good, you're listening. We are short on time, so I need you to pass through screening and continue to your gate. Everything will be fine. You will have no trouble at all, I assure you."

"But there's—" I began just as the line went dead. I stood there for a while with the receiver in my hand, gazing at it dumbly. People again were looking in my direction, so I replaced it on its hook. What's worse, two security officers, beefy guys in black uniforms, were milling around the entrance, listening agitatedly to their earpieces.

I am not sure what made me join the screening queue, perhaps it was the horrific thought of what the nebulous "they" might do to you; I was convinced that they had been in our house. By any measure I was not in my right mind that morning. Sweat trickled from my armpits and down my spine and probably stood out on my brow as well, though I was unaware of it. I kept thinking that these people were trained to observe passengers, to note and monitor anyone exhibiting nervous or erratic behavior. The whole procedure became much more civilized after the TSA (now when anyone says "TSA" he of course means the Taiwan–Singapore Alliance, the newest member state of which I was about to visit; even that acronym surely would prove ephemeral, as a name change would become the first order of business once some measure of stability had been achieved) was disbanded four years ago. Still, I was a wreck by the time my turn came. I had great difficulty placing my bag on the conveyor, and the first time the attendant asked me to walk through the detector I simply stood there. I was on the verge of bolting when a gruff "It's your turn" from the annoyed passenger waiting behind propelled me into black uncertainty.

I passed through the apparatus without a blip and waited for my luggage with clasped hands. As it crept through the X-ray machine, the bomb was plainly visible on the technician's screen. No one said anything. After I picked it up on the other side, I remained by the belt, looking at the technician, a young north Asian man with a stubbly beard, perhaps for guidance. I adjusted the telescoping handle, aware of the congestion behind me, not wanting to provoke another comment from the ungracious fellow. As I turned to go I caught the technician's eye, and I swear, Tanya, that he winked.

* * *

On the plane I fared no better. First I passed my seat and had to work my way back against the flow of passengers, to the deep irritation of all. Then I was unable to hoist my bag over my head to place it in the bin. I could get it to waist height with no problem but failed three times over at the subtle buck and squat needed to send it soaring to its perch. Acutely aware of the stares of those seated and the shifting and throat clearing of those still standing, I prepared to enter my full Zhabotinsky routine but was spared that final embarrassment when an enlisted man in dusty desert wear spotted me by seizing one of the wheels. His eyes widened at the considerable heft, but together (yes, he did most of the lifting; so what? It would have shifted and fallen without my slender fingers on the seam) we sent it sailing to its berth. We grunted at one another and took our seats, I with the Cavanagh tucked into the breast of my jacket. I was in the window seat, and the two to my left were mercifully unoccupied. The soldier slouched in the window seat two rows back, miserably confined. He quickly donned his Sony specs and hid beneath the brim of his cap, a satisfied smirk developing; I assumed that he was watching hardcore pornography.

I waited in my seat, belt fastened tightly across my lap. My hands were clasped on my left knee, and after a few minutes I became attuned to their white-knuckled grip. I willed myself to relax and appear innocuous, if eccentric. As the line of boarders dwindled, my anxiety grew. Despite my early impressions, the flight was rather densely populated. The stragglers cast their unhurried gaze up and down the cramped rows. It seemed increasingly likely that I was to have company. A wrinkled Asian grandfather in shades of brown and his chubby grandson in a sharp navy school uniform halted on the periphery, the elder's bleary gaze fixed on the tiny plaque designating the seats.

"What does this say?" he asked the boy, voice thick with effort.

"This is it, pops," the kid flippantly replied. Or so I surmised from their body language. They were speaking a curiously high-pitched, nasal sort of Cantonese that I could not even begin to follow.

Grandfather sternly motioned for the boy to take the center seat. The grandson stiffened, and for a moment it appeared that an intergenerational argument was imminent. The old man's shrunken frame shuddered, and color rose in his cheeks. The intransigent whelp deflated and flounced hard into his place without removing his slim backpack. Something inside crunched under the strain.

I returned to the Cavanagh, holding it before me as a shield. I attracted a number of curious or derisive looks from the cabin at large preceding takeoff. A few senescent passengers may have been reading, obnubilated orbs slack behind their shiny specs (more likely they were watching reality television, cooking or home improvement shows, insipid animal videos, or even an uninterrupted stream of advertising), but certainly no one else brandished a paper book. Katrina, the sole scintilla of the humane artistic impulse yet to surface in the novel, had made no appearance in the current chapter. The author rather dawdled away his daily quota (oh, I can see him there beaming at the gnarled low board of some storied tea house on the slopes of

Alishan with a tiny floating window showing the project targets on the periphery of his laptop's screen, knocking it out sip by recrudescent sip of sweating nacreous anisette, pointedly spurning the deservedly famous oolong in his insufferable hipster manner) on the simpering maundering of uninteresting, ignominious Branford, the protagonist, yes, but a character in thought and action more gormless habitué of the tight-laced 1730s than savvy navigator of the blithely technocratic corporate oligarchy of the near future.

Well, I could stomach only so much of *that*, and when the first beverage service came around I gratefully stowed the Cavanagh in my seat pocket and accepted a cup of frothy matcha and a loaner pair of integrated display spectacles, some Thai knockoff brand of which I had never heard. After enjoying the tea in the prescribed relaxed yet attentive manner, I slipped on the IDS and surrendered to the cowardly anesthetic of the in-flight movies.

Two

After my fitful sleep on the flight I was disoriented. Gathering myself and my belongings (the rolling bag with the aid of two others) and trundling through the spirit-soiling processes of disembarkation, declaration, and immigration check contained any wild excitement or even worry about my indeterminate immediate future. Once I was free of the airport, fear reasserted itself, and I made my way without hesitation into the howling myrmecological dark below. I had become strangely possessive of my secret, weighty burden.

Bodies, bodies, bodies disgorged from the suppurating maws of the airport terminals pressed me forward into the close interior of the waiting subway car. An attendant tweeted shrilly on his chromed whistle, the sound wetly impeded by the viscous accumulation of his earnest puffing. He gave the impression of a man nearing the exhausting end of a very long shift.

Nevertheless, his white-gloved hands pushed people into awkward corners of the car, packed flesh upon flesh with officious efficiency. I became keenly aware of the unfamiliar odors of my neighbors' panting exhalations. Ding-dong, ding-dong, out slipped the attendant, offering a slight bow from the solid safety of the platform as the metallic doors slid shut. A momentary expression of panic rippled over the visages of even the old-timers, driven away by the sudden, welcome motion of the train. We closed our tired eyes and grimly endured.

My limited knowledge of the shockingly fresh East Asian milieu suggested that the cheap accommodations still were to be found in Kowloon. A certain hotel stuck in my mind because its scandalous back-channel sale by the Boy Scouts to a Saudi construction group lately had made the news. Some ugly stuff transpired, to be sure, but my primary impression from the short, tightly produced video exposé was of the clever modern design and impeccable cleanliness of the little rooms that packed the property's twenty-five floors. To this somewhat sure aerie I winged my weary way, autopilot engaged.

The young clerk at the desk was deeply suspicious of my arrival. It must have been unusual for an international guest to appear so late without a reservation. My smoldering stare brought him short, and at the end of the highly involved check-in procedure

he offered a seemingly genuine apology for his imperti-
nence. Maintaining a flat expression and saying nothing, I sharply accepted with my middle and index
fingers the timidly proffered key card. I shrugged off
the breathless offers of assistance from the eager bell-
hops and pushed my way into the dark-paneled elevator and pressed the cool glass face of the gilded
button for the twenty-fourth floor following a moment's hesitation caused by the numbering beginning
at 0; for the gently humming and swaying duration of
the skyward ride I was blessedly alone.

* * *

Once inside the room, I bolted the door and just
stood there for a few breaths, my left palm resting on
the telescoping handle of my rolling bag, the right
hovering over my heart. The interior was close. I admired the design in person that I had seen on the
Web—this was no bait and switch—but the size of the
place prompted a reaction closer to the ancient terror
of the suffocating velvet darkness of a sarcophagus
than the modern celebration of an ingenious use of
light and space. I pushed my luggage into the narrow
channel between the bed and the wall and stepped
into the bathroom to refresh myself.

The lavatory was ridiculously diminutive. I
bumped my bottom on the shower door when I bent

over the little metal basin to wash my face. It was like being in the facilities of an airplane, train, ship, or any other construction or conveyance for which circumstances dictate that comfort and dignity not be of primary concern. The milled soap was nice, though, of good quality and scented lightly with lemongrass. The frosted green glass was stately, the cabinetry of dark, fine hardwood reassuringly genteel and solid. Every surface was impeccable in its cleanliness. I dabbed at my cheeks and brow and twisted dry my fingertips with a tightly stitched embroidered hand towel of smart design. The loose skin of my face tingled slightly from the fragrant oil of the soap.

Out in the room I sat on the edge of the bed, gazing absently at the textured ocher wallpaper. I was good for nothing. I had slipped into an in-between realm of existence. Exhausted by travel and worry, I could think about things only abstractly and from a great distance, buzzing in close enough to bounce roughly off the turbulent surface at the very height of effort; nor could I sleep—my body eventually would succumb, but there was nothing I could do to hasten happy oblivion, no exertion of will could flip the switch. I decided to go for a walk.

The desk clerk and the doorman displayed reproving looks at my going out at such an hour. There was no one on the steaming street, and I wondered briefly whether I was breaking some curfew. It certainly was not out of the question, was likely even, given the recency of the split and the political emergencies that it had engendered. The convenience store at the next intersection was open, however, and a few customers moved languidly about its aisles. I entered and went to the humming refrigerators, scanning the unfamiliar cartons, bottles, and cans of fermented tea, cool grass jelly, sweet papaya nectar, and the like. I settled on a box of soy milk before realizing that I held no local currency.

The cashier read my body language with a practiced eye and motioned for me to approach the register.

"U.S. dollar OK," he said. "Euro OK." After a bit of eye rolling and a flurry of counting on his fingers, the cashier wrote the figures on a small pad: 1€, 5$.

I was not confident in the fidelity of the smiling merchant's calculations, but I did have a five dollar bill in my wallet and was very thirsty. I handed him the worn note; he opened the register's drawer and pressed it onto a thick stack of its kin. We stood beaming at one another over the counter, lips twitching. I expected at least a small amount of change, but clearly none was forthcoming. I shrugged and exited the convenience store, the sliding glass doors parting smartly with an electronic chime. I sat on a bench on the sidewalk, detached the small straw from the side of the soy milk carton (I have always enjoyed the snap produced by the hard but brittle adhesive that manufacturers use for attaching such straws) and threaded it through the foil of the hole on top, noticing for the first time that a manga cat was printed there, glancing over its stylized shoulder with a mixture of trepidation and longing, tail half-bristled as the angle-cut point of the plastic tube penetrated its anus.

The glass doors of the convenience store whooshed open, and the clerk shuffled over to my bench. He sat next to me, looking up at the sky. He then peered intently at his shoes, buffed away a bit of grime on the toe of the left member of the pair. Finally he turned toward me and extended his right palm. With the index finger of his left hand he slowly counted—one, two, three, four, five, six, seven, eight. 8 Hong Kong dollars. He flipped his hand over, making a fist, and nodded for me to take the coins. I held out my left hand to accept the sparkling, tinkling cascade. I put the money in my pocket and waited for him to depart. He sat there, leaning forward slightly with his hands on his knees, gazing at the bright sign above the sliding glass doors. I was parched and had not had a sip of the soy milk. The sweating carton cooled my right hand, promising wonderful things to my hot mouth and darker corridors, but the cashier's presence unnerved me so that I could not drink. When a customer inside the store walked timidly up to the unmanned counter, he hurried inside.

I sucked a deep draft through the straw and was taken aback. It was chocolate soy milk. Adjusting my expectations, I finished the carton and deposited it in the recycling bin adjacent to the bench.

* * *

Back in my hotel room I prepared for bed. The red, aggressively bright digits of the alarm clock (too large for the tiny bedside table on which it rode, a strange oversight in this carefully designed space) read 2:48. Whoever had rummaged through my belongings to make room for the bomb had been perverse in his attention to detail; no bit of clothing left to me seemed to match any other. I had a worn checkered pajama top but no bottoms, a rumpled umber henley, crisp navy slacks, three white undershirts, the pair of socks that I wore and those cushioning the bawdy cryptid in the sinistral balmoral, and, crushed rudely against the bottom of the gleaming cylinder, a single fresh pair of boxer briefs. I removed everything and arranged it atop the small dresser. I wanted desperately to change my underwear, but I knew that I would be better served by having a pair ready to go when I woke at midday (fates allow me to sleep so long) and that I would rather buy ten new scratchy, ill-fitting pairs than wash the single one with the dainty bar of lemongrass soap in that omphalos of a sink. I settled for performing a quick undercarriage wash, which led naturally to weary masturbation, slipping on one of the white t-shirts, and, after contemplating going without and rejecting the idea because of some vague need for security, re-donning my sweaty, musty drawers.

In the semi-darkness, tossing on the impossibly hard mattress in the hope of finding a somewhat tolerable position, covers kicked to the foot of the bed, pillow above my head, pillow below, a third, smaller pillow from the closet between my knees, I saw in the depths of my standing, open bag the blue LED leap to sudden, shocking life. The rays that it cast rendered a coldly surreal diorama straight out of Kubrick. I found the secret showing to be deeply calming.

"Yes, I always thought that it was like this," I murmured, drifting off to sleep.

Three

I slept well into the afternoon, but when I woke I rose immediately, vigor spreading like spring sap through my long, ligneous limbs, groggy glutted head clearing in subtle stages. I cupped my hand over the row of LEDs on the metallic cylinder to ascertain that last night's light still shone. It did, and the others remained consolingly dark. I made short work of my morning grooming and navigated my way to the street. The humidity had been sucked away to reveal bounteous blue sky. I connected these two things, the clearing of my head and the clearing of the heavens. The air was almost pleasant, warm enough to remind one of childhood vacation days, not too warm for sannyasin ambling. Here, Tanya, is what I wore: the unmolested boxer briefs, a clean white undershirt, the henley, the slacks, the selkie's socks, and the balmorals. Go ahead and laugh.

You will think that my first thought would have been of sustenance. If you substitute *should*, then you show some primitive level of understanding and draw us closer to our gimbaled golden mean. You are so damned practical, dear. Do not fret, for it is a trait that I value still. You have been my bedrock. *Really.* Anyway, I went first to a tailor's shop (after popping into a bank—in the nick of time; for some reason they close quite early—for some local currency). The poor man partially parked in the glandular gloaming beneath his couturier's key seemed to be in the late stages of shuttering his shop, but he tentatively took pity on the dejected gray gwailo loitering listlessly on his threshold and thus unlatched the door.

The still, cool, dim atmosphere of the shop reminded me forcibly of my maternal grandmother, who did her needlework until the last and even insisted on operating her great clacking loom in the stone fastness of the former dairy. The smell of dyes and elderly fabric laced the air, and the presence of so much soft material enforced a mortuary hush. The aged proprietor led me to the back, with gestures bade me stand before five eighths of an octagon of tall mirrors, with some effort and a positive click pulled down a lever that caused the sodium lamps of an ornate overhead fixture to warm to yellow life. Two bright halogen floor lamps with umbrella reflectors he activated with foot switches, creating in the central space some ideal

Asian expression of light. The configuration did nothing for my complexion.

The tailor withdrew a tape from his jacket pocket and measured me thoroughly, gently caressing every area he passed. It was more touching than was necessary, to my mind, but the man seemed intent on his task, sure in his routine, absolutely confident that this time-honored approach produced superlative garments. It is embarrassing to admit that I was mildly aroused.

Following the measuring, the man brought out bolts of fabric for me to scrutinize with eyes and fingertips, smiling and nodding to indicate his favorites. I selected a fine dark tyrian paduasoy. Next the tailor withdrew from a brocade chest large laminated cards demonstrating a variety of cuts and styles. I flipped through them quickly and settled on fitted trousers and a jacket of medium length with flared cuffs and a mandarin collar. The old man raised his eyebrows slightly but moved on to the shirts, fanning a new deck before me. I rejected the wait staff-looking plain and lightly embroidered cards for a stark tau cut with a dandy's hint of lace for the throat, down the front, and at the cuffs. The tailor's penetrating gaze sent me reeling a step. He held me thus for a moment, shrugged and turned to a jade-handled drawer for his color swatches. Perhaps he thought that I was some dirty foreigner, intoxicated or worse, out on a lark, having a go at him. He relaxed his mien slightly when I selected ivory, looked alarmed once again as I held up three fingers, stared openly in disbelief as I chose a vivid cherry blossom print and held up my index finger. He recovered quickly and made a note of my requirements, brought out a calendar thick with Chinese chicken scratches, and gave me a questioning look. Grinning sheepishly, I pointed to the square for the sixth. His eyes went wide, and he snatched away the sheet in silent fury.

He pushed his way through a curtain into some dark recess of the shop, and I heard from there a muffled clanging, as of a rhinoceros walking slowly across a thick mattress covered with pots and pans. When he returned, he held what looked like a horse whip in his left hand and an abacus in the right. He placed the abacus on a low table and began urging the beads aggressively along their wires while flicking the dusty air with the crop. When the tailor finished his manipulations, he bent beaming over the apparatus making clucking sounds. My dim recollection of a junior high mathematics lecture giving a brief history of such counting devices and a demonstration of their use rang clear Poe's brazen bells. As the proprietor turned smugly in my direction, no doubt ready to see the back of me after his fine performance, I surprised both of us by nodding my head in acceptance of his terms. He stood stock still for a moment, then held up three fingers, tapped the face of his watch with them, held them aloft again.

On my way out of the shop I made a note of the address in case I had trouble retracing my steps: 40–128 Chatham.

* * *

Blinking in the sepia light of early evening as chaotic traffic swarmed the intersection, I realized that I was very hungry. Military police attired in pitch black uniforms and armed with automatic weapons moved among the crowd. Had they just appeared, or had I, head-down in my mulish focus, simply elided their previous presence? Ducking through sheltered byways, I searched for food. I stopped at a street vendor's stand for the compelling honeycomb of an egg waffle, something I remembered from the visit with my father. It was served piping hot in a brown bag of just the right size and shape that was smartly punched with an appealing pattern of steam holes to keep the contents from becoming sodden. The waffle was the perfect provender for me at that moment, crispy exterior yielding to the light yet concerted application of mandibular pressure, spongiform interior releasing its deep flavor and inviting through consistency and warmth the probing tip of one's tongue, and I consumed it nodule by nodule with relish.

Prompted by the nostalgia wakened by the taste and texture of the transcendental egg waffle (as was Proust by the distinctive properties of his fair madeleine), I yearned to revisit past experience, to delve into the somewhat dim—made naturally so by time or willfully repressed—psychic territory of those years, to discover whether something of worth, of artistic merit, lay buried there. It was the sort of thing for which you regularly chide me. I made it my pursuit, my project. Perhaps *this* was what the whole strange journey was about. I strained toward the park in which I had spent so many happy hours but perceived right away that nothing would be the same by dusk or full dark, as all my intervals there had been passed straining through a vaporous atmosphere candidly refulgent. Tomorrow, then.

* * *

Instead I walked the waterway for pleasant hours, heeding the gulls' keening cries as a sea of people gathered against the railings for the nightly spectacle of light and sound that soon would play out on the architecture of the opposite shore. As the throng accreted to a level well outside my zone of comfort, I sought refuge in a basement jazz club, above the beckoning door—deep black backlit by an intense blue aura, reminding me forcibly of last evening's intimate display—of which glowed a neon cat in a top hat puffing soulfully on an alto saxophone. The semiotics of the signage were unclear to me. Were the twitching lines near the mouth of the cat meant to represent air or whiskers? Their cognates below above the mouth of the instrument, at least, clearly were intended to signify sound waves. With this slight buzzing puzzle occupying my thoughts I entered the club.

In the smoky darkness of the small bar five heads turned to me then turned away. All the men—the stolid bartender and his four suited customers—adopted a dismissive stance. There was an empty stool at the end of the bar nearest the door. It seemed a kind of mute challenge, an only slightly evolved school yard dare, that I take it. I planted my mismatched slacks firmly on the smoothly concave seat. The rough roust tottered, one starkly descending leg sadly shorter than the others.

My sidelong swivel as I sat had informed me that whisky was the what of this sad itsy scene. Beneath the sparse saloon lights David Sylvian banged from bass-heavy black uprights around which the bartender maneuvered with a disturbing lack of gentleman's grace. I rapped my knuckles firmly on the scarred, blackened board and issued a guttural provocation of my own: Ardbeg Corryvreckan, neat. Eyebrows elevated, Tanya, I assure you, but a nearly brimming bottle, dusty and diabolically consigned to the staid space back the blackly tumid lip of a veneered lower ledge and next to the disregarded Glen Grant belied the bartender's boorish beat. When the sparkling crystalline snifter arrived, I, staring steadfastly to the fecklessly foreign fore, poshly pretended to selfishly savor my every infinitesimal sip.

Well, then. You can imagine how agreeably my affronted effectuation carried. I would forgive you for assuming that my fellow patrons, regulars context made clear, called callously for their tardy tabs, gruffly made good, and quiescently quit the premises. Not quite the case, love, not quite the case. The jukebox wound wheezingly down. The salarymen arrayed stiffly on my left sipped fiercely their stale selections, exchanged subtle shrewd nonverbal messages. As they finished, in some secret sequence speaking to the informed of social standing, each ordered not his accustomed soda with a careless splash of Johnnie Walker Black but a scintillating snifter of Al-de-be-ge, no ice, you dirty son of a monkey. I will give credit where it is due: they swiftly downed them, to the last, pocked poker faces almost imperceptibly puckered. But then they sullenly withdrew.

The bartender turned treacly genial in the salarymen's sudden absence, puckishly provisioning the jukebox with a buoyant American set and slyly suggesting some of the establishment's more obscure stock, leaning heavily on French and Japanese labels.

44

Only once did he pause in his ministrations to answer a shuddering cell phone, a recent model with a large flexible screen. As the evening wore on, I deferred to his judgment, now that we were on the same grainy plane, and obligingly ordered some sautéed prawns to accompany wisely my simpering host's worldly rotgut regimen. They came hot and head-on and were indescribably delicious.

Salty seaweed salad and bland blanched peanuts accompanied my later libations. When I was sure that I had had enough (and, obviously, that really meant far too much), I held up a hand and settled square, leaving an outrageous tip in pointed variance from the regular crowd. The bartender smirked behind the board in his splotched black apron and bowed me disingenuously out the door.

Halfway to my hotel I became apprehensively aware of the sinewy shadows following leisurely my faltering steps. Now, I had always thought of these entities, the soulless Asian accountants, traveling salesmen, glorified secretaries, and general yes-men of the commercial establishment as fundamentally chthonic. It was my unshakable impression that they toiled their days away in dim cubicles, groped innocent lithe co-eds on the shimmying subway, drank grimly to their inimically enhanced capacities and beyond in small, dark venues such as the cat bar, then wended their ways widdershins to conspicuously bare patches of earth, such as those afforded by fresh construction sites and neglected small city parks, to there in their serpentine susurrus slowly subside. Instead they ambushed me in an alley and beat me within an inch of my life.

Four

I awoke in the late afternoon in a clean, quiet hospital room. I lay in a slab-straight bed that was dressed with blue and white linens. Everything hurt. I myself wore a teal gown and, from what I could see, which was not very much because my left eye was swollen shut and the vision in the right was blurry, a great many bandages. A moment of panic came when I found that I could not move. It subsided somewhat when I discerned that I was strapped to a board. A nurse call button on a wire lead was within reach of my right hand, and I pressed it hard with my thumb, pinching the back against my curled index finger.

A heavy white curtain was drawn down the length of the room along a track in the ceiling, so I did not know whether I had a roommate. Warm sunlight streamed through partially opened blinds on my left, slashing my bedclothes with bright bars. My little

partition seemed suddenly safe, blissful. I thought
that I could stay there for quite a while with no com-
plaints. A small sigh escaping my dry, bulbous lips, I
closed my eyes.

* * *

Nighttime. The gloom wrapped around me, a faint
line at the base of the white curtain the only point of
contrast. I felt chilled. Groping the covers, I became
increasingly distressed as I failed to locate the nurse
call button. Had I dreamed my earlier lucidity? In
frustration I clawed and pulled the blanket, rattling
the metal bars at the sides of the bed. I tried to call
out, and a terrible high sound like the bugling of a
rutting bull elk emanated then fell away as I gasped. I
heard footsteps somewhere on the other side of the
curtain. I closed my right eye and concentrated on the
sound. Yes, someone was approaching. I strained eagerly, if weakly, against my bonds, producing a rhythmic creak. The footsteps halted. The person was near,
perhaps was standing in the door of the room. My
breath came rapidly and my pulse was high in my
aching eardrums. Footsteps again. No! It was hard to
be certain through the scratchy espalier of the gauze
and from the isolating depths of the morphine's still,
dark pool, but my perception was that they were re-
ceding. I pulled again at the bunched covers and suc-

ceeded in feebly rattling the bars like some enraged shaven lab animal, track marked and bloodshot, like some raddled filthy criminal sure of his own guilt but indignantly desirous of his freedom anyway. For minutes I panted in the darkness. My attenuated airways' back scores of spiracles felt terribly clogged.

The footfalls returned, moving quickly and echoing as off the sinuous surface of a long stone tunnel. No, these were not they. This was a gathering, a small group, a field doctor riding bravely a diminutive donkey to the blazing hell-horror of the front lines, two intrepid interns trailing, stomping along flatfooted in their ill-sized scavenged combat boots and carrying stoically shapeless drab bundles.

Light burst forth. The glittering ommatidia of my dextral optical array shot searing warnings along strained axons to my sputtering synapses. The pale curtain screeched half the length of its runner, and a doctor in his white coat, a nurse in a pink and white uniform, and a flat-faced man in a brown suit crowded close.

"Excuse me, Mr.—" began the brown-suited man in heavily accented English.

"You'll get your chance, inspector. Kindly wait in the hall," said the doctor. He sounded almost native, probably took his schooling in the States.

A stare-down ensued, which the unflappable physician, drawn up to the height of his authority and looking thoroughly at home in these sterile surroundings, quickly won. The other man walked slowly away half bent, muttering and holding open his jacket with his elbows.

The doctor leaned over me, brusquely businesslike. He ran his right hand up the rear of my nearest leg, under my gown, all the way up; my cerci twitched at his touch.

"He's doing better now," he said to the nurse, who was holding a clipboard. She wrote something on the paper it held in place. He withdrew a pen light from a wide pocket and shone it all over my face, making me shiver in discomfort. He even pushed open my mouth with his thumb and forefinger and thrust the light up in there.

"I can't move," I tried to say, but I produced only the same awful high sound as before. The doctor held an admonishing finger to his lips.

"You're in room 8040 of Kwong Wah Hospital. Today is Thursday, the sixth of October. The time is ten fifty-seven p.m.—"

"I'm late for an appointment," I attempted to convey, thinking of the precious suit and its accoutrements, but nothing was working right and I could not manage even the cervid screech.

"I have contacted your spouse …" he trailed off, and we spent a moment in embarrassed silence, looking steadfastly away from one another. "And arranged for your belongings to be brought here from the hotel."

At this point I flapped about in protest, and I think that he mistook my display for anguish. The nurse, who had been busy at a cabinet in the corner, carried over a shiny tray holding a syringe, as if they had penned this little play in the prep room hours ago.

"I'm going to give you something for the pain now," the doctor said matter-of-factly. "It will also help you sleep."

I remained quite groggy from whatever they had given me before, but in my condition I could not resist. There was a chitinous pop as the slender needle penetrated my defenses and slid softly within.

Five

In slanted sharp sunlight a squadron of black military helicopters chopped the air. No, that was not it at all. An echo of some film I had seen, perhaps. Focus came slowly. My mouth was achingly dry, and my lips cracked as I swallowed. The light fell through the thick blades of the white horizontal blinds at the industrial windows. It was midmorning light, I guessed from my earlier glimpses of the room. My bed was jacked up, and I found myself reclining in a terribly uncomfortable position. It came to me quickly that this new inclination meant that I was no longer lashed to a batten. I flexed my arms and legs, sat up a bit farther and immediately wished that I had not. My head swam with the pain. I turned to the window, as the change of perception reminded me that the sound that I had taken for a helicopter vanguard in my half-conscious state persisted. Confusion whipped in sagging sections across my countenance, I am sure. In my dream the reassuringly professional doctor of the evening before (I certainly hoped that no more time had passed) had transmogrified into another Asian man of medicine, Hong, the dark villain whose license rightly had recently been revoked, to whom my nemesis Cavanagh practically was wedded. He kept me sedated for weeks in some far cloister of his creepy compound, slowly replacing my protuberances—fingers, toes, nipples, nose, penis—with carefully crafted porcelain facsimiles.

"I'm glad to see that you are awake," said the doctor from before, the real man, not the dream figure. How long had he been standing there on the periphery of my distracted gaze? "The grounds crew is mowing the lawn," he continued, obviously having observed my contorted straining.

I nodded in annoyance. A suddenly aware victim of nocturnal penile tumescence, I well wanted to hold his attention with my serious scowl. He gave me the once-over regardless.

"Can you move everything?" he asked.

"Yes," I stunned myself my enunciating clearly. His eyebrows lifted.

"Good. And that's a positive sign," he continued, motioning toward the apex of the pole of the tent. I turned to the window. "A nurse will be by shortly to take your vitals and order breakfast, and then a *gen-*

tleman from the police will see you." The doctor took his leave.

The nurse, this one was a young, buxom beauty, Tanya, I will not lie to you, arrived readily, and I could not have willed my wood away for anything. She held an ironic smile for the duration of her needlessly thorough examination. It is shameful that I tried to chat her up at the end (I was addled yet) as she with pink manicured nail pointed insistently to the American-style breakfast on the brief bilingual hospital menu and I acquiesced simply to please her; it became apparent right away that she spoke not a lick of English. She looked nervous as she waved goodbye, a girlish overhand cupping of her left mitt as the right tugged down her short, pleated skirt. A dour detective pushed into the room and antagonistically rounded the unoccupied first bed, causing the exiting nurse to step savagely to the side. He flashed his badge as he reached me.

"Some question," he blared, smelling of seafood. I recognized the man now. He wore the same brown suit as before. Maybe he had dozens of these up-jumped workman's outfits, but did he really toss them into the street during rush hour to sully and rumple them so? Had he been sitting in the hallway the entire time, frightened at the prospect of reporting to his precinct without a statement? "Do you know the man?" he asked, haltingly.

"Which man?" I rasped, a tickle in my throat.

"Man who hit you," he clarified.

"The *men* who hit me," I corrected with gentle emphasis. "Four of the louts set upon me. I see them clearly still."

"Hmph." I was not sure whether he doubted my assertion or did not understand it. "Four?" he eventually followed, holding aloft an equal count of calloused digits, which I found oddly reassuring.

I nodded energetically.

"What you do in bar?"

"I had a drink."

"No, what—" he cut himself off. "Why you go in there?"

"To have a drink."

He had produced a pad from his jacket pocket and was filling out the columns of a complicated form. It was hard to be sure since I did not understand the characters, but it appeared to me that his handwriting was childish.

"No other person inside bar?"

"The four men were there, seated when I arrived. A bartender, also a man, served us. I saw no one else, but there must have been kitchen staff. I had food. The bartender went into the back to get it, but he certainly was not gone long enough to have prepared it."

The detective stared perplexedly at his pad. He screwed up his eyes and scratched behind an ear with his pen. Facial contortions clearing, he brought the pen down swiftly and added something to one of his towers of testimony. It was done so quickly that he may well have produced a single character. He had lifted the pad to his chest, so that I could no longer see its face. He tapped the pen against his smooth chin.

"Okay. Tomorrow I come again. You suitcase outside. See you. Bye-bye."

"Detective!" I called after him in a squeak, but he did not slow. I wanted to ask his name, whether he and his cronies had searched my bag and room (I was sure that they had), and several other perhaps impertinent questions. Also, his use of the word "suitcase" had reminded me again of my tardiness with the tailor.

It turned out that "outside" meant "outside the room," as in standing in the hallway. The nurse returned wheeling my bag and gripping a strange curved plastic container under her arm. She brought the luggage up hard against the foot of the bed, and the sudden thump accompanied by the fanning of her starched skirt quickened my sluggish circulation. She moved around to my left side, pulled at the cords to raise the blinds, sending small clouds of dust into the air. She frowned at this and ran a finger along the sill, grimaced at the residue of the act. Turning to me and clapping her hands, she spoke.

"Nao pi."

"I'm sorry, but I don't understand you," I said.

"Nao. Pi." she repeated, somewhat sternly.

As I sat in baffled silence, she pulled away my sheets and urged me to roll onto my side, facing her and the window. She pushed the odd plastic container in against my left thigh.

"Nao pi," she said, hands on her hips.

I shrugged my shoulders as best I could in my current position and widened my eyes to convey bewilderment. I searched the smattering of Chinese that I had casually acquired. The words sounded more Mandarin than Cantonese to me, but I had to admit that I knew next to nothing about either. It struck me that *nao* could mean "brain," a remnant of some puerile rhyme I had composed about a mangy but smart temple cat of abnormally small size. But *pi* ... At that point the nurse bent backward slightly, slid her right hand to her pelvis, mimed with her fore and middle fingers spreading the meatus, and with her left pinkie traced the ambitiously high arc of the imaginary, illustrative urine stream, ending with a light tap on the wan interior of the plastic container.

As you can imagine, Tanya, I turned seven shades of red, mortified by the impropriety, which you harangue me for speaking of compulsively as you, despite your upper-crust provenance, care for such things not a whit. While I was caught off guard, the nurse reached through the slit in my gown and extracted my penis, leaving it dangling limply against the rim of the container.

"Now pee," she said again, hands balled into fists on her sturdy hips.

* * *

Breakfast, and it certainly was *eastern* western breakfast food—overcooked scrambled eggs, thin strips of desiccated bacon, perfect toast—was delivered without ceremony at 12:02 p.m. by a fashionably coiffured young man who had the air of one with better things to do. Using a ridiculously tiny plastic knife of incongruously appealing design, I lightly smeared the toast with (thankfully) room-temperature butter and tangy marmalade. Suddenly aware of the depth of my caloric deficit, I consumed the toast with gusto and with decidedly diminished enthusiasm nibbled the tail of one of the shards of bacon; the mere appearance of the eggs set my stomach roiling, so much so that I hastily covered that section of the tray with the stiff institutional napkin I had been issued. I really wanted coffee but had been given chilled water and apple juice. I went with the water, the juice reminding me uncomfortably of recent events. The fortified yielding solidity of the toast had done me good, but I had reached my limit and was aloofly grateful when Mr. Cannot-be-bothered sullenly returned to collect my leavings.

In the late afternoon the doctor again appeared, and observing an interaction with an orderly I finally got his name. Dr. Sun, presumably fresh off a troublesome shift, was amusingly punch-drunk. A shrewd negotiator when I apply myself, though even then never without a shiver of liberal remorse, I pressed my advantage.

"Mr. Sun," I began, a little stridently and, for some reason, stubbornly refusing to employ the greater honorific. "I have some questions for you. And there are a few non-medical matters that require prompt attention."

"Yes, Mr. Makarov," the doctor said, eyebrows arched, hands aflutter seeking the capacious pockets of his white coat, "you have my full attention."

"Well," I stammered but quickly regained my drive and forged ahead, "first there is the matter of the police."

"What of them?"

"Not in any way to impugn Hong Kong's finest —"

"Are they taking the investigation seriously, do you mean?" he asked, moving toward me with obvious excitement.

"Something like that, yes. Strangely enough, I feel little animosity toward my assailants, I mean I wish I had never been beaten, of course, but it just seems like—"

"You were in the wrong place at the wrong time?"

I nodded. If he kept interrupting I would turn very cross indeed.

"*Something like that,*" I continued, hoping that the emphasis was not lost in some cross-cultural chasm. "I have given the specifics minimal thought. It could have been a Triad meeting. Or even a gathering of apparatchiks from the mainland."

The doctor pulled over a wheeled stool with a shiny green top and seated himself on it, one leg over-lapping the other in a slightly effeminate manner. His dark eyes shone.

"Whatever the circumstances," I went on, slightly flustered by the sudden intensity of his inter-est, "an incident of this nature, a brutal attack on a foreign national ..."

"Is a delicate matter, right? An unwelcome thorn in the paw of those concerned with portraying the strength and goodness of a nascent nation, for those striving for legitimacy on the world stage."

"Quite correct," I muttered. I was not sure where to go with my inquiry, now that it had taken this turn. The doctor clearly had a horse in the race. Was he the scion of some important family? A knee-jerk supporter of the separatists? A concerned Confucian scholar-gentleman who was cautiously optimistic about the prospects of the present situation and wished to shepherd events in a beneficial direction? I had no way of knowing and wanted to avoid causing myself more trouble. I became reticent.

"I have prints of the photographs of your injuries here at the hospital and in a fire safe at my cousin's house," Dr. Sun spoke animatedly, seemingly oblivious to my change in mood. "There are also digital copies on flash drives in various locations. The photographs will go on the Web if the authorities try to bury this episode."

Something about the way he said "episode" sent a chill down my spine.

"Well, good," I said brusquely. "I would like copies of the photographs and my medical records as well."

"Of course," the doctor answered with a distracted air, sensing for the first time my frostiness. "Of course."

He sat and I lay in stony silence for a time.

"Well, if that is all—" he said, standing and replacing the wheeled stool.

"No it is *not* all," I interjected, savoring the moment. "There is a personal matter of some importance that I would like to discuss."

"A personal matter?"

"Yes. I have made arrangements with a local tailor for a jacket, trousers, and four shirts—"

"On the city isle?"

"No—"

"Not one of those Indian tailors under the bridge near the ferry—"

"*No.* A Chinese tailor. The address is on a scrap in my jacket pocket."

"Surely he will wait. Tailors are used to—"

"It was a rush order."

"I'll see what I can do."

The doctor took his leave.

* * *

Deep in the night, when I was sure that the late shift nurses were broodily settled at their station gossiping over slimy cup noodles and sappy period dramas and that the glum orderlies long ago had shed their scrubs and gone home, I made my move.

In the early evening a graying stern physical therapist in a thin and tight gray sweater with big buff buttons had had me up. I learned from her the way to work the rails that rose at the sides of my bed, though she frowned when she caught the vector of my gaze, assuming that I instead was ogling her pert little breasts. They weren't, in fact, half bad.

Now I with careful flicks of my thumb unlatched the butterfly switches along the line of the frame, congratulating myself quietly for getting it right on the first attempt. I slowly let the left rail slip to its resting place. Here I hesitated. If my reckoning was correct (and there was more than a shadow of a doubt whether some of my previous visitations had been real or imaginary), I had at best 96 minutes to pull off my caper. That seemed like a long time, but the earlier session with the physical therapist had proved excruciating. Unconsciously a bodhisattva's supernatural stillness had crept over me as I dwelt in abject misery in those first flashes of cognizance and since had endured as an act of sheer self-preservation, but the paces through which that harridan had put me shattered such shields with insouciance. I doubted whether I could manage what I had in mind on my own and whether I could for the duration withstand the screaming bright fire of my taut attenuated nerves. Regardless of these deep misgivings a separate, unstinting will animated my limbs, which like crepuscular, dull litter-bearing beasts of ancillary burden crawlingly conveyed my reluctant trunk inch by shuddering inch toward the fearsome promise of the freshly exposed precipice. My plan was to balance there, gripping the edge with my buttocks while sliding a leg to the floor, then swing across the other leg and, both feet planted firmly on the tile, ease myself into a squat with my back propped against the side of the bed, there to rest and reassess, to move forward into a crawl if necessary. Instead I badly misjudged the springiness of the mattress and the slickness of the sheets and pitched forward off the bed onto the radiator beneath the window.

The sudden contact with my tender ribs rudely withdrew the air from my lungs, and I bent there for a time clinging to the cool metal of the grille. Once I had caught my wind, I was pleased to understand that I had come out relatively unscathed. I tried the kind of steady one-foot-in-front-of-the-other gait that the therapist had insisted on, keeping a firm hold with my hands in case one or both legs gave way. I moved with some pain and stone stiffness but surprisingly little true difficulty to the end of the bed. My luggage was not there. Someone had moved it whilst I was distracted or asleep. I cast my crippled gaze over the dusky shrouded lumps along the walls of the room, all rendered suddenly mysterious and fey. I could just make out the extended handle of my bag in the farthest corner. After listening carefully for any sign of movement from the hallway, I gritted my teeth and began my sorry progress.

Panting and sweating and generally feeling my battered, diminished state deeply, urgently I slumped into the corner, resting my forehead, right temple, and right shoulder against the solid channel of the sharply meeting thickly painted cinderblocks. Abruptly aware of the ticking of the clock—the insistent sound seemed to echo in the seashell whorls of my hairy ears—I got down to business and laid the bag out gently on its back, with trembling hand unzipped the main compartment. I knew before I saw (from the ease with which I was able to handle the vessel's weight) that the strange cylinder was gone. What surprised me was that the clothing that had in Boston at some point in my fugitive peregrinations been removed now was folded neatly in its former place. I pushed my fingers deep into the interior to make sure, but there could be no doubt. A secondary blow was the absence of the bawdy mermaid brooch. I felt consumed by loss and in a daze made my way back to the haven of the bed, not bothering to right the suitcase or even to re-close the zipper.

Six

"Good news," beamed Dr. Sun from atop his stool at the side of my bed. "I am authorizing your release tomorrow afternoon."

I offered an ambiguous grunt.

"Will you be returning to the hotel from which the detective retrieved your things?"

"I think not."

"Wise, probably. Where will you go?"

"Somewhere on the city isle. It was always my plan."

"Do you need any help making arrangements?"

"No, thank you."

"I could ..." he hesitated. "I have a large family. I could put you up somewhere safe, somewhere comfortable, if you would would like."

"No, thank you."

"If money is an issue—"

"It isn't."

I turned to the window and closed my eyes. After a few minutes I heard him wheel the stool back to its place and exit the room.

* * *

After lunch I made a flurry of telephone calls. My energy was returning and with it came a keen awareness of my responsibilities. First I spoke with Caroline, explaining where I was and what had happened but eliding any motivation for my globe trotting. She was unperturbed, asking right away whether my review and introduction would be ready by our deadline, whether I was set up to edit what she had compiled so far for the issue, to vet the layouts, assign revisions, to damn well do my job. I assured her that I was not in dereliction of my duties and that all would proceed to schedule. I added that I would likely be away for some time (and here I may have invoked your father's name, insinuating that I was traveling on some business, some whim of his) and that—and I thought of this only as I said it—having an editor-at-large reporting in and making pronouncements from cities far and foreign might give *Lit* an international boost, regain a bit of cultural cachet. I was aware that we had been coasting. By the time I rang off, Caroline seemed to be feeling my angle, was quiescently considering the possibilities with her accustomed verve. What would I ever do without Caroline?

Next I called Jim at the printers to inquire about a waxy cover that I was considering for our upcoming special issue. He assured me that as long as my check did not bounce he would obtain an adequate supply of the material, but he urged me to make my decision soon so that we would not be surprised by a dip in availability or a change in cost. As it was this little extravagance would cost a pretty penny of your father's money, though not enough for him to take notice, of course. As we said our goodbyes Jim invited me to join him for a Reuben and a beer the next time I was in Hoboken.

Thinking that it would be a good idea to consult someone who knew what was going on in East Asia, I tried the last number that I had for Cesar Wood, written in cheap, faded blue ink on the lottery number (15 21 7 2 1 57) side of a yellowed fortune cookie fortune. If I recalled correctly, it was for his Kyoto residence. An angry-sounding Japanese woman answered, and I could not make myself understood. Her rising intonation spoke of rising agitation, so I mumbled some weak platitude and terminated the call.

Finally, I called you. I lay there with the phone on my chest for quite some time before I dialed our number. I do not know why I had not called before then. It is not something that I can explain, even with all the fine words at my disposal, even after prolonged contemplation. Put simply, it was as if from the time I boarded the jet at Logan to the time Dr. Sun somewhat sternly mentioned my wife you had completely ceased to exist. So obliterating was whatever quirk that caused the absence that when you popped back into the picture at the doctor's insistence I could not be sure whether he or I had not invented you.

"Anatoly," you said without even a greeting, having glanced at the caller ID, I assume, and before I could utter a syllable. Then through the light interference of our international connection came quiet sobbing. You seemed very real to me at that moment.

"Tanya," I began but was forced to bide my time while you mastered yourself. "Tanya, I'm in Hong Kong." I had a lot of things to say, but the pressure on my chest was overwhelming.

"Why?" you asked in a small voice.

"I will explain, Tanya, but I cannot do it now."

"Is someone with you?"

"No. I'm in a hospital room, I—"

"Yes, I know. Dr. Sun called." So he had handled the matter personally.

"They are releasing me tomorrow."

"Are you okay?"

"I am recovering. I can walk short distances, and the swelling around my eye has gone down enough for me to see some blurry shapes, and—"

"What?"

"I'm getting better. They would not release me otherwise, right?"

"You could barely walk? Dr. Sun said that the accident was minor, that you were shaken and maybe had a concussion. They were going to observe you overnight out of an abundance of caution." So he had not called right away, and when he had phoned he had lied through his tea-stained teeth.

"What accident?"

"With the rickshaw."

"Rickshaw? What exactly did the doctor tell you?"

"Well," you hesitated, and I caught a hint of something sour, as if you would prefer to believe the doctor's words. "You misread the signals at a busy intersection and stepped into the traffic. Luckily you only got as far as the bike lane, where a rickshaw bumped you …"

"Tanya, I was set upon by hoodlums in a dim alley. They beat me severely."

"That's," you stammered, "not what the doctor said. Is Dr. Sun really your doctor?"

"Yes, he is."

"Why would he lie?"

"I do not know, but I intend to find out."

"I don't know …"

"What don't you know?"

"What to believe, I guess."

"Believe me, Tanya."

"I'm having a little trouble, A." I was simultaneously disheartened by your hesitancy and buoyed by the familiar form of address.

"I'll call you tomorrow evening. I should know more then, and I will be somewhere more private."

"Promise that you will."

"I will call," I promised. "And Tanya, one sees rickshaws in modern Hong Kong only in museums and night markets."

Seven

The orderlies had me up early in preparation for another session with the physical therapist. The harried nurse who stepped in briefly to take my vitals was evasive when I asked to see Dr. Sun. She said on her way out that she would relay the message.

The physical therapist remained her dour self, brusquely demonstrating the various movements I was to attempt. She wore what to my good eye appeared to be the same thin gray sweater as before. As she hurried to my side to smack away the hand with the curled fingers of which I was gripping the seam between two cinderblocks for better balance and support, I realized that the scent of camphor that I had been catching emanated from the sweater itself. The session was long and arduous.

* * *

Lunch was lavish to the point of arousing suspicion. The spread included pungent gai lan, delightful bursting xiao long bao, nested firm yi mein with succulent crab meat, and an artfully arranged half chicken stuffed with glutinous rice and surrounded by glistening wood ear mushrooms. Mild toasted barley tea accompanied the meal, and a salty-sweet cinnamon and sour plum decoction ("good for the digestion") was served afterward. I felt like a death-row inmate on the fraught evening of his penultimate day.

By the time the leavings of my lunch were cleared away, the soft, bright light filtering into the room had taken on a decidedly lazy-late-afternoon aspect. I wanted nothing more than to curl up on the soft grass and spongy moss growing languidly in the shade beneath a suitably majestic and aged tree in the corner of a verdant and seldom-visited park, there to alternate happily between snoozing and reading. Instead I watched inscrutable period dramas on the room's small silver television and waited impatiently for some word of the doctor's nebulous whereabouts, my impending release, and the availability of the custom clothing to the foppish idea of which I lately had become barnacled. It was a trial, Tanya.

The last came first. A young man with a boxy head and big ears brought the suit, and it was as divine as my sartorial imagination had dared to dream. Through vulgar hand gestures—rubbing his fingers together, flipping out ghost money—the lad conveyed that he expected payment right then in cash. This presented a problem, as I had planned to stop by a bank on my way to the tailor's shop and thus did not currently possess notes in any currency that could meet the agreed upon extortionate sum. I shrugged my shoulders and mimed the turning out of pockets to demonstrate my predicament. The fellow did a good impression of a greedy carp, gaping there halfway between my bed and the door, then he turned abruptly on his heel and moved swiftly away. I slapped my hand hard against the Formica plane of the bedside table. He turned. I knew that I had mere seconds to make my case.

"Look, I'm a wealthy man," I desperately began, beseechingly holding out my white arms. It was clear that he did not understand me. A nurse, the one who earlier had helped me to urinate, entered and looked slowly from the oafish boy to my distressed figure and back.

A rapid-fire Cantonese conversation erupted. From the way the nurse kept glancing in my direction and nodding, I felt that she was vouching for me. The errand boy, still looking dubious, pulled out a slim cell phone and speed-dialed a number. After a barked introduction, he passed the handset to the nurse. She spoke sharply, now appearing somewhat annoyed, and again turned her gaze to me and nodded. She handed the phone back to the young man and reached out for the cluster of hangers. He pulled away reflexively and a half-hearted tug-of-war ensued. The lad caved rather quickly and as the nurse stood holding the limpid garment bags he wrote something on the receipt, crumpled it, and thrust it into her cleavage. She shouted him out the door and down the hall.

The nurse followed my pointing, grasping, beckoning gestures masterfully, and soon the suit was hanging from an IV stand wheeled up next to my bed, where I could admire it in the light, reach inside the plastic sheath to savor the rich texture of the fabric. Out of the corner of my eye I caught the nurse performing a funny little genuflection as she left the room. Something about the ensemble called for a cane (and a top hat or a bowler, but fortunately I checked immediately that impulse), and for weeks I would *need* one. I started a mental list: cane, monogrammed stationery, quality fountain pen, good black ink, notebook computer (since I had lied to Caroline about being set up for work), sundry office supplies and domestic appurtenances, living quarters. Well, some additions and refinements would be necessary, but it was something to work toward, an appealing plan of action.

Afternoon had begun its slide toward evening, and I became concerned that my release papers would not materialize. I summoned a nurse with the call button and inquired about the location of Dr. Sun and the progress of my manumission; she fetched another, younger nurse who spoke a little English. The second nurse seemed largely to understand what I was getting at and departed with purpose in her step. In an hour she returned and informed me that Dr. Sun was not in the hospital, but he had signed my papers that morning and left them at the front desk and I was therefore free to go at any time. When I asked her where the doctor had gone and why, she met the many formulations of my questions with school-girl deflections, hiding her mouth behind her cupped hand. When I persisted she simply fled. The twitch of her bottom reminded me of the hula, and that of Lili'uokalani, last monarch and only queen regnant of the Kingdom of Hawai'i. For some reason I remembered that she ascended the throne in early 1891. Terribly sad what happened after.

Since my papers were clear and I would have no chance to wring answers from the doctor, I prepared myself for departure. I took a shower, which was excruciating, and changed into my own clothes—the mysteriously returned clothes, a black button-down shirt and trendy jeans, not the fancy new ones. My nerves screamed with pain, but being up and about and nearly free felt wonderful. I did ask one of the nurses for a few packets of analgesics, and she obliged me after only brief hesitation. Once my wits and effects had been gathered, the orderlies insisted on pushing me down to the lobby in a wheelchair. My retort, that I would not be allowed to take the chair with me and thus would have to stand on my own two feet and work my stiff legs in mere minutes anyway, did not sway them in the least, if they half understood it. Young men both, one pushed the chair slowly with his head bent over mine, his shuffling gait rasping down the hallways. The other walked beside pulling my luggage with one hand and dangling the garment bags from the other. He meandered quite noticeably, so that he could match our progress without feeling that he was dragging his feet, I assumed. Both men seemed to be singing quietly, and it took me a moment to discern that it was the same song, likely some popular Internet tune, something they had been listening to in the break room, taken in parts; the shuffling and wandering fell into the rhythm of the track. I felt a sudden paternal fondness for these guys.

In the lobby the analog clock over the reception desk read 6:02, not as early as I had hoped for my escape, but not too late to settle into a comfortable hotel in Hong Kong proper, have a nice supper, and solidify my plans. The woman at the desk did not give me any trouble about the paperwork and promptly called a taxi for me when I asked. As the driver pulled away from the curb, I waved at her and the two orderlies, who had hung around to help me into the cab

and, I suppose, slowly take the wheelchair back up together. When he asked me where I wanted to go I told
him to stop by an ATM and then take me to the Four
Seasons in Central. He seemed to get the gist.

* * *

Checked in and reclining on the downy bedclothes I
felt kind of smug. My slumming was at an end and
my mad caper to the East was forming up in my mind
as a very positive fillip for the reputations of myself
and *Lit.* I was so afraid of everything that had happened up to my stay in the hospital that I had wanted
to travel incognito, to throw any pursuers off my trail.
Also, I reverted to my former self, the one before *us,*
to a degree in the grip of my adrenaline rush, and in
that state my native frugality prevailed. You know
that I came from nothing.

Though I first felt as if a part of myself had been
removed when the bomb went missing, I now breathed
freeing air. The heady shift was so welcome that I
pushed important questions—Who had planted the
bomb in my luggage? How had this been accom-
plished? Who had taken the device? Who were the
men who had assaulted me? Was there any connection
among these things? What of the doctor's strange behavior? Why me? Why this? Why? Why?—out of my
mind. It is how I always am when I have caught the

scent of a new project (yes, often to the point of abruptly abandoning whatever last had stirred me). Anyway, my brain was awhirl, and not with the strangeness of recent events. I decided to turn in early to plan and dream; I would take my supper in the hotel restaurant. Trying on my new outfit like a fresh skin, I spritzed my neck with the thoughtfully provided eau de toilette and caught the elevator down to the sixth floor.

I was in Hong Kong and should have opted for the Cantonese restaurant, but I chose instead its French sibling on the grounds that I was yet in a delicate state and there would know what I safely could order. The maître d'hôtel paused for a beat at my battered appearance and shuffling step but recovered quickly after giving my finery a surreptitious once-over. Nevertheless, I was seated in a quiet corner where the aftermath of violence might not put other diners off their meals. I understood, though I simultaneously felt the absurd urge to get right up in their faces and boast loudly about how much better I now looked in comparison to the day of my admission to the hospital, to tell them how very fond I was of any territory where a foreign traveler could be treated so courteously from the very start of his stay.

All the rich fare was terribly tempting—I wanted desperately, in fact, to order one of the tasting sets—but even reading the ridiculously overblown descriptions made me nauseated. The options for light dishes were surprisingly few, and I nearly made a series of special requests. When I looked up from the fussy menu (parchment limned in gold foil, curly letterforms in India ink, no prices), however, I noticed that a small pack of staff was regarding me askance. I settled on consommé and a saffron risotto. The waiter fairly snatched the menu from my grasp when it became clear that I was ordering no more. When he thrust the wine list within half an inch of my patrician nose without so much as consulting the sommelier, I waved it away with a disdainful sniff. The food was utterly unimpressive, the consommé had been simmered too long with a raft of too many egg whites, the risotto was disgustingly wet. I was still hungry when I quit the dining room after only a few mouthfuls of each, which I am sure is exactly as the management intended.

Back in my borrowed bed, before removing my flâneur's dress (and suddenly desirous of a crushed velvet cape) I called room service and had them bring up a glass of warm milk. Sipping it did wonders for my constitution, and undressed to my skin and wound in the sheets I slept peacefully for many hours.

Eight

Bollocks to my early start, then. One's health must be the primary concern in such cases, of course, so I did not *really* feel like I had squandered half of the day in rest. I was merely impatient.

I grappled with an urge to have lunch—breakfast and, sadly, even brunch were ruled out by the late hour (and at any rate it was not the weekend)—at the hotel, in my room, even. The impulse was not entirely insular but was born of a desire for expediency, which unfortunately did not stand up to scrutiny. In the first place, I was not yet very hungry. Further, as we seasoned travelers know, morning or midday room service is notoriously slow because the guests are far less likely to be intoxicated and, therefore, to tip well. No, those ancient Greeks had it right about a task well begun. I hurried through my grooming ritual and got out onto the street. If there was a spring in my step, then it had been taken from the tortured groaning mattress of a 1,031-pound Midwestern couple deep into the thirtieth year of its corn-fed diabetic coma.

I had asked at the reception desk in the hotel on my way out for the address of a reputable dealer in antiques who was known for both the size and the diversity of his collection. My request certainly sent those smartly suited girls scrambling, but in the end I was presented (from a cupped two-handed grip accompanied by the slightest bow ever to crease coccyx) with a sheet of hotel stationery bearing the names and addresses in Chinese characters, pinyin, and English of three auspicious-sounding purveyors. I chose the middle man to visit first.

Rightly I should immediately have settled matters with the tailor, but were I to walk into his den in the absence of attire compleat I would have lost somewhat the moral authority of the persona created by such fuss and expense and found myself thus stripped taking the tine end of exploitation's tarnished utensil. I insisted it be otherwise and hobbling, sweating, and swearing clingingly climbed the vertiginous heights (the famous escalators had begun their siesta, you see), providing, if the sudden appearance of faces at windows was any measure, welcome comic relief on what was turning out to be a long Monday afternoon for everyone. May I never lose my philanthropic streak.

When I reached what I was reasonably sure was the correct tier, I spent quite a lot of time—an alarming span, proving that I was dangerously rushing my recovery—panting beneath a patisserie's maroon awning. A light touch on my arm drew my attention to the presence of a young woman in a maroon head scarf and apron, the latter emblazoned with the pink brand of the shop, a dancing panda. She was offering me a paper cup of hot green tea, which I accepted so as not to appear rude, though it was the last thing I wanted. I took a few sips to signal my appreciation. I was far less sociable when she produced a sour-smelling rag and attempted to mop my forehead with it. She gave me a terrible, wounded look as I reeled away. To make the misunderstanding a tad less embarrassing for both of us, I pulled out the paper from the hotel desk and pointed to the address of the shop that I was seeking. She gestured vaguely up the lane. I thanked her and set off straight away so that neither party would feel further obligation.

Not all the shops had boards that prominently displayed their numbers. I did quite a bit of stiff walking back and forth along the segment where I felt that 9600 should lie. Eventually I was rescued by a stroller, tall for a Chinese and a fellow dandy by his dress and demeanor, who asked me what I was looking for with such forceful self-assurance that I mutely handed him the slip of paper. He determined immediately which address was in the vicinity and pointed upward, tapping his finger with hollow thumps twice against the pipe of his audacious silver hat. He returned the paper and led me gently to a narrow door between two shops and held it open, revealing an equally narrow staircase ascending at a steep pitch. I thanked the man for his assistance, and he gallantly doffed his hat and, smartly replacing it with a practiced tug, stepped back from the threshold, leaving the door to close with a bang. I stood one step back from it in semi-darkness. I was left with the impression of the helpful stranger's powdered high cheeks and waxed Confucian mustache.

There was a peculiar odor in the stairwell, though it was in no way unpleasant. I closed my eyes and stood musing for a moment until I arrived at a tentative identification: cinnamon-infused lamp oil. Pondering this curious confluence, I began my climb. The trek was rather easier than I had anticipated, owing to the facts that the same narrowness of the passage that left me feeling a little heavy in the chest allowed me to grip the thin handrails on both sides and therefore to do quite a bit of the work with my upper body and that my destination lay only a level above. At the top I pushed through a split canvas curtain and stumbled into golden light.

The shop resided above not only its downstairs neighbor but also the establishments to either side.

Windows in the wall facing the street rose from floor to ceiling and presented a formidable spectacle. I am not sure how I missed such a thing from outside. The glass of the many square panes was thick and mottled and was the color of warm clover honey. The old dark wood lattice into which the glass was set provided a stern counterpoint and spoke of history and care. Swallows nested in the upper reaches. Residing in such sunny pools as the bubbled glass cast must have had some effect on the constitutions of all inhabitants. Surely over time the amber pall would become annoying or oppressive, but for the moment it performed Midas's parlor alchemy on the contents of the wide and airy space. I did not immediately spot the proprietor, but I suddenly was in no hurry. I was absolutely certain that here I would find that which I sought and much besides. I flicked my tongue against my incisors with satisfaction.

The merchandise, and I hesitated to think of it as such for the displays were arranged with the loving gleam of a curator's eye rather than the cold glare of a marketer's glassy orb, formed something of a meandering maze, and I browsed pleasantly down the first branches to which I came. Most of the items there arrayed—lacquered bowls, ivory chopsticks, jade figurines, folded silks—I lacked the knowledge to appraise. Nonetheless I found every item lovely, and the whole of the arrangement imparted a very fine impression indeed. Be that as it may, by the time I had taken two further turns through branching corridors of inscrutable goods I was feeling keenly the need for a walking stick. I decided to curtail my lingering amble and sally forth with purpose, at which point the shop-keeper appeared as if summoned.

He was a short man and elderly. My brain kept supplying wispy white hair that his bowling ball head and wrinkled brown face did not possess, a remnant of watching too many wushu flicks during my difficult teenage years, no doubt. He held a slate up to his chest. In hot pink chalk carefully was printed some English:

> Hello! I am Mr. Hu. I do not speak English, but I am sure that with good will and friend-ship we can conduct business successfully. Thank you for coming to my shop.

Some perverse part of me wanted quite badly to break out stridently some of the vulgar German from my college days; maintaining the self-control for which I am infuriatingly (according to you) known, I simply nodded my agreement. Mr. Hu set down his slate on a little wheeled cart and clacking the frames together selected another from a pile. It read:

> Are you looking for anything in particular?

Again I nodded and mimed an old man walking with a cane. Unsure of my performance, I held my hands apart to emphasize the length of the object in question, made a circle to indicate the circumference of the shaft, and played out the charade a second time, pointing to convey the object's role. Mr. Hu gave me an up-and-down look and his cheery face took on an expression that could mean only, "Well, of course!"

Pushing his noiseless trolley he led me quickly to a fine selection. Consummate trader, he insisted on handing me particularly suitable candidates and waiting with clasped hands while I took a turn up and down the aisle. As I rejected rod after rod, his mirthful expression deepened. Finally he shrugged his shoulders as if to say, "I suppose I cannot help you after all." Half-turned he held up a finger to pin me in my place. He went slowly past the three-high rack of canes and opened a man-sized black sea chest. He set aside the deep velvet-lined top tray that was spilling over with pearls of every description, and from the shallow tray below drew forth one of six quietly ostentatious props. He slammed the lid of the chest shut, causing me to shuffle back a step, and twirled his prize skillfully from hand to hand. He brought it down hard between us, the silver spike on its earthward end embedded deeply in the runneled planks of the shop floor. Mr. Hu pulled his hands away as if stung. The yellowed ivory skull with its dull yet enticing cinnabar chip eyes swayed slightly atop the oiled mahogany haft. We both laughed with undisguised boyish delight.

Unlike the tailor, the antiques dealer accepted credit cards. After swiping mine he kept tapping its face and trying to tell me something, but I did not have the foggiest idea what he was getting at and willing my face to remain blank merely nodded politely.

* * *

Later I visited a small corner bank branch with unmissable red awnings over its windows and door and withdrew enough Hong Kong dollars to settle matters with the tailor and fuel my shambling street life for a few days. The manager, the utterly unexcitable sort of man with oiled hair, a forgettable face, and perpetually compressed lips, handled the transaction himself with quiet dignity.

It took far longer than I had anticipated to travel to the tailor's shop. On the deck of the ferry (I am not overly fond of tunnels that pass beneath bodies of water) foul sulfurous wind washed over the passengers, causing many to bring to their faces kerchiefs scented with spices and bergamot. Boarding had been interminable because a cadre of police in dark blue uniforms had insisted on checking everyone's identification.

On the other side I stopped a moment in the fading sun to get my bearings, then set off for my dingy destination, clicking my cane on the cobbles. The tailor was waiting at the door, for someone else it seemed from his look of irritation at my appearance. I started to take a turn for him, to show just how becoming his work was draped on my frame, but a twinge of disgust turned down the corner of his mouth, stopping me short. I realized that I was holding my left hand limply and carelessly in the air. The old man was not about to budge from his door, so I counted out the crisp colorful bills right there in the street. He took the stack one-handed and wadded it peremptorily into a pocket of his apron. Business finished, his gaze shifted past me, resuming whatever vigil he had been keeping until my arrival. I felt a little put out, partly because I had just handed him so much money (really far more than his expertise demanded) and partly because in some cobwebby corner of consciousness I had viewed him as an accomplice in effecting my novel persona. Stung by his studied indifference, I walked slowly back to the launch.

Waiting for the ferry, I experienced the oddest sensation: I could virtually feel the humming of my cells, the fervent activity of my body reconstructing itself. Because contemplating one's inner workings too carefully inevitably leads to exhaustion (and to the certainty that such personal-scale bustling must one

day, could any day cease), I went faint and sought the
support of a concrete pylon. In a flash someone was at
my side, gripping my right shoulder firmly in one
white-gloved hand, the other bringing something right
up under my nose. Given my recent history on this
side, I feared that I was under attack and reflexively
jabbed the head of my cane into the assailant's abdomen. An explosion of sharp sensation raced through
my brow, and as the glove pulled away from my face I
saw that it held a little faceted green glass bottle of
smelling salts. The man—the dandy whom I had encountered outside of Mr. Hu's shop, I now saw—held
up the bottle with two fingers and a thumb, turning it
around for me to see. I felt abased by my panic, but
luckily our bodies had been too close for my blow
with the cane to do more than surprise or inconven-
ience him. He shrugged his shoulders as if to say,
"Feeling better now?" I nodded. I could see at this
range the tell-tale sheen of spirit gum at the edge of
his mustache; the pancake makeup seemed thicker and
slightly smeared, as if it had been hastily reapplied.
He pointed to my cane, gave me an enthusiastic
thumbs-up, turned on his heel and joined the crowd
disembarking the ferry, which had just arrived. I
briefly entertained the idea of attempting to follow
him, and he did seem to be glancing over his shoulder
with every other step as if curious whether I would,
but daylight had fled, I was tired and hungry, and the

lights across the water seemed to be beckoning me home.

Nine

After an early start I made my way to the park in which I had read for hours while waiting for my father to finish his business all those years before. I wanted nothing more than to read the same books I had read then, but I had made a lot of promises to Caroline about all the work for *Lit* that would bubble forth from the rejuvenating fountain of my Oriental project and had therefore to finish the Cavanagh.

I sat in the park on a low red-brick wall held together by a very dark mortar that was flecked with tiny black snail shells. The morning sun was behind me (obliquely, not searing the pages) and a light breeze tickled the hair in my ears. I felt refreshed and at ease, though I looked ghastly as my bruises were going yellow. A few matrons beneath a bower on the other side of the open space were gossiping and stretching ahead of their tai chi routine. The rippling bright purple folds of their exercise outfits and the easy music of their quiet banter set a pleasantly lively scene.

In the novel the narrator's tone had changed yet again, moving through the complicated genealogy of the estate's hounds with grandfatherly disregard. I made a note of the digression on hotel stationery and soldiered on. Oh, for the love of shivering Donskoy! Cavanagh was going on about the kitchen staff again, like in that terrible Altman film we saw projected poorly at some charity event on the Esplanade. I did something then that I only ever do to express contempt: I skimmed several paragraphs. A further page pulled partially over by unconsciously curled pinkie revealed a welcome chapter break. I reseated my improvised bookmark and clamped closed the covers for a time to bask in the waxing warmth of filtered photons. An unmistakably crisp edge honed the gently whispered breeze, asserting with quiet force that even here slither-scything autumn waited in the wings.

Following their languid warm-up the women entered seriously into the swanning motions of their transcendental script, accompanied by the thin straining of a zither-like instrument played over the compact speakers of a fold-out portable audio player, the white plastic of which I could see even from my distant perch had become streaked with urban grime. I wondered how often that low-end piece of consumer equipment had made the journey to the park (probably daily for at least a decade, I decided) and what sort of batteries it required. Despite the unpromising mundanity of their unhurried preparations, the women moved surely and with touching grace as the music took hold. I set aside my book and crossed my legs to watch the routine in its entirety.

As the final note of the song screeched skyward, the women twisted up onto the toes of their right feet, those of the left braced hard against the opposite thigh, heels tucked to cunni. Their left hands cupped beneath their right breasts while the right shot straight to the crown of heaven in some strange salute, thumbs pressed fervently into palms. They held position for excruciating bars as the sour note succumbed slowly to a dull electric hiss. I stood partly because their performance unexpectedly had moved me and partly because my right leg had fallen asleep. After breaking formation, the women moved loosely to their duffel bags, there letting down their hair and producing small taut towels which they ran over their lightly moistened skin with obvious pleasure. Their utter disregard during this action drew me in, and I felt my heretofore forgotten member stiffening. As the women started packing up and quietly saying their goodbyes, I sat back down in embarrassment, tugging at my trouser leg in the hope of shifting my sex into a somewhat less painful arrangement.

"Good morning, sir!" the one with the audio player called, standing in front of me and beaming. She wasn't going anywhere.

"Good morning, madame," I replied with a measure of reluctance.

"How are you finding the park today?" she asked.

"Lovely, thank you. It reminds me of my youth."

"Oh, did you spend a lot of time in parks as a boy?"

"I did, but I was thinking of some hours I spent in this particular park."

"Oh! Did you live nearby?"

"No, we were traveling on my father's business."

"I see."

A silence followed during which we both watched a crow hop across a grassy expanse to pick at something (a rodent carcass, I guessed) near the end of a hedgerow.

"I am retired," the woman said, squaring up to look me right in the eye, "but I am looking for something to do, something involving English. Even though I have studied with tutors for quite a while and have reached a conversational level, I do not feel like I *really* know anything. When I want to say something, I always have to overcome a little hitch, to convince myself that I have the right to voice the words, if you know what I mean."

"I think that I do."

"Anyway, I'm looking for something part-time to keep me progressing with the language, to keep my mind sharp, not that I'm losing it or anything. Do you know of anyone who might have an opening like that?"

I had been toying since my arrival with the idea of hiring an amanuensis. There was something terribly appealing about it, about introducing someone that way at a soirée, for example. I also had been dreading getting into the nitty gritty of renting appropriate office and living space, and having a local in my employ would help tremendously in that regard. I could delegate.

"In fact, I have some need of such service myself," I replied, grabbing my lapels and puffing out my chest.

"Really?" She looked as if she did not believe me.

"Indeed. I am the editor of an American literary magazine on sabbatical in Hong Kong. I plan to keep up the majority of my duties while charting the future of the publication, reinvigorating the pages with fresh and foreign perspective to refresh and expand its readership."

This seemed to be too much for her to swallow, and she started making small movements, as if to flee.

"Well, think on it a while," I said evenly, writing my name, room number, and the title of the magazine on a sheet of the hotel's stationery. "I'm just getting set up, and I really could use some help. Give me a call at the hotel to let me know whether you are interested."

She took the sheet and scrutinized it with tight brow.

"It doesn't pay very well," I warned with a smile.

"I'll let you know, Mr. Makarov," she said. "Thanks for listening."

She seemed shell-shocked as she walked away, and I thought immediately and unpleasantly of Hiroshima, of her nice skin turning silvery and translucent and falling off in curls like vellum and rising over the harbor on the wind.

Ten

On Saturday, 12 November nothing much happened.

I remember the stultifying tedium of the day because of an unfortunate association. On that date a significant number of years earlier you met my mother. Your father drolly was administering one of his themed soirées when, fashionably late in the evening, a gleaming white carriage pulled up in front of the Copley (where he had rented the ballroom, thankfully, rather than hosting the event at home). The white horses wore plumes and everything. Out of this contrived conveyance stepped unsteadily Ayelet. I despised the shabby performances required by these throwback "happenings" but once again had been pressed into service and stood as amiably as possible among the throng in the atrium in a ridiculously inauthentic period costume. Ayelet was deep into her Zelda persona already, clutching shoulders for support and asking loudly where the *fun* people had gathered. As she pushed her way through the crowd, her gaze fixed on me for a moment, held my line of sight so that there could be no mistake. By the time she reached your father, she had gone so far in her act as to affect a southern drawl. True to his nature, your father was charmed by the display, while your mother betrayed her mortification only through the slightest crinkling of her sharply defined nostrils.

Here was Ayelet's mode: she flitted off to Europe, played the damsel, reeled in a lonely old gentleman whose ready money could finance a string of avant-garde productions at her small theater in San Diego. She directed these productions and invariably reserved for herself a prominent role, if not the lead. Attendance was sparse, but she had become in her way a fixture of the community, and no doubt one day soon a Hollywood scout would take in a show. Eventually these sad old men would tire of her pernicious behavior and return home to sit in comfortable silence among the dust and ruin of their ancestral estates. And my mother would start again. She was engaged many times but to my knowledge married no one other than my father, and even all these years later I am not sure whether they ever properly divorced.

While I knew that since her arrival I had been waiting—I caught myself holding my breath—for the other shoe to drop, I never expected the critical moment to arrive in such a literal manner. The tension had risen in my system with her every sip of champagne. Her husky voice became louder, her abrasive laugh brayed with greater frequency, innuendo darkened slurred sentences. A song that she liked struck up, and she cocked her head in a queer and characteristic manner that I knew meant that Ayelet was about to dance. She kicked off one shoe with a rough force that upset a white-jacketed waiter's silver tray and sent him sprawling in an attempt to contain the damage. The other she slipped off in more ladylike fashion and held before her as a microphone, crooning and swaying to an old-fashioned swing number. When the song was over, the band did not start playing another right away. Everyone looked around the hall in nervous silence. Ayelet appeared perturbed briefly (she had expected applause, I think), held the shoe out to her side as far as her slender arm would stretch and dropped it from shoulder height. Its impact echoed impressively. She pushed aside a platter, sat down in the middle of a long serving table, and spoke through her disheveled tresses: "Now I want to meet the girl."

Well, you know how the rest of the evening went, and I don't want to think about it any more.

Eleven

When my alarm went off at 8 a.m., I shut it down rather than fingering the snooze bar. The twisted sheets showed that I had been thrashing around for a while. I sat on the edge of the bed and thought about the pieces that I needed to write for the magazine. Midday I got dressed and truly began feeling sorry for myself. It was with a measure of chagrin that I, after lolling around by the phone the day before with occasional lonely breaks in the dark hotel bar, admitted that the woman from the park (I had not secured even her name!) was not magically going to appear to take care of the messy details of my business. I decided to return to the low wall with the curious mortar in Kowloon and remain doggedly on task until the Cavanagh was put to bed. There also was the possibility that the woman frequented the park or lived nearby; it was where she had fallen into my lap—

101

metaphorically of course, you're so damn touchy on the subject of women—in the first place. As I left the hotel, I calculated that in three days' time I would have to send my new suit to be dry cleaned.

The journey enervated rather than invigorated me, for whatever reason. Callous reality crashing down on my laureled, weary head, you would say, have often said. Despite a general bottled-up loathing and sorrow I completed with little bother the strange commute. On that squat wall, its miniature crenellations stippled more or less permanently into my bottom going by sense memory, I strove like the Bard of Avon to persever, and there my will (and stomach) proved strong. Cavanagh be done be damned.

Looking around with blinking eyes, putting away in my jacket pocket the swaybacked book, the spine of which I had given quite a workout with my derisive flexing, I half expected to see across the paving stones the collimated lithe form of my shadow amanuensis. No one was there. I got up and really felt the damage I had done by sitting cross-legged for so long. A faux-antique clock face mounted incongruously on a modern metal utility pole showed that three and a half hours had passed. Needing badly to stretch and not yet ready to face the return trip to Central, I walked deeper into the park. Since I had no idea where I was going, I quickly fell into the practice of following the arrows on the park's rustic signposts denoting the turns leading to the aviary. Suddenly I was climbing, every turn the opposite of the last, ascending a steep hill through a series of switchbacks. As I rose the temperature seemed to swell around me, which was welcome at first as earlier I had been chilled but rapidly built to the level of discomfort. I was sweating profusely, cursing mildly, and waning constitutionally by the time I crested the butte. An expansive flat top spread out before me, with narrow paths winding among gigantic cages painted in a green-brown crosshatch to disappear somewhat among the foliage, I supposed. Benches dotted the winding ways, and I on autopilot sought one. The first supported a snoozing salaryman, who was sprawled in an improbable position, mouth wide open in the blissful grip of little Thanatos. I edged past his jutting unlaced brogues and secured the next bench, well down the path. I was seated opposite one of the enclosures, and therein squawked and flailed a motley of waterfowl.

On my side of the cage lay a pond, its far edge a pleasingly artificial arrangement of chipped stone. In the water front and center a white flamingo attempted over and again to stand, each try marginally less successful as the bird's strength and will seeped from its body. The head described wobbly little halos in the fetid air, the feathers clung in sparse tufts to its oily, bumpy skin. Two of its kind, slick feathers lightly blushing, stood to either side, screeched and fanned their wings. I at first mistook their excitement for some dim form of concern, as one witnesses among elephants; when they began circling with slow sidling steps, pale green eyes intent on their target, I recognized animal bloodlust. As my gaze broadened from the dramatic dance of the flamingos, so broadened my perception of the scene. The deterioration and back-biting were not merely a set piece at center stage but constituted a terribly generalized condition. Listing egrets, miserably floundering terns, and raucously squabbling ducks (normally so adorable and dignified) kept wary eyes on roving, strutting comrades of dubious loyalty. All was suffering in that infernal pen. Whatever gripped the fowl was in its end absolute, a question only of time. Strains of overheard newscasts, of the nervous chatter of fellow travelers, of the curt instructions of the highly alert guards at the infrared body temperature spot-check upon arrival at the airport came crashing to the fore. Was a new round of avian influenza wreaking havoc? I became convinced of latent memories to that effect.

In a blind rush of primordial fear I descended rapidly the slope, the clicking of my cane increasing with my heartbeat, the dolorous cacophony raging at my back. I kept it up right through the park and out into the thronged streets, presenting a farcical figure I fear. Finally I collapsed onto one of the pylons at the ferry terminal, wheezing hard for oxygen, taut nerves on fire from heel to crown. My vision swam. No one offered succor, even though a casual observer would have been forgiven for assuming that I was going into cardiac arrest. Over desperate minutes the panic subsided, the world subtly realigning itself all around me into some semblance of the everyday.

* * *

Back on the city isle among the evening crowds, I found myself wrung out and in need of comfort. Only one thing—two things taken together, really, but I think of them strictly as a unit—would do, and when I name it you surely will understand why since I on our thirteenth anniversary shared with you as an anodyne to our pre-dinner argument the buried vignette explaining its importance. Or maybe you have forgotten that evening entirely; you always did have a memory like a sieve and rarely carry grudges, thank goodness. At any rate I was in the grip of a mad craving for Dux soda crackers and Allowrie butter in their white and gold, tall and short tins. The problem was whether such prizes were easily (or at all) obtainable in Hong Kong. I decided that wandering indiscriminately but hopefully was at a late hour unlikely to end in happiness and instead pointed my lustrous, aching toes in the direction of the Four Seasons with the thought that the desk staff, though not exactly forthcoming, would perhaps prove capable of assisting a foreign guest with such a petition.

When I entered the building, some secret communication passed between the stiff doorman and a younger, more relaxed bellhop standing just inside. He in turn gave a hurried hand sign (gripping twice with his left white-gloved hand the top button of his uniform just beneath the crimson-slashed V of the neck cut) to the sharp middle-aged woman placed front and center behind the reception desk. She practically vaulted the board in her haste to intercept me. Her name tag, slightly askew I noticed right away, read "Dorothy."

"Mr. Makarov!" she panted. "You have a visitor."

When I raised an eyebrow to prompt her for more information, she did not at first catch the cue. I felt more and more adrift clutching my lapels and holding the arch as she came to her senses and responded.

"Over there by the fireplace," she said, pointing to an overstuffed chair supporting the woman from the park. "She has been here for a very long time, since shortly after lunch."

"Thank you for alerting me, Miss," I said and brushed past her on a clear vector. I had pinned too many hopes on my fair amanuensis to allow her to slip through my grasp again. As I approached the chair, I saw that she was engaged in some kind of stitchwork.

I stood, somewhat impatiently, at a discreet distance to allow her to become aware of my presence.

Without any indication that she had yet seen me, the woman folded neatly her nascent shawl and placed it gently into her large handbag. She smoothed her skirt, inspected her fingernails, stood with an almost inaudible grunt, and turned to face me. I thought that I saw a hint of a smile at the corners of her small mouth.

"I have decided," she said, hands held palms together beneath her breasts.

I waited with bated breath for her to continue, but she seemed to be playing some sort of game, arranging her features as serenely as possible and leaning forward slightly so that I could not ignore the dark pools—black on black, almost—of her almond eyes. Finally I broke.

"And?"

"I will help you."

"I'm thrilled, just thrilled!" I said, reaching out to shake her hand, which she steadfastly did not extend.

"We need to talk about the specifics."

"Of course, of course," I stammered, looking around for a place comfortably furnished but well out of earshot of others.

"Let's go to your room," she said and with a little nod started walking toward the elevators.

I was quite a few steps behind by the time I got moving and leaned on my cane more heavily than usual, thinking of a tactful way to suggest that negotiating somewhere else might be more appropriate. By the time I reached her an elevator had arrived, and she stepped quickly inside and held the doors for me. I puffed out my cheeks and, shoulders slumping with the sigh, hobbled into the confined space.

* * *

"If I am going to work for you," she explained, the two of us sitting side-by-side on the large bed with our hands in our laps, "it is important that you trust my instincts. I have a special method of divining what needs to be done that I have developed over the years through practicing meditation, contemplating ancient sacred texts in a strictly secular manner, experimenting boldly in large- and small-scale business settings, and playing competitive mahjongg. It may seem strange at first, but it really works. It is also important that you see my bare breasts."

"Now, wait a minute—" I gasped as she stood and began unbuttoning her blouse. Before I could do anything more, she was pulling open the front; she was not wearing a bra, so there they were. My mouth may have hung open a beat.

The breasts were remarkable, and not in the way you probably are thinking, dear, so hear me out. The left one drooped pendulously and was terribly wrinkled, looking for all the world as if it belonged to a much older woman. Around the edges the mottled skin even gave the impression of having been ravaged not by time but by fire. The right breast was smaller, the skin taut and smooth. A large, dark aureole surrounded the long, pert nipple. This specimen would have made any sorority initiate proud. She buttoned up before I had gawked to satisfaction, and as she did I noticed that she was not wearing a bra because her blouse was specially adapted to her condition, with a sturdy sling on the left and a padded cup on the right anchored by straps around the torso and across the shoulders. When cinched up, this mechanism gave her bust some semblance of symmetry. I wondered whether even her tai chi outfit was thus reinforced.

"Do you understand?" she asked.

I nodded, worried that she might insist on some sort of exchange, flesh for flesh or secret for secret. And I did feel that I understood, that her deformity, whatever its cause, *said* something profound about her as a unique, capable person, conveyed a deep sense of trustworthiness and an inexplicable aura of comfort. Asked to explain then or now *how* the experience of viewing her disparate breasts elicited those complicated thoughts and emotions, I surely would fumble.

She sat back down next to me on the bed. In one of the adjacent rooms, a drunken salaryman was singing "99 Bottles of Beer" and sobbing uncontrollably.

"All right," she said, drawing from her bag a small pad of dun paper with an attached bamboo pen. "Let's make a list. What do you need me to help you with first?"

"First," I began, glancing at the alarm clock, "I need to know whether two food items are available in Hong Kong and, if they are available, where I might find them at this hour. Tonight."

"Go ahead," she said, cocking her head slightly, pen poised to write.

"Allowrie butter and Dux soda crackers. They come in—"

She put away her writing gear and grabbed my hand.

"Come on, we have to hurry."

Twelve

My amanuensis went by "Mabel" and would tell me no other name. She gave me a business card beset with mysterious characters but also featuring prominently "Mabel."

"But what if you aren't around and I need to find you? Or what if there is an emergency?"

"Call the number, ask for Mabel."

She would not hear another word on the subject.

"First we need to get you set up to work," she said, going over our list. "You stay here, have a big lunch, keep your health up. I'll go shopping, bring back some of these items. Give me some money."

"I have not withdrawn much cash ..."

"Give me your credit card, then."

I felt uncomfortable being railroaded like this, but she stood there with her hand held out so expectantly that I complied with a defeated shrug of my shoulders. If she disappeared, then I would just have to cancel the card and instruct Caroline to order a replacement. And, I reminded myself in morning's cold light, I had decided just last night to put my trust in her. Without further comment Mabel left my room.

She had not spent the night, I suppose that I should get *that* out of the way right up front. When we had left the hotel, she had hustled me into a taxi and instructed the driver in barking Cantonese. Traffic was heavy, but we reached our destination, an upscale market known as Jason's, just before closing time. Blessedly, Mabel's intuition had been spot on and I— the final customer of the evening—left with a crackly waxed bag containing the two sought after tins (plus a small, fat jar of herring in yogurt and a tall, skinny one of pickled capers). She put me into a taxi and said that she would see me the next morning for an early start. On the way back to the hotel, I could not help myself and opened both tins, spreading satiny butter onto dimpled cracker with my forefinger. The driver was not pleased at my behavior and glared into the rear-view mirror rather than keeping his eyes on the road. When we arrived I paid strictly what the meter read.

My new assistant had not been fooling around about the early start. I was lolling about in my pajamas still when the sharp rapping came at the door. I could sense her impatience as I fumbled around with rumpled clothing, brushed my teeth, and splashed a bit of aftershave on my stubble-strewn neck. She said nothing about my disheveled appearance when I finally opened the door but pushed her way straight inside and got down to business, leading our little discussion and departing with my platinum card. After latching fast the heavy loop of the safety lock, I immediately shucked my stale raiment at the foot of the bed and got into the spacious shower.

* * *

It was 2:24 p.m. when Mabel returned to the hotel pushing a hand trolley laden with brightly colored boxes. It was a bitch maneuvering the thing into the room through the tight turn created by the arrangement of furniture around the entry door, but following considerable effort it occupied the space between the foot of the bed and the closet door, which I would no longer be able to access. My assistant assured me that if all went well this afternoon I would be checking out the very next day. I had trapped myself in the narrow space between the bed and the window and had to clamber across the wide mattress to gain the corridor, a terribly undignified business, and with Mabel looking on.

The gilded hands of the ornate clock in the lobby read 2:48 by my quick reckoning as we scooted through the revolving door and into a waiting taxi. I was having trouble keeping up, a hitch remaining in my step, and soon would have to be stern with my amanuensis (demote her to "secretary" even, if only in my mind and manner) if this relationship was going to work. She seemed to sense a change in my demeanor and was quiet for the first few minutes of our ride. As the taciturn driver made slow progress through the city, she suddenly began telling me—in a newly deferential way—what she had purchased to aid me in my work. I nodded as she ticked off the list. She had not gone too far beyond what I myself had suggested, and everything seemed sensible enough. She informed me that we were now traveling east, heading for a sliver of low-rise mixed-use buildings squeezed between a public park constructed over a disused waterworks and an expansive warehouse district, which was slowly consuming the old buildings despite their protected status. When we arrived at the property, I at first was certain that we were in the wrong place. Mabel, however, after scooting across the leatherette seat and settling up with the driver came around to my side, widened her eyes solicitously, and coaxed me out of the back of the cab. The neighborhood looked rough and unwelcoming, and I admit to feeling the beginning strains of panic as our erstwhile driver turned a corner and was lost to sight.

As my assistant fumbled with the lock—a large antique type requiring a curious tubular key—I took in the activity on the street and was calmed somewhat by its gentle rhythm. The sense of decay that had first seized me was fostered by the history of the buildings, which by their very nature had been constructed and expanded as resources allowed. The clusters leaning on one another in seeming commiseration, most rising two stories, a few an ambitious three or four, were ragtag, perhaps, but definitely not ramshackle. The people going about their business here were unlike the city folk to whom I had become accustomed. Instead of dashing thither and yon to some schedule of retrenchment airdropped from the heights of gleaming towers of late-capitalist influence, they ambled peaceably from door to door, in a pleasant, communal habit of profitably passing the days; all were old, I noticed, older than I at any rate. With a startling clack, Mabel attained entry to the property.

"We'll need to oil that if I decide on this place," I remarked as we sat in the vestibule on the raised floor of the main room to change into the slippers that my amanuensis withdrew from her bag, still in the plastic.

"No, there's a trick to it," she said. "I'll show you later."

The remainder of the first floor was at first blush unpromisingly abbreviated. A shop counter filled the back of the room off the vestibule, with barely enough space for both of us to stand before it. A small bench with embroidered cushions occupied the nook of the large front window. The plane of the counter ran from wall to wall, one of those hinged segments covering a narrow gap to the left to allow the shopkeeper to slip in and out while keeping customers in their place. As Mabel lifted the moveable segment and gently flapped it over onto the stationary span to allow us passage, I studied the grain of the wood and found it pleasing. Some fancy led me to decide that it was spruce, but as you know I am absolutely awful at identifying materials. I looked around at the walls, floor, and ceiling and noticed a very pleasant, woody fragrance in the air (a bit of mustiness, too, since the place had been closed up for some time). The floor planks were knotted and ancient looking, of a darker wood than or at least treated to a different finish from the slab of the service counter. The wall panels were carved with a geometric design that varied its step subtly just when the eye began to rebel against the uniformity. The ceiling was high, relieving claustrophobia if one would simply look up now and again; it seemed to be carved as well—the design was difficult to discern in the dimness—and was made of a very dark, almost black wood or had had a deep finish worked up in layers.

Mabel coughed into the sleeve of her jacket ahead of me in the short, narrow hallway straight back of the cut-out. I at first thought that she was trying to push me to view the building to her schedule and was annoyed at her presumption, but it turned out that she had inhaled some dust and choked on it. Her eyes watered as she showed me the little half-bath on the right and the ample storage closet on the left beneath the stairs. She opened the back door and gestured for me to take the lead.

Passing through a vestibule similar to the one in front but smaller, we entered a screened L-shaped walkway that enclosed a delightful little rock garden, which looked by its swept lines and lack of debris as if someone had been taking care of it. Two round doors, one in either arm of the walkway, opened onto the garden. The space felt like a temple annex because the walkway was constructed in miniature pailou style (like the gate at the entrance to Boston's Chinatown but painted bright red and carrying brick-red tile on its roof rather than mirroring that structure's green and white scheme). We lingered near the back door, running our palms over the smooth wood of the handrail as we looked into the garden. It was a very peaceful space, even if sounds of machinery could be heard, and speech seemed inappropriate.

When we went back inside, Mabel pointed out a small door that I had missed in the gloom of the vestibule. It led to a narrow kitchen overlooking the courtyard. I had noticed the windows from out there, but somehow it did not register that they must have belonged to an as yet unseen room. The utilitarian nature of the pleasant little space and the wear evident on some of the appurtenances made me think that it probably was the earliest of the additions. I moved to head back into the building, eager to see what awaited upstairs, and was startled by my assistant's wiggling backside. She was rummaging in the cabinets below the burners of the stove. Before I could object, she produced a cast iron kettle, filled it from the tap left of the burners, which were arranged in a row, placed it on the leftmost trivet, and turned on the gas. While the water was heating, she measured scoops of matcha into two ceramic bowls and set out a bamboo whisk.

* * *

I went into a sort of trance at that moment, when the little whisk clicked gently down on the oiled butcher's block of the counter. I traveled back in time. What had seized me was the memory of my first visit to the house on Beacon Hill, well after we had decided that we were to marry. I was—quite understandably, I am sure you will agree—terribly nervous about the evening. As I paced up and down the slope of the wide sidewalk before the magnificent gate, uncomfortable in my newly purchased suit and reeking of the

Spanish musk that you claimed your mother liked, you brought my peregrination to a halt with a deft cupping of my right elbow and whispered into my ear (it tingled, there in the small kitchen of the prospective property in Hong Kong, even as I experienced the memory in its terrible strength) that they probably could see us. Right, then. I gave my lapels a stern tug, stepped up to the intercom, pressed the button, and, despite being expected at the very hour and despite your claim that the masters of the estate were well aware of our presence already, announced myself in an awkwardly formal manner, taking my cue from the tone of the dogsbody whose electric voice on that first eventide seemed so commanding. With a hyperbaric pop the gate-cuff loosened, the imposing iron obstruction swinging just enough for us to squeeze through without snagging our finery.

"Theater," you murmured wryly. "Like the rigmarole in the antechamber of an ancient Egyptian temple. Meant to put the petitioner in a mindset of supplication. It opens wide for an automobile, of course."

You looped your arm through mine and leaned in as we slowly traversed the central cobblestone way of the front gardens. It was late summer, and the faint sine of fading cicadas accompanied our languid walk. The air smelled of heliotrope, and the cooing of nightbirds promised that much lay hidden in the carefully tended boughs and the webwork of roots. That would have been enough for me, the moonlit walk and a hasty return to the cozy nest of our small apartment on the edge of campus. Instead we pushed forward toward the light of the many fixtures surrounding the grand arch of the entry, you straightening into a proper posture and summoning that blank but brilliant smile that your mother and governess had championed from a tender age. You returned the overly familiar greetings of the footmen with good grace and a hint of flirtation.

I was overwhelmed. I knew what to expect, but the reality (or more precisely the practiced way in which everything was entirely unreal but no one deviated a syllable from the script) of the opulence and depravity and entitlement pummeled me into stupefaction. Your father—well, you are his daughter, of course you know him—was *mean* in both of the common senses of that adjective. He insulted me and my family from the moment I entered his halls. You seemed disappointed in me, on several levels, but I could not make myself care about performance under such withering and entirely unprovoked assault. I blanched and was, by the time we were seated in the parlor with figs and brandy, on the verge of violence for the first time in my life.

Your mother defused the situation, through insistence on decorum rather than due to any measure of fellow feeling, steering the conversation toward our academic progress and casting subtle reproachful looks at your father as he fussed with his pocket handkerchief in the cool grooves of the ancestral andirons. When one of the maids (you later told me that these people were basically actors, that your father employed but a single full-time domestic servant and the coachman, putting on this grand illusion anytime guests were to be entertained; you also said that *everyone* knew of the charade) entered with the aim of moving us to our next station, your father made a great show of scolding her over the state of the fireplace, how it could not possibly be particularly difficult to keep it clean during the summer. For a moment the maid's countenance took on a hard veneer, and her hands flew to her hips. Before she could say anything, your mother dismissed her with that expert kind but curt delivery that is worse than a flailing. It was at that point that I withdrew into myself, only to process the remainder of the evening in the safety of our nest, with the aid of your patient, wry deconstructions.

* * *

The tea was ready. We quietly sipped it and nibbled rice pastries that Mabel produced from a small decorative box. Her handbag clearly was a place of mysteries. She mentioned between sips that rumors were swirling that Chinese agents had compromised the water supply; obviously she scoffed at such scaremongering. When we had finished our serene collation, she gestured for me to take the lead as we left the kitchen and climbed the narrow stairs to the sleeping quarters. I confess that despite my condition I took the steps two at a time.

The upper floor was quite snug, a trait that I at first blush counted against it. A gentleman, after all, is expansive, needs rambling room. As I stood mulling the arrangement—there was not much to mull up there, a modest bedroom, a very small room that probably had been used as another bedroom, perhaps for several children, and an attractive bathroom of respectable size (the whole family had been crammed in there at times, no doubt)—I began to notice the details. The intricate carving, representing years of close work and telling a story of that if of nothing else, that I had noticed on the downstairs panels covered practically every surface. Occasional whimsical touches—a frilly dragon in the alcove in the smaller room, a little troll family behind the commode, fanciful growth marks at the head of the staircase—spoke of the fun that the craftsman had had with his children. A companionway, which Mabel urged me to ascend once I had discovered it, led to a nook at the apex of the building. The peaked room was for lounging, tall enough for a man to stand only in the center. A comfortable-looking mat was placed next to a large round window overlooking the twisting side street. Low shelves ran down the walls at the point where one would have to begin crouching to proceed. I was not sure what they were for but imagined that they had once held netsuke or the like. The place was made for the sort of reading and writing requiring quiet contemplation. And the shop level and garden were perfect for the more journalistic sort needing engagement and bombast. All in all, a most fitting atelier. I stayed in the pleasant space for some time, alone as my assistant had wisely not crowded in behind me.

When I had descended the smooth rungs of the ladder, I was happy not to see my amanuensis. It had been next to impossible to stop my derrière waggling in the confined space. I found Mabel in the front vestibule, barking instructions to a young man in a blue jumpsuit. Glancing in my direction, he gave her a weird kind of salute and scurried out the door.

"It's suitable, Mabel," I said. "But what is the rent?"

"Surprisingly reasonable."

"Well ..."

"Well within your means," she said.

"Good, I'll take it. Have—"

"I told the agent this morning that you would be renting the property. A carrier is fetching your things from the hotel, and a delivery of linens and sundries has already arrived. You will sleep here tonight."

I was dumbstruck and not a little affronted. True, I had given her the task of finding, as quickly as possible, a place that fit my specifications. I had told her that I would trust her judgment. But this usurpation of my authority stung, the more so because her reckoning had been dead accurate. I decided to leave any discussion of the matter for another day.

Thirteen

I was terribly disoriented in the morning. Mabel had made sure that I possessed everything that I needed to get through the night and have a reasonable start to the day. She insisted that we get the place whipped into shape over the weekend so that my first work day would be auspicious. She was going to bring lunch from a stall at the end of the street. Still, it was my first morning in a new place, and I stumbled around like a drunkard, making a hash of everything from brushing my teeth to steaming pork buns and making coffee. There was so much novelty to take in and process that I felt overwhelmed and sat glumly on the bench after breakfast and watched the street life through the streaked front window. Lunch could not come quickly enough.

When my amanuensis arrived she sprang onto the scene in a most comical manner, shuffling in ass backward and sitting with a heavy sigh on the little platform next to the step up from the vestibule. I went to investigate.

"You're quite a sight!" I exclaimed, a little punchy from my unsettled forenoon.

"Take this top one," she grunted, with a measure of disgust. I could now see that she carried a stack of graduated boxes that must have come close to toppling as she messed with the door, so she had bent to trap the cargo between chin and thigh. I felt bad because of my attitude and hurried to comply with her request.

The top box contained the new (to me) notebook computer that I had requested. I immediately took it to the counter and scored the tape seal with a key. I pulled at the front flap, and with a pop the upper panel flew wide. The computer and its charger were packed in a nest of crumpled brown paper grocery bags. I impatiently pulled the components free from the batting and turned them over in the light.

"The battery is no good," said Mabel coming into the room.

"It's all right. I'll keep it plugged in."

"That was very hard to find. Why do you want to use such an old computer?"

"I cannot abide the newer models. Glossy 3-D touchscreen bullshit, always leaping out to demand one's attention. Keyboards with keys like almond slivers, can barely tell whether one has been pressed ..."

"Instead you get all this: ugly as sin gray and white plastic body, battery that doesn't work, thing's probably slow, too. Heavy as well, almost four pounds. Without the charger!"

"Where did you find it? A specialty dealer? What else did he have?"

"Junk shop," she said, rolling her eyes. "I'm going back out for our lunch."

I got into the other packages while she was gone. All contained rather commonplace office necessities, but I was determined to arrange the supplies to my liking to encourage the relationship with my employee back into the vicinity of its natural railbed if not exactly onto the tracks. The matrix of pigeonholes behind the counter made categorizing and storing the supplies a simple, almost pleasurable pastime. The situating of the computer proved more problematic. My first inclination was to set it up on the counter, where I could sit or stand as the mood took me, where I could watch the life of the street between bursts of typing. But then, whither Mabel? Confining her to the narrow kitchen would seem like punishment. The garden was spacious enough, but the weather would not always be clement. The upstairs was to be for living, my private quarters. Plus, the phone connection was next to the counter, and sources, clients, delivery people and other visitors might come to the door. No, clearly the secretary belonged up front, as was customary. Because of the system's condition, I could not roam but needed a station at which to work; by the time the tinkling of the front bell signaled the arrival of lunch, I still had not decided and was feeling a little foolish about insisting on such an antique.

We ate lunch—plastic tubs of some provincial soup consisting of a lovely light broth (made from a whole small chicken, two pig's feet, and a duck head with neck, Mabel explained) bobbing with small meatballs and dumplings, a pleasantly springy plain steamed bun wrapped in foil on the side—standing in the kitchen looking over the garden. We did not speak. I could tell by the ease of the arrangement that this would become our habit.

When we had finished, Mabel with a curled arm swept our leavings into an oddly shaped orange refuse bin that she had stashed next to the small refrigerator and at some point fitted with a liner. Just like that the galley looked as if we had never dined in it at all. We washed our hands and returned to the front room.

"We will set the computer up on the counter, there at the corner," I suddenly decided. If my amanuensis were to pay for herself, to truly earn the title, then there was no other way. "You will need a tall chair that is also comfortable. I will pace back and forth here in front of the window and dictate. Have you ever taken dictation, Mabel?"

"Not in English, but I'm sure I can manage."

"Good. We'll get started this afternoon."

* * *

It did not go well. I, unaccustomed to giving dictation and prone to digression, meandered and backtracked until the piece—a long introduction to the issue explaining the freshness of matters doctrinal, latitudinal, and the like—was a complete mess. Mabel, for her part, kept substituting familiar but incorrect words for the admittedly obscure, sometimes archaic polysyllabic phraseology with which I season my speech and writing (in just the right proportion, of course, and never enough to slip into the sesquipedalian) to lend it the appropriate gravitas. I sent her home and finished the work myself, sipping tepid green tea well into the night, sidling up to the keyboard in canny feints and determined advances continually. I transmitted the introduction to Caroline, the sting of whose crop I at this point felt keenly, shortly before midnight and began work on the Cavanagh review after a restorative stroll around the dusky rock garden.

Fourteen

Again I woke in confusion. Soreness gripped my limbs and some emotion, that which you accuse me perennially of lacking, played havoc with my slowly forming morning thoughts. The room, still strange, seemed to arrange itself around me as I swam toward consciousness. When I sat up, I lost my equilibrium for a terrifying moment and felt the nearness of the abyss. I shuffled into the bathroom and splashed my face with cold water, brushed my teeth with an odd, purplish toothpaste that tasted of licorice. I had grown accustomed to my altered appearance, had grown even to like it in a mysterious, ghoulish way, and thus noted with a twinge of disappointment that my most prominent bruises had faded further. The pain had fled almost entirely, and at this point I could use my condition to startle others into silence or to drink in their sudden sympathy (or so I imagined; I had tested the supposition only by walking up and down the street in front of the office). I did a few light stretches on the floor of the bedroom. My loose pajamas facilitated these, so I liked to perform the routine first thing before heading down to the kitchen.

As I gazed out over the garden while waiting for the tea to steep, I came to the ineluctable conclusion that I would have to ring Mabel to apologize. She had said, after all, that the plan was to outfit me with office supplies, to get everything set up for a proper start on Monday morning. Instead I had launched directly into the tasks on my list and had kept her there with me well after normal working hours. She had not uttered a word of complaint, but since I knew next to nothing about her I had no idea whether she had had to cancel plans with friends, whether family might have been waiting for her, relying on her. I let out a sigh that fluttered my slightly distended lips.

The tea was very good.

* * *

Fortified by a large bowl of abalone juk and two additional cups of oolong, I hunched contentedly over the whirring laptop and read at my leisure and with sharp pleasure last night's scholarly evisceration of that punk Cavanagh. The review was long at 6,212 words, but this morning's reading confirmed that it did not require further editing. I forwarded the piece to Caroline and answered some of her messages, making executive decisions with a dispatch that I had been unable to muster in the Boston office.

Remember how we started out at 615 Boylston, in that low-ceilinged room above the copy shop? As I signed my John Hancock at the feet of the introductions to those early issues, I stared through the thick smoked glass at that architectural monstrosity across the square. It took me a year and a day to convince your father that such modest digs were not appropriate for a literary magazine of scope and ambition. When we finally moved to a spacious suite on a lofty floor in one of the barbs of the High Spine, I felt it a personal triumph, that we could at last project our voice, have some meaningful influence on the culture. What I was building for *Lit* in Hong Kong felt of similar significance.

I put off calling Mabel until late afternoon, and when I dialed the number on her card, ring after ring came down the line. No machine answered, either, so I left things as they were. I had made an honest attempt.

* * *

Evening found me suffering from cabin fever. Worse, though my larder was stocked it was full of unfamiliar ingredients, and I had had my fill of the exotic and, frankly, of cooking for myself. I set about searching the Web for restaurant reviews and was miffed to find a good many sites that required a newer browser than my computer was capable of running. In the end, I jotted down several options that were near one another, changed into my on-the-town clothes, and summoned a taxi.

The first establishment was dreadful. Upon passing the somewhat tasteful, entirely hopeful rattan-and-pitch entry, my senses were assaulted by a cacophony of electronic sitar twiddled over the top of a relentless wubba of bass and a thick haze of cloying patchouli smoke. In the dim vastness of the interior, colored lights strobed and bodies writhed. The desperately enthusiastic swarthy greeter informed me that the food was *modern*. This hopelessly current fare he, while wringing his hands like a car salesman, described as "world cuisine, with a tantalizing hint of the Indian subcontinent." Please, he implored, let me take you on a culinary journey. I turned on my heel and beat as hasty a retreat as I could manage, cane clicking along the uneven flagstones. The driver chuckled as I ducked back into his cab, shaking my head.

The next restaurant on the list was an Italian joint, and having experienced dismal Asian interpretations of Italian-American standbys of life-altering magnitude, having heard well the hushed horror stories of experienced fellow travelers at uptown literary soirées and in cramped airport martini lounges, I came close to instructing the driver to pass it by. More the fool I. Something about the understated exterior presentation, some old-fashioned quiet confidence, prompted me at the last moment to deign to reconnoiter. And what a scene I discovered! The receiving room was very nearly as sterile as a hospital's. A dignified gentleman in white tails said not a word as I approached. I sensed immediately that this hardened quality was calculated to turn away those who did not belong. I stepped past the guardian, who broke character and betrayed a hint of surprise at my audacity, and peeked through the heavy curtains into the intimate dining hall. At myriad tables finely laid with the crispest of starched white linen supped fanciful characters of centuries past. Cutlery rose and fell in practiced rhythm, held delicately in pinkie-up hands poised carefully at the curves of daintily turned wrists. I even glimpsed a monocle in the subtle clamor, if I recall correctly. I instructed the man in white to settle matters with my driver (shoving into his gloved hands the fare plus a ridiculously inflated tip), and when he returned promptly I discreetly slipped him a letter of introduction, that is a blue bill of outsize denomination. He pocketed it deftly with a professional's composure, not as much as an eyebrow hair out of place, and passed me off to the maître d'hôtel, a formidable silent androgynous figure in soft scarlet with agelessly smooth skin and a real-or-not pencil mustache.

Beneath the veneer of genteel refinement lay a tell-tale decadence, the singular component of the hoary class system that does not on solitary contemplation cause my skin to crawl. The expressions forming on the floating faces of the diners were orgiastic, transcendent. Some sucked hard black brothy mussels, others with their tiny tridents speared surreptitious tastes of slow-roasted pigeon, more still covered deliciously puckered lips with index knuckles between stimulating sips of Prosecco. About a third of the figures were non-Asian. I was led to a small table at the front, quite close to the stage, which at the moment stood empty, its center fuzzed with soft golden fill from the barrels of the anodized spots above. I was seated not facing the platform, but on the left side of the small table. The shifting of attention was gradual, decorous. You know that I have an uncanny ability to read a room, so I felt as a rippling prickling of the short hairs on my tense neck the collective movement. The newcomer here was not common, clearly, but the strange, unaccompanied male also was not unknown and provided just enough of the *other* to titillate, a pleasant disruption of the evening's routine festivities. That sentiment could just as easily and quickly turn in the opposite direction, I knew. My face became as sculpted wax; I focused on the grosgrain texture of the stiff tablecloth, which warped slightly in the glow of the freshly lighted candle in its blue cup there at the center of things.

As is my custom when first visiting a restaurant, I ordered very little (the proprietors despise this, and how their staff handles the situation quickly reveals the worth of the establishment)—a bowl of bagnun and a glass of Barbaresco. The waiter betrayed no discomportment and whisked away the scant menu with a curt but deferential inclination of his neatly pomaded head. While I waited, and I knew from the data collected thus far that the wait would be substantial and worthwhile, I folded my hands in my lap and allowed the world to shrink to a single candela boundary. The murmur of dinner conversation ceased abruptly, leaving me moored happily in a sphere of terrifying specificity. The trick was one that I had learned in adolescence; it had served me well in countless trying situations, but there was very real mental danger in lingering in such a created space. On this occasion I, like a subject seemingly forgotten overnight in a German university psychology department's antiquated isolation chamber, forcefully regressed.

* * *

Your father's offer caught me by surprise. I for months had been applying like a fiend, regularly falling asleep at the kitchen table over mountains of paperwork, for every position in Boston and New York that related even tangentially to my MFA studies. You will of course remember, everyone of our generation will remember, how scarce jobs were during that decade. Your father, wealthy and insulated, knew nothing and attributed the unemployment epidemic to a serious lack of gumption on the part of these green-as-fairway-grass youngsters. As the months wore on, my situation became an acute embarrassment (your subsidized charity endeavors, of course, were entirely within bounds; why should *his* daughter ever have to work?) to him at the club.

The invitation was innocuous enough, a terse message that bing-ed into existence on my phone one Wednesday afternoon requesting the pleasure of my company at brunch the following day. He did this from time to time, summoned me for a brief audience, so I thought nothing of it beyond minor and reflexive annoyance. The engagements were usually for show, opportunities for word to get back to you that he was *concerned*, that your satisfaction was still at the forefront of his expansive thoughts, little princess. I donned the black mantle of duty time and again, enjoyed despite myself if truth be told the respite provided by the sumptuous meals and the refined atmosphere of their languid consumption. I had prepared myself—shaving thoroughly, smiling into the mirror until my face ached, downing seven ounces of coconut rum, the last bottle in the cabinet—for the encounter, but that Thursday was to be dramatically different.

I should have known right away from his reticence. We need a word far stronger than "uncharacteristic" to describe how anomalous was his behavior, but I was so preoccupied with surviving the afternoon that I did not at first take notice. He had ordered for us, as was his wont, before I arrived, but this time the courses were varied and strange, almost as if he had chosen each dish by the roll of a die. Small dun steamed clams presented a common enough point of entry, but the tangy lemon-asparagus risotto that followed startled the palate. After a few forkfuls apiece, we placed our delicately curved silver utensils tines down on the upper edges of our gilt plates. When the waiter arrived, with a dubious expression on his face, it must be said, carrying the black pudding, your father waved him away with irritation, that ridiculous Super Bowl ring flashing in the slanting light. Finally he broke his silence.

"Anatoly," he began, "I've been thinking. Well, that is to say, Irina and Sophia have been pestering me about philanthropy. They think that we don't do enough. You know that I do not buy into that white

guilt nonsense, or the class warfare stuff ... but anyway, you know how the women must be appeased
from time to time."

This last he said with a knowing smile, and
raised his eyes to meet mine, seeking confirmation of
our trials with the weaker sex. Not knowing where
this was going, I did my best to meet his expectations.

"So I've been thinking," he continued. "I'm sick
to death of the videos of vacant-eyed children in dark-
est Africa with flies on their lips. And the last time I
gave a sop to those vile greenies, they turned around
and used it against my mining interest. What I'm saying is that I'm tired of that shit. I'll not do it any-
more. Our aims are at odds, and that will not change.
I give them money, but they never give me anything.
I'm finished with that. Done. No one will meet me
halfway, it seems. So I'm looking toward the arts."
Here he paused dramatically. He seemed to expect
something from me. I sensed nothing beyond disaster
but tried hard to appear intrigued.

"Go on," I urged.

"I considered sculpture. You know how Irina
loves it. But some of it would end up in the garden, in
the conservatory. We're full up with little marble
pricks as it is, you know. You've seen them! No, that
would not do. Nor would Irina's various other artistic
interests, which all somehow come back to roost in
our home. This time it should be my decision. It is my

139

money, after all. I have always admired the written word—as much as I admire any such thing, I mean—above the other fine arts. The sort of education that one squanders in its pursuit has always seemed more noble, more useful than that of the competition. So, I am going to fund a literary magazine. Sophia tells me that so many have folded over the last twenty years that it is a rather small world. I could make quite an impact under such circumstances with a surprisingly modest outlay, don't you think?"

* * *

The soup and wine were transcendental. So pleased was I that the band's preparations passed unnoticed. Their blaring trumpet intro caught me utterly by surprise. My leg jerked, knocking sharply against the underside of the cleared table, spoiling the serenity of my postprandial drifting and, I feared, lessening to some degree my cultivated foreign mystique. When the waiter came by to refill my wine glass, I tried to wave him off, content with the satisfying and lingering balance of my recent intake.

"Service," he whispered as he filled the vessel perilously close to its rim. I knew that in East Asia the word meant that the pour was complimentary. My resistance evaporated.

I enjoyed very much the band's first few songs. The singer, who also played the alto saxophone competently, had the stage presence and style that is so often absent in the younger musicians. The range was narrow, light jazz and pared big band standards, but with age I have learned to accept succor where it is offered without worrying too deeply whether my blushing pleasure signals a loss of edge. When the second (tall!) glass of Barbaresco took hold, I experienced that shift in consciousness that means it is time to go home—the music was suddenly too loud, the stage lights too bright, the cigarette smoke thick in my nostrils, the table conversation, which I had been successful in ignoring, crashing around me.

I summoned the waiter and paid the bill. As I swiveled in my chair to stand, which was difficult because my legs had gone numb, I noticed a small card in the center of the table. The very plain envelope was addressed to me, using my full name. I slipped it into my breast pocket as I rose.

Fifteen

Since I had been quite tired when I left the restaurant and had worried needlessly about making myself understood to the taxi driver, the envelope had gone unopened until midmorning. Not that I lazed around or anything, Tanya. In fact, I felt a deep obligation to be ready to work when Mabel arrived at seven. It was during the first tea break that I remembered what lay in the pocket of my jacket that was draped over the armchair in the corner of the bedroom. Once we had finished our modest but delightful collation, I excused myself and mounted the steps two at a time, pulling myself upward with the aid of the rail.

The plain envelope contained an equally understated invitation. The pleasure of my company was cordially requested at a midweek secret floating ball. I was to arrive at pier 131 on the west end of the harbor at least thirty minutes prior to the launch time of

2:55 a.m. on Thursday. I put the note back in the pocket of the jacket after I read it.

I did not mention the invitation to Mabel but had her commission as a rush order a fresh dapper outfit at the shop of a tailor whom she trusted (decidedly not the intemperate fellow with whom I earlier had dallied) and put her on the trail of a capable milliner. That digression put to bed, we whiled away the afternoon like workers in a real office, devising healthful and shrewd directives for the stalwart crew back at *Lit.*

Sixteen

Your father has often accused me of lacking staying power. Knowing how all men feel about their daughters, I have often fantasized about rejoining, "Not true at all! Just ask our dear Tanya." An exaggerated mummer's wink or a lascivious car-salesman grin would necessarily follow. (Calm down! I have never actually been so impertinent.) It is true that once I have a project well underway my enthusiasm dwindles as I begin searching for the next big thing on which to focus my burning attention. Despite this tendency, which many entrepreneurs would regard as positive indeed, I have never shirked my duties.

Thus I found myself flailing a bit in the grip of a vague dissatisfaction. *Lit*'s new direction boldly scripted and impressively launched, I felt like a boy with a stick who had goaded a hoop over the crest of a gentle hill and now needed only to poke at it occasionally when it wobbled to keep things on their course.

I thought suddenly that what I needed—what our little Hong Kong office suite desperately needed—was a samovar. Though I appreciated quite deeply the quality of the delicate green tea that Mabel brought and prepared (and even the occasional somewhat more substantial late-day "red" tea that she seemed to hold in reserve as a minor reward), I longed for a good black cup, strong and bitter. It was a trifle to find some export Caravan, which my secretary looked down upon as "adulterated oolong." I told her that I wanted to go to the antique shop from which I had purchased my walking stick to inquire about a samovar. She evinced skepticism, having heard through whatever network she cultivated that the proprietor was a charlatan. I remained firm, and she sulkily arranged our transportation.

* * *

Mr. Hu was conspicuously disconcerted by our arrival. He hemmed and hawed behind his counter, wringing his wrinkly brown hands and shifting his weight from foot to foot. Eventually he made some show of clacking around with his English placards, throwing them down in disgust as my assistant stepped up to my side. He perfunctorily excused himself and pushing through a vaginal parting of heavy yellow curtains gained the stockroom. He was back there so long that I began to suspect that he had escaped down a pope hole. When Hu emerged, he hissed something at Mabel that to my ears sounded thoroughly malevolent. Her hand flew to her mouth, and I at first assumed that she was shocked and offended by the antisocial behavior and reached out to cup her elbow, to guide her straight out of that venomous den. Soon it became clear that she was attempting to conceal a soft smile.

"He apologizes for his indigestion," she whispered directly into my ear.

When questioned about samovars, Mr. Hu led us directly to his small selection. One was sheathed in chrome, which you know I cannot abide. Another was ridiculously ornate, and initially I was drawn to it. The interior, however, suffered from shocking neglect. It would have taken a concerted effort to remove the thick green scale and bring the vessel to a more or less neutral aroma. The third and final specimen was as utilitarian as they come, stainless steel and of somewhat ugly design. Inside and out it was spotlessly clean and presented no disagreeable bouquet. The price—hastily inflated by at least a token percentage, going by the sudden shifting of Mr. Hu's eyebrows when he was queried—was reasonable. After asking hopefully whether I might be interested in other items for the home, the proprietor carried the bulky samovar to his counter to wrap with paper and stash inside a sturdy and voluminous canvas bag.

While Hu performed these workaday tasks, Mabel and I casually wandered the maze of goods, she frequently commenting under her breath that any given item was readily available and probably a third of the price at a regular market, I keeping my mouth shut. It was pleasant in a homey way to listen to her grumbling while clicking along the time-worn boards. At the flaring nub of a dead-end aisle, I was confronted by a sight that made me drop my stick. It smacked heavily against the floor, startling several small sparrows from their hidden nests in the gloom above. A shaft of flaxen light from the large front windows fell upon a garden pedestal supporting a curiously out of place and terribly familiar object: the bawdy mermaid brooch from your jewelry box, lately of my rolling luggage.

"This, this, this," I sputtered.

"Yes?" asked Mabel, puzzled by this behavior but clearly concerned at my sudden high dudgeon.

"This is mine!"

Mr. Hu came over to see what was causing the commotion.

"Where did you get this?" I demanded, rounding on him furiously.

He gave a helpless, unhappy look as my secretary translated this and the following questions, delivered in rising intonation and ending in a sort of feral shriek.

"He says that it has been in the shop for years —"

"He lies! Liar! This was stolen from my bag while I was in the hospital! Where did you get this, old man? Who sold it to you?"

"He says that he doesn't remember ..."

I picked up my walking stick and stormed lividly to the counter, where I wrapped my arms around the samovar in its rough sack and proceeded imprudently down the stairs without the aid of cane or rail. Mabel was hot on my heels, trying unsuccessfully to wrest the package away from me. Her quick hand kept me from falling the last few steps.

"You haven't paid for that," she said.

I badly wanted to walk away with my parcel, to steal something from those who (even if indirectly) had stolen from me. In the end sense prevailed, as I had had enough of Hong Kong lawmen and their Eastern perception of justice, and I handed my wallet to Mabel and sent her back inside to pay for the samovar *and* the brooch, which she brought down in a royal purple velvet pouch held in front of her like a fine handbag.

Seventeen

This day was not a day of work. I paced and fretted as I am inclined to do when anticipating a gathering of even minor importance. Worried that the tailor would not come through with a timely delivery or that some sartorial disaster would require alterations for which there was no margin, I pinged around the place all morning in a dark mood.

For her part, Mabel sorted and filed the papers and correspondence that I had allowed to pile up on the countertop. I had warned her not to touch them, but since I was giving her no direction she became determined to do as she damn well pleased. I still had not told her anything about the party, gave no hint as to the cause of my agitation. Though she looked perturbed and obviously was aware that today things were quite different around the office, she refrained from prying.

We took a silent but civil lunch of baguette and kippers in the stone garden. The air finally carried a hint of the autumnal crispness that awakens my blood. A perambulation of the neighborhood would do me great good, I resolved.

My secretary came to the window as I hastened down the street after having but mumbled "out for a stroll" from the vestibule before making my escape. I had become something of a recluse, feeling safe and whole embedded in the constructed miniature universe of my home and office but bewildered and fragmentary when assaulted by the lively otherness of the surrounding streets. I had been meaning to address this imbalance that threatened rapidly to become mode, but time and again the impetus eluded me. Well, the kick in the backside had come from unexpected quarters!

At the first intersection, I experienced a mild panic attack. It was one of those weird confluences of ways that led to wedge-shaped buildings in the interstices and chaotic conflict between conveyances attempting to take one or another of the confusingly labeled turns. The possibility of losing my way on this little jaunt had me patting down my pockets. My wallet was with me, and in it was the scrap of paper with my address. If worse came to worst, I could get a cab driver to return me to my rightful place, assuming that I could find an avenue from which to hail one.

Bolstered momentarily, I selected a spoke more or less at random and continued my walk.

Not far up the lane that I had selected sparkled the appealing front glass of a little convenience store. It did not seem to be very busy, a condition for which I always check by pressing my face in at the side opposite the register before entering any such shop with narrow aisles, so I entered and searched the small newsstand for an English daily. It did not take me long to choose between the two options. The paper was free and thin as the surviving print rags all are these days. Feeling too self-conscious simply to grab my prize and go, I bought a chilled can of espresso, the first thing my eyes encountered in the refrigerated case. The can was a deep chocolate brown and fit in the palm of my left hand in a very satisfying manner, sweating out its cool. In lighter brown was depicted a listing gentleman in a bowler, who seemed to be winking as he slumped to the pavement. I thought passingly of Poe.

What I needed was a park, or at least an out of the way bench near a tree or shrub. Down the avenue to my left, four serious-looking young louts in mirror-shades and the helmeted black uniforms of the military police were bundling a confused elderly man into an unmarked van. I set off in the opposite direction at a brisk pace, swiveling my head to catch the views between buildings down the side streets. I was hardly using my walking stick and marveled at how little stiffness remained (I would, of course, continue to carry the cane, as I adored it as an accessory and had resolved to keep it always about my person). Blocks passed in comfortable reverie. The cries of gulls pierced my consciousness, and turning in the direction of the sound I discovered that a narrow but lovely esplanade had opened up beyond the buildings to my right. I hurried toward the sparkling water.

I had to walk some way up the cobblestone path to find a suitable bench, one made of wood rather than concrete, nicely shaded by a mature bauhinia, and set well back from the metal rail that kept pickled promenaders from tumbling into the sea. I unfolded my newspaper, which had spreading ink in spots as a result of my switching the coffee can from hand to hand, and placed it beside me on the acacia slats, as much to discourage anyone from sitting there as to foster a pleasant reading environment. After wiping the rim of the can with my shirtsleeve, I pulled the tab and took an experimental sip. On the front of the palate, the coffee tasted fine, surprisingly good for espresso from a can. As one swallowed, however, a strange bitterness like that of Seville oranges asserted itself; following the firm depression of the epiglottis that this prompted, a curious, incongruous flood of quite distinct grapefruit tang filled the dilating debouchure. An interesting potation experience under laboratory conditions, perhaps, but not something I would care to repeat.

The lead story dwelled indecently upon the shocking death toll—193 and counting—from an illegally overloaded Bangladeshi ferry that had capsized late at night. Apparently the drunken, unlicensed helmsman had steered the vessel straight into the broad side of a barge carrying drums of depleted uranium down the crowded Meghna River. The photo spread following deeper in the A section was predictably a close study of wailing and the gnashing of teeth, the tearing of hair and cloth, the muted anger brimming the eyes of the bereaved. I had had enough of the news.

I leaned back against the gently tilted plane of the bench and laced my fingers behind my head. A sharp pain, a hitch yet in my abused muscles, rilled across the middle of my back. I closed my eyes and bore with it until the sensation subsided. A great weariness overtook me, progressing like thick paint downward from my temples. I was suddenly uninterested in my impending outfit, uninterested in the distraction of attending the floating fête, which seemed in my present mood to be the sort of high society idyll —an excuse for wealthy men to sip champagne, snort cocaine, and plow one another's trophy wives in an environment safely isolated from media and law enforcement—that I should have expected it to be all along. I wanted nothing more than to fossilize on that park bench, to become a perch for pigeons and seabirds, a curiosity for harried urbanites dipping into the serenity of the esplanade, taking a few restorative steps to the sound of surf, fleeing the city without actually leaving it. It could have happened, Tanya, through some hiccup in the cosmic ordinances. I felt *this* close to unfathomable infinity. And then I was rudely jolted to quaking vitality by the arrival of Zero.

The bench was of heavy construction and I, no lightweight after years of consolatory delectation, was seated firmly on it, but the entire apparatus moved a good few inches when he sat forcefully on my newspaper. He was young, early twenties maybe, and wore faded blue jeans, tattered black sneakers, and a lurid new pink T-shirt with a large stylized naught on the chest. 0. Kids these days! He leered across his left shoulder, just daring me to say something. I did my best to ignore him, knowing that feeding such desperate wild youths (from having been one myself, naturally) simply prolongs their maladroit flagellation. Zero, however, was not so easily thwarted. He thrust his long legs out in front of him in a wide arrangement, bumping against my right knee as he settled into his practiced slouch, and rested his occipital protuberance on the top slat of the bench's back. He did not remain long in repose but soon enough began alternately arching his back and slamming it against the slats, rocking the bench alarmingly with each blow. My paper crackled beneath his gyrating bottom.

Why have a contest of wills with this imbecile? My instinct is never to back down, but what would it have served? The whelp's education was not my responsibility. I stood and, with as much dignity as I could summon, straightened my jacket, adjusted my hat, brushed my sleeves, and turned to go back in the direction from which I had entered the esplanade, my fearsome cane brandished before me and a sharp look of disdain lasered down the steep piste of my aristocratic nose at the air above the hooligan's glistening spiky hair, where the dark pools of his eyes should have been had he been sitting properly. A smirk of triumph creased his taut young physiognomy.

In the abstraction of my black mood, silently fuming as my soft soles whisked the sidewalk, I had no trouble retracing my steps and soon found myself clattering into the vestibule—tiny! suddenly it seemed so cramped and mean—of my home and office. I shouted for Mabel but received no reply. I looked around for her with mild irritation, expecting to espy her deliciously occupied in the kitchen or garden. I discovered not even a note.

* * *

The new outfit arrived shortly after four o'clock. The winded lad who stoically bore his burden knew not what to do with the handsome tip I tendered into his sweaty slim fingers and stood shifting on the threshold for some time. I rid myself of him finally by slowly closing the door in his face, then watched secretly through the front glass and thrilled to the naive exuberance of his developing frame as he loped up the street seeing visions of hope (the base hope represented by rice liquor, cigarettes, hookers, and ma que, no doubt, but one can expect only so much from poorly educated unskilled laborers). I hurried up the stairs to model for myself the party raiment.

Not bad. Somehow clothing never looks covering my slightly overstuffed dermis quite how I imagined it in the shop, but the richest fabrics, most vivid dyes, and highest quality design and tailoring succeed in moving the eye and mind in a positive direction. I was tremendously relieved that sartorial disaster had exited the picture and resolved at once to shift my nervous preoccupation to matters more urbane: compiling witticisms to suit the occasion. Though I desire always to give the impression of being capable of repartee, the fact is that without a near supply of bons mots I flounder, thinking of the perfect line far too late for it to be of use. To my ready stock of Wilde I would need to add something with Eastern flair (nothing as obvious as Confucius, of course), something

156

American that would be at least vaguely recognizable but that was not utterly embarrassing, and something drolly nautical, whatever its provenance. In short, Tanya, I had work to do, real work, and I bent to my task of assembling beguiling courses of words with the gourmand's gleam.

Eighteen

I did not at first recognize my alarm and allowed its shrill, stretched bleating to continue for several minutes, thinking that the sound was coming from the street below. As I sat on the edge of the bed rubbing my eyes, I felt old and fat and lonely and wanted simply to crawl back beneath the covers. Instead I sprang directly into action, turning on every lamp in the place, stoking the samovar, and emptying my bladder into the kitchen sink. Taking a seed cake with me to nibble, I stepped out onto the back walkway to gaze upon the moonlit rock garden.

The cake was on the verge of going stale, just as I like them. I also liked the little line of crumbs that I left on the railing, and I slipped into a partial squat— still some tenderness there—and squeezed my eyes almost shut to form a slit scene with the crumbs hyper-real at the fore and the background an unfocused smear of red, green, gray, and brown, some remote woodland tableau, perhaps, today tamed only by the narrowest of margins, tomorrow to fall into uncaring wild riot. A dark form moved on the roof tiles across the way, one of the scrawny cats from the nearby shrine. Always they lurked on eaves and in secluded corners, hoping to gain through exploitation, scoring an easy handout or a quick and larcenous procurement. People were afraid to do anything about these half-feral invaders because of their affiliation with the shrine. Blasted superstition. And in the modern era! Normally I removed every trace of a meal or snack from the walkway or garden, disposing it scrupulously in the kitchen bin, but deep in the black heart of that special evening of wretched excess, unaccompanied and (I thought) unobserved, I left the crumbs; let them eat cake.

I went inside for a shower and pomade, after which my humors seemed much more in balance. Dressed in my new outfit, cane and hat in hand before the mirror glass, a measure of confidence and self-sufficiency returned to me. The carved capering figures on the walls seemed not, as I sometimes perceived, to be mocking me but to be encouraging the slightest movement of mind or body, cavorting with animal excitement at the prospect of my aged after-hours escapade. I was feeling rather chuffed by the time I had prepared fully to quit the premises.

* * *

The street was creepily quiet. Now, our little pocket of the city, on the edge, out of the way, and with wisdom and reserve stalwartly fighting its losing battle against global capitalism, was hutong-esque and therefore experienced lulls. But the first large street that I encountered a block and a half farther was deserted as well. Was there a curfew? I cursed myself for being so aloof from mortal affairs. Of course there was a bloody curfew, given the political situation, the recent earth-shaking shifts. I recalled thinking just this when I first arrived, marveled at how rapidly such an important recognition had fled my consciousness, moved aside by *larger* concerns. Art! I equivocated conspicuously on the curb, came to my senses and stepped into an alley to continue my analysis.

Prudence counseled turning back. If taxis were scarce or absent, I had a long walk ahead of me through unfamiliar districts. You well know how quickly I become dogged in such circumstances, have identified and frequently enough commented on my perilously committed "broach no argument" face. Stiffly I walked on in what I felt was the right direction. An arrest at this juncture would have been a badge of honor; I had not been hauled in since the Occupy protests, and that night spent in a large pen with enthusiastic singing college students had provided a (largely vicarious) thrill, reminding me of previous brushes with the entrenched forces of fascism during my own student days, when dissent of any sort was terribly out of vogue.

I had progressed not three blocks before an automobile, running nearly silently, pulled up beside me and came to a halt. Though this car was painted black instead of the expected red and had tinted windows rather than the usual astonishingly clear panes, a dully glowing sign reading "Taxi" was affixed to its smooth, polished roof. The rear passenger-side door opened slowly, invitingly. Hydraulic, you know. These Asian cabs are tricked out, their driver-owners spending unconscionable hours entombed in the supple leather and brushed ox-hair interiors, often with a soundproof barrier, breached only at the operator's behest, separating the two worlds, allowing for bifurcated climate control, for soothing light jazz in the back and Cantonese hip-hop in the front. Anyway, they open the two rear doors (passengers *never* are allowed in front) with a button or switch when a prospective fare approaches. As I moved reflexively to enter, a slight hesitation perturbed my stride, and the hitch came not merely from stiffness, from abuse. Before its cause could properly register, I was sliding down the curve of the broad back seat, the door closing a tad too eagerly behind me. Then it hit: the partition glass was as heavily tinted as the exterior panes.

This most certainly was not a commissioned conveyance.

I had a hard time telling whether the vehicle was moving. The windows, you see, here in the back, here in my box, were as nearly opaque from the inside as from without. No doubt the driver was not likewise encumbered, but that thought was far from comforting. When has such an arrangement, such a *design* ever propagated for the benefit of the person in my position? I don't know, maybe it has somewhere in space, some time in history, for would-be grooms to "kidnap" the object of their affection, for example. Surely I have many admirers, but the possibility of a pleasant surprise at the end of this ride seemed distressingly remote. I pushed the switch that should have lowered the window, but of course nothing happened. The handle likewise did nothing, swinging freely on its pivot.

We stopped briefly, at an intersection perhaps, so I could tell at least that we *were* moving. I leaned in close to the thick glass of the window to my right, hoping that I would be able to discern outlines, or at a minimum the blur of the city in motion. Nothing of the sort presented itself in any way to orientate me, but I did notice that very small numbers were etched into the glass just above the rubber sheathing of the window well. I strained to make them out: 67 255 255 255 255 255 255. Well, that meant exactly nothing to

162

me. I am not sure what I expected. Likely it was some sort of serial number or watermark, an anti-theft measure, which, given the circumstances, suddenly struck me as hilariously absurd. I laughed out loud, and the driver, obviously caught off guard by the outburst, jerked the wheel slightly, causing the vehicle to wobble. I was reminded of Ron, an acquaintance in graduate school. I think that you never met Ron. He was corpulent, stretching alarmingly even the "big and tall" clothing that he despised buying ("I will kill myself before I resort to a mu'umu'u" was one of his wry lines), but he had the most insouciant manner, had flowing locks that even a woman or Frenchman could envy, had a way that was his own, was admirably comfortable in his skin, despite it all. He was a photographer and railed again and again about the cavalier attitude that his customers evinced regarding his copyrighted works. He also had a car (Toyota Corolla) fitted with a twelve hundred dollar sound system. Most of the back seat was occupied by paper sleeves containing CD-Rs burned with pirated music. Right, this reminded me of that; you'll have to forgive the digression.

Eventually we stopped. Truly halted, I mean, for a significant span. I had no idea how long I had ridden in that rolling prison, since I carry no timepiece, no phone. That thought gave me pause. Surely my captors knew my habits as well as you do. Had I carried a phone like most people, I could have called emergency services. No one frisked me, no one inquired. Perhaps some jammer was in effect and I had no way of detecting it, but that silent confidence impressed upon me the former possibility: a fat file of my foibles furnished someone's afternoon doldrums with a satisfying sense of superiority. The door to my right slowly opened.

Stiffly I emerged, determined to betray no alarm at my predicament, to stand tall of my own will, under my own power and with dignity intact. We were on the access road above the quay. The driver had, after all, delivered me to my destination. The door smoothly closed, and the sedan pulled away. Not even the pretense of a fare? Noted. I straightened my clothing, gripped my walking stick, and took my first steps —not nearly as sure as I intended—toward the ship. What a vessel it was! Derelict, rusting, hulking, groaning gently as the filthy water lapped its hull, presenting patches and flourishes of Disney cheapness, certainly not actual indicators of its condition. The subterfuge was, however, quite effective to the casual eye. The craft did not in any way appear seaworthy. A gangway clanked with the movement of the ship, but no one stood near it or occupied what I could make out of the interior. I must admit that I was having second thoughts. I walked closer, straining for any snatch of merriment issuing from the belly of the beast. I heard nothing beyond the groaning of the ship itself. I had made it right up to the launch, the toe of one shoe on the gangway. The wall just inside the opening was decorated, painted with a troll-like creature that was bending over to look backward between its legs. Steeling myself either to plunge into the unwelcoming unknown or to navigate the treacherous streets back to my bed, I became aware of movement on the edge of my vision.

In the shadow of a quayside building, two figures seemed to be embroiled in an argument. The one on the left gesticulated wildly, betraying profound exasperation. The one on the right was untouched by the display, stretching languidly with hands on the back of the head in a devil-may-care pose. The figure on the left held something forth, beseechingly pressed it to the other's chest. Something was said, calmly, a serious threat or final offer. I moved a few steps toward the building to get a better look, while doing my best to stay out of the light and their line of sight. The figure on the right, a young man I now could see, snatched the item, tucked it between his knees, shrugged out of his jacket, handed the jacket to the other figure, and began stripping off his shirt. I was no longer sure that this was something I wanted to watch. The item that had changed hands was a different shirt, which became clear as he pulled it from between his knees and shimmied into it. He turned around and held out his arms, and the other figure stepped into the pale light and helped him into the jacket. The other figure I somehow recognized. It was dressed like, *exactly like*, the dandy I had twice encountered but was otherwise all wrong. The height was wrong, the posture was wrong, the movements lacked the refined grace that had left such a deep impression. The figure jerked and withdrew into the shadows, I assumed as a result of my approach. The lad of the quick change strutted directly toward me, chewing his gum prominently and weaving his head from side to side.

There was no way for me to outrun such a fit young guy, so I planted my cane before me and stood as solidly as my quivering legs would allow. The lout came right up on me and rammed his shoulder into mine as he passed. In such intimate arrangement, I noticed two facts that startled me grievously. The first was that this fellow was the same one who had harassed me on the park bench earlier in the day. The second was that the shirt he was wearing, the shirt into which he recently had changed, was my own, one of the items of clothing taken from my luggage when the bomb was planted, returned when it was stolen. Apparently this migratory garment was once more on the wing. To lose one's shirt, indeed. Well, not again! I set off after the young man, shouting and waving my stick.

He embarrassingly quickly left me behind, heading away from the harbor up a narrow, slanting lane at the same fast walk at which he had rammed me. My agitation and hotness fled as I struggled for breath, glancing warily from side to side in sudden fear of ambush, of being cornered and beaten a second time. I could not endure it again. Something had been taken out of me, permanently lost. The darkness was very deep. Even though the night was not especially cool, I shivered uncontrollably, chattering my teeth. A chill had seeped into my marrow. The sudden attack —the way it felt like a reversal of fortune, a setback of sharp significance—made a great impression upon me at the time, but I did not really know what bone cold was then. I do now, as I write this. I do.

At the next intersection the fellow (and he was by that time far enough ahead of me that I was not sure I was still following him rather than some shadow-snipe) took a slight left. When I arrived huffing at the crossroads, which to my relief was well lighted, I knew that the chase was finished. The new street was wider and dotted here and there with lamps, but it rose precipitously. My quarry already was far up the slope, his pace not having slackened in the slightest. I thought I heard him whistling. Just then, as I had given up getting any answers about why my meager possessions were so god-damned interesting and had resolved to linger in the penumbra of

the intersection's pool of light to catch my breath before plotting my next foray, a long black car screeched
to a halt in front of the cocksure lad, causing him to
jump half out of his skin.

The tinted driver's window—despite knowing the
score, I often still expect it to be on the other side of
the vehicle—slid smoothly down, and a barking Cantonese argument commenced. It was hard to be sure
from my vantage point, but I thought that the driver
was the faux dandy from the docks. Something about
the figure's body language, the person was really letting go, struck me as both feminine and familiar. That
I was the subject of the altercation was not in doubt,
as the lad kept turning and, with his hands behind his
head in that insufferable display of arrogance, staring
deeply into the liminal space in which I, obviously incorrectly, thought myself concealed.

"Slow the fuck down, youngblood. You're losing
him," the driver's hands seemed to convey, alternately
presenting the impassive vertical plane of a metaphor-
ical barrier and fiercely clawing the air between them.

"Shut it, bitch. I've done my part," the kid's
erect, admonitory finger replied.

As the pantomime progressed, I withdrew from
the scene, backing slowly down the midnight corridor
of the original slanting lane. When I reached the point
at which the curve of the way would throw a building
between me and the now small figures on the hilltop,

the lad shucked off my much abused shirt and passed it through the window to the driver. I turned and hurried recklessly back toward the harbor, clicking my cane along the pavement like a blind man.

By the time I reached the quay, the ship was pulling away, the number 248 stenciled across its aft in white. I trotted to the end of the pier, waving my arms dramatically in the yellow light of the sodium lamps. Perhaps they would send a dinghy for me. Minute by minute the vessel slowly progressed into the bay, and I dropped my burning limbs and leaned heavily on the death's head of my rod in utter exhaustion and despair. I was all in. Fagged out. Weary almost to the point of preferring a terminal plunge into the toxic dark water of the harbor to facing the prospect of trekking back to my place of residence, if I could even find it. In profound sorrow I slumped to the concrete, noticing only belatedly how filthy it was, and sat cross-legged with the cane spanning my thighs. I pulled my hat down over my eyes and leaned forward into red-black oblivion.

* * *

I woke in perfectly perplexing dubiety. I was wearing my nightclothes. The pajama top was horribly rumpled, and the upper sheet twisted around my torso like a constrictor. In stages I remembered the fiasco of the morning's wee hours, came to understand that I was now and by unknown agency in my own bed. And Mabel was there. We were lying back to back, she still in her work clothes.

I know what you must be thinking, but please believe me at long last: It was only the one time, and nothing really happened. Rosaria was unaware that I had returned a day early from that dreadful conference. Thinking she was alone in the house, she went about the usual tidying and cleaning that was her job. Now, for some reason she was doing it topless. I do not know whether that was her usual mode or anything about her motivations for doing so that day or any day, but there you have it. I was soaking in the bath, trying hard to forget the imbecility of my peers. I had used one of your bottles of bubbles, the pink stuff that produces mounds of self-colored suds and is supposed to smell lightly of rose petals but to my senses comes off as steamed aubergine. An inoffensive lather, at any rate.

Anyway, I was ignorant of Rosaria's presence and she of mine. I was far down in the water as is my custom, in a pit of bubbles scooped out around my face, nose and eyes protruding, ears submerged. The overhead light was off. I leave it that way when bathing because otherwise it glares in my eyes in a manner that is not conducive to relaxation. The only illumination in the bathroom shone feebly forth from the dim bulb of the night-light plugged into the top socket of the outlet box to the left of the sink. While thinking of nothing, attempting at least to find the void enveloped in the warm water and deprived of the workaday armor of sensory differentiation, I stroked gently my penis and testicles, pressed firmly and rhythmically against (but did *not* penetrate!) the firm ring of my asshole. I may have been humming. I do that because it helps blot out the world beyond the tub, and because I like the sensation of the taut water surface vibrating against my skin.

Rosaria did not hear the humming, if indeed I was doing it on that particular occasion, because she was listening to music on her electronic player using those "ear raper" buds that I so deeply despise. That is also why she did not hear you, stopping home unexpectedly for lunch—the slide presentation on the shocking ill health of the starving children in India's slums had put the guilt in you about the leftover chicken salad you had been on the verge of tossing—on your way across town from one charity's office to another's, enter by the garage door.

When Rosaria in her natural progression reached the bathroom in which I was ensconced and flipped on the overhead light just as I approached the point of sweet release, the sudden flare startled me so that I sprang to my feet, fearing first, I think, that we were being burglarized. I gave a garbled grunt, a wholly in-

voluntary vocalization, and Rosaria, likewise auto-
nomically I believe, ripped the buds from her ears and
moved to place them and the music player to which
they were attached on the counter next to the sink.
But her shaking hand came up short and she dropped
the player on the floor tile, bending quickly to retrieve
it. That is how it came to pass that you, hearing the
odd sound I had made, walked down the hall and with
a quizzical expression peered around the doorframe to
take in the scene of me standing in the tub with penis
erect and dripping clumps of pink bubbles and our
maid kneeling before me in a state of partial undress.

I watched from the front window as you caught
up to Rosaria (now wearing her blouse) at the end of
the driveway and made a big show of taking your
checkbook out of your purse and writing out a check
for an outrageously large sum—"Final Payment for
Services Rendered" I later saw in the memo field when
I peeked at the duplicate—and flourished it in her
face until she snatched it and ran crying down the
sidewalk. I remember feeling after that incident, after
things had calmed down, I mean, that I theretofore
had underestimated you. Perhaps I had underestimated poor Rosaria as well, for she never cashed the
check.

You never even pretended to believe that events
unfolded in the way I explained them, in the way I
have set down here; reading over the words now, I am

forced to admit that it all seems pretty unlikely. The point is that nothing happened that time, and nothing happened in Hong Kong with my secretary.

Nineteen

At breakfast Mabel was unusually circumspect. For my part, I felt terrible from the stress of overexertion and from having gone down to the kitchen and drunk a rather large amount of claret after waking upstairs with no recollection of how I had got there. I had no intention of goading her into speaking of my curfew-breaking folly. If she was willing to ignore the incident and her own part in it, then I was more than willing to meet silence with silence. As I cracked open my soft-boiled egg with a delicate spoon, she stepped out to fetch a few mundane items for the office and an exotic tonic for my head.

When Mabel returned, I dropped into my lap the paper-thin slice of fish from the lacquered tips of my chopsticks. Her face was stricken. Gone ashen, many writers would have it, though I have never actually seen that happen to anyone. She definitely looked both pale and strained, however. Without speaking she slapped a newspaper onto the counter. It was the better of the two English dailies. The lead story's headline leapt to the fore in a garish, inappropriately cinematic typeface: Pleasure Cruise Turns Deadly. I smoothed the paper and began reading, though the huge photograph of smoking strewn wreckage and oil burning on water told the tale plainly enough. Just out of the harbor the ship had exploded in a spectacular fireball. Bodies, 41 of them by the time the story had been filed, had been recovered. Evidence discovered at the scene suggested criminality.

I made it to the small oddly shaped waste bin and there purged my breakfast.

* * *

By midafternoon the death toll had risen to 46. I did not have the fortitude to keep up with the news and instructed Mabel to brief me periodically. The sunny office with its high windows and broad bar suddenly felt terribly, dangerously exposed, every movement on the street causing me to jerk my head up from my laptop's screen, hands poised crabwise above the keyboard. Finally I retreated to the attic atelier, where I felt more secure and was able to make some decisions about work that I was evaluating for *Lit*.

Lit was much on my mind, in fact. I was thrilled with the way that this impromptu Asian sojourn had freshened the magazine's content and image, even if only for a single issue to date. It had done something for my own reputation as well, and after my brush with fate such things seemed more important than I had previously allowed them to be. I was making vague plans to gracefully quit Hong Kong, not right away, that would lose me some cachet, but soon enough that whatever I had narrowly avoided might not catch up to me, soon enough that I might move among America's cultural elite while my star was still rising.

It would not have done to make any hasty resolutions in my mental state, however, and I had presence of mind enough to realize that. Something was looping around in my skull about the nature of the danger that pressed upon me and about the nature of the fathomless danger I had felt the morning I left our house in a blind rush. The threads of my thought were not entirely rational. I felt that the two dangers were intimately connected, that I had with my panicked flight drawn this vortex of ill intent away from you, from our home, and that if I could somehow throw it off my scent in the Orient I could safely return to my —our—former life with a mysterious bulwark of certainty that we would never be troubled by such intrusions again. There was also the corollary possibility:

that I would *not* be able to shake off whatever importunate power had attached itself to me, that once the underworld touches a man he is marked from that moment forward.

Deep in the night, still in turmoil and feeling rather puny, I called you. You were short with me and I found it infuriating. I knew that you were not really angry, that your manner was dictated by your usual public reserve. It was, after all, the middle of the day before for you, and you were surrounded by judgmental women of charity. Since I had not shared with you all that had happened to that point, you surely felt that my whispered parting words, that I was trying to find my way home, that you must be steadfast, must wait there holding open the door so that I would be able to return, seemed out of character, inappropriate. I cannot blame you if this conversation did not cheer you in the least, if instead it brought to the fore all that stony disapprobation that your mother and father for so many years had strongly implied, that I was unreliable, not practical-minded, not money-minded, beneath you. You surely worried for my mental health and probably even began pulling away then, testing in your mind the tender possibility of a new life, the flavor and texture of which I am sure would have been much altered. I consider all this only now, belatedly. At the time I felt that I had done a proper job of encouraging you, of letting you know that our bond was still strong, the beating heart of our life together my sustaining rhythm.

(You may have noticed—oh if you are reading this then of course you have noticed, you are sharp as a tack—certain discrepancies in what I have written here and what you remember. For instance, I know that I did not call you when I said that I would after being released from the hospital, though I no longer remember the reason for the delay. I also know that I did not leave you hanging for many days as this narrative has it. And some of what my memory has placed early on, regarding my work especially, surely happened in later days if at all, but speed is of the essence as I record these events, and I am starting to suffer bouts of lost time and mild hallucinations. Then there is the cold. It has crept into my recollection despite the fact that Hong Kong weather is mild even in winter. I cannot remember warmth! When you learn what was done to me, what I have been through, I think that you will understand and forgive any such lapses. Fields of lavender, just like that. I can see—and smell, vividly—them when I close my eyes, an endless rolling French horizon like that summer in Alsace. Life is but a dream.)

Twenty

At the unusually circumspect insistence of my amanuensis, I found myself on an early ferry to Macao. Mabel was lumpy, indistinct, swaddled in motley serape, headscarf, and pantaloons. She wore outrageously oversized sunglasses and many tacky plastic bracelets. The straps of a large straw bag sat heavily on her left shoulder. That morning when she entered and found me in the kitchen (no, she had not stayed the night), she presented a bundle of clothing for me to wear. I was not sure what she had in mind, but cowed by recent events I grudgingly obliged. I looked like the worst sort of tourist in red sweat pants and shirt, a navy windbreaker, and a black Yankees cap. Very white tennis shoes. I was forced to leave my cane behind and was instructed to take an arm when I thought support was required. I held to the rail for the passage.

We scaled a high hill overlooking a narrow beach littered with flotsam. The view on the opposite side was of the backside of a large casino. Mabel produced a thick blanket and doubled it up on the springy, slightly moist vegetation that seemed to crawl down the slope when the wind changed. We sat on the blanket and stretched out our legs. *These are kind of old person ankles*, I thought as my eyes drifted toward sudden activity at a back door of the casino. A minor argument had erupted between line cooks or dishwashers—it was hard to tell at that distance—and seemed to resolve itself quickly and without bloodshed.

"My sister works in that casino," Mabel said.

"Oh?" I hedged, unsure whether this was an entrée or a throwaway fact.

"Yes. If you ever find yourself in trouble, and I'm not around, then you can come here."

"What's her name?"

"What? Oh, just say that you are Mabel's friend at the front desk. Tell them that you would like to speak to her sister. They will take you to the right person."

I was not sure how to respond, so we sat in silence for a long time.

My father was such a taciturn man that the odd glimpse of his primitive wildness invariably took observers by surprise. Looking around the marginal landscape I was reminded of a verse he once bellowed in such a rugged place, one he claimed to have composed.

> It is good to marinate the body well in slate-dark oceans' briny swells, to cure it high on windswept hills.

A few of these up-jumped aphorisms were collected in a diminutive pocket book, titled *What Is Good* in loopy script, that he kept about his person; most of the tiny pages were blank. He had proceeded to strip buck naked, spread his legs wide, stretch his arms to the sky to let the salty air wash over him, no doubt thrilling to its tickling touch in his private regions, then had raced (kind of awkwardly, really) down to the lonely shore and pitched into the surf. He made a great show of splashing around without a care, seizing the day as it were. When he grew tired he stood, the jade-green water rising to just above his navel. He looked at me expectantly, this entire outing, this display meant as a life lesson of sorts, a typical outcropping along the sparse headland of his attempts at proper parenting. I did not join him. Rather, suddenly possessed of my long-gone mother's haughty petulance, I turned and erected my easel facing not the sea-scene that I had come to paint but the bland scrubby hills marching away in the opposite direction.

"In the past?" said Mabel softly with a sidelong, wistful look. "Me, too."

For a couple of hours we sat watching gulls sweep the sky. The occasional activity at the rear doors of the casino provided a welcome interruption, the human figures laboring uselessly there distant enough to be someone else's problem. The past, Mabel had said, but it was not just the past. I became unmoored in time, sliding Sagan-like serene and ageless down an alien starscape detached and more-or-less eternal. Of what concern is this? Of what concern is anything?

Later we shared a picnic of sardines, rice balls, and saké. It struck me that doing things like this with Mabel was exceedingly comfortable, the relationship exhibiting characteristics of the quiet rapport that exists between very old friends.

As the afternoon slipped toward evening, the sky trending to purple behind the stolid rectangle of the casino, we packed up and descended to the launch. Despite sitting for many hours I was fairly limber and found the walk exhilarating. It was quite late when we returned to the office. Mabel was stopping by to take a quick inventory of office supplies and to see me safe to roost, she wasn't staying the night.

* * *

The place had been ransacked. I leaned wearily over the counter in the kitchen and stared out into the garden as Mabel steeped some green tea.

"Call the police," I commanded as she handed me the small cup.

"You can't be serious."

"Damn straight I am. I've reached my limit with this bullshit. Call the police. Do it now."

"They're probably the ones who did this!" she said in exasperation, holding out her hands in a beseeching manner.

It was a distinct possibility, I had to admit when I allowed myself a little space for calm reflection.

"We'll tidy up. Let's do it right now. Make everything look just as it did, like nothing ever happened," she suggested.

I could not think of a better plan on the spur of the moment and shrugged my shoulders in acquiescence. The clean-up took hours. We both had pretty sharp memories, and by the time we had finished we were reasonably sure that nothing had been taken. Was someone desperately looking for something? Was someone simply sending a message? Maybe I had been subjected to gaslighting for some time and only recently had the perpetrators cracked against the blank wall of my nature, oft-oblivious to matters mundane. It was decided with no prompting from me that Mabel would stay over. She set about creating a makeshift bed behind the counter. It looked very cozy by the time she considered it adequate, and I was a little jealous. As a child I loved to find tight, unexpected spaces in which to curl up for a nap. Perhaps the recent trauma had caused me to regress. Mabel moved the phone down next to her pallet and put her cell phone on the shelf beneath the counter for good measure.

"I'm a light sleeper. I'll call for help if anyone tries to come in," she said, trying to reassure me.

"Whom will you call?" I asked with a cocked eyebrow.

"The police," she said sheepishly.

I went up to my bedroom. There had been no sign of forced entry, so I was not at all confident that we would hear a thing if the vandals returned. As I readied myself for sleep a tiny thought niggled, a black patch in the weave of meaning my brain was attempting to pull together. Had I opened the front door with my own key, or had Mabel used hers? I kept mulling it over as I brushed my teeth and washed my face. It came to me that it had not been necessary for me to produce my key to lock up when we left in the morning. I had become accustomed to leaving such mundanity to my secretary, charging ahead on my important business while she scurried around without complaint to set things right in my wake. I sat down on the toilet for an overdue movement, still trying to fit events into a tidy chronology, to remember clearly the fine details. I disliked using the upstairs toilet because the mirror above the sink, which the commode faced, was at such a level as to reflect my head from just below the eyebrows to the crown. The cutoff point was truly *just* above my eyes, making the space of flesh appear too elongated, as if eyes should be there but were missing, a nightmare face with orbless sockets covered by smooth skin. All around the mirror and basin the little carved figures cavorted, ululated, fornicated with bestial glee.

And there it was. Near the floor to the left of the sink's pedestal the troll bending over to peer backward between its legs that I had seen on the wall of the doomed ship stood slightly apart from the other graven zoomorphic forms. I stumbled forward from the seat onto my hands and knees, pajama trousers around my ankles, and crawled toward the wall, leaving the task behind me half-finished. I gazed intently at the vulgar image. It matched the version in my memory in every way. I pressed my fingers into the deep grooves of its outline. The wood was very smooth. When I rounded the hump of its back, the panel on which the figure was carved gave a bit. I pushed harder and the entire sheet of wood tilted like a transom window. I saw that it was mounted on a clever pivot and would slide easily up into the low roof of the small space behind. I crawled into the cavity. It was a very tight fit, my shoulders rubbing the fragrant walls and my bare bottom bumping the smooth ceiling if I did not remember to lean forward far enough on my elbows. It did not go back very far, and I could see in the dim light that something was there at the end. It was quite dark all the way in, with my body blocking much of the illumination from the bathroom, and I could not raise my head high to peer down my nose at the object. I stretched out a hand and felt the cool metallic surface. I would come back with a candle (more conspiratorial) or a flash-light (undoubtedly safer) tomorrow for a proper inspection, but I knew what it was.

Twenty-One

My mouth was terribly dry; I remember that clearly. My tongue felt like an old scrap of boot leather, the black aftermath of a whisky bender, though I in this case had been practically abstemious the evening prior. It took a few terribly unsettled moments to come to terms with my situation. I was in the atelier, sitting up amid pillows, eiderdown, dirty clothing, a slightly damp towel. On this textile patchwork some mere measure above the unforgiving floorboards I apparently had passed many uninterrupted hours, given the curiously tidy lines of the near rectangle definition in which my senses kindled. When my blissful confusion fled, fear returned; it was, however, of a distinctly different timbre to that of the night before—some aspects now seemed more remote to my person, more manageable.

I stood and whirled my arms a few times, performed a couple of slow squats. I went to the large round window overlooking the alley. The view appeared the same as it did every other day. I poked my head down the cutout through which the ladder rose but could see nothing because of the thickness of the joists. I considered calling out to my assistant and immediately felt silly. Just get it over with. I turned and clambered down the sturdy rungs.

Calcutta. Why Calcutta? My father had loved the city. Well, you know that I was ill at ease for the duration of our painfully extended Indian adventure. Previously I had thought that the nadir of our explorations was and would remain some hideous amalgam of the confounding streets of Hanoi and Da Nang. Menace lurked around every corner. Every meal was delicious in its setting, bowel-wrenching about four hours later. And then India. I thought I'd seen filth, thought I'd experienced danger. The leavings of the English were hard-nosed and whip-worn, quite unlike the occasional surprising remnant of the French. You laughed it all off, said I was being paranoid, provincial. The tension, that dread hunted feeling that never left me there must be what echoed round my Hong Kong sublet. Nothing had been disturbed. The dummy me lumping up the coarse linen was not convincing in the light.

I expected to encounter Mabel in the kitchen, had braced myself for her pale green tea. She refused to touch the samovar. If I wanted something dark and bitter I would have to brew it myself. Therefore I usually suffered her partially cured hay infusion. High summer in a tiny porcelain cup. The kitchen was dim and still, the rosy fingered child of the dawn having not yet thrust its miserable pudgy digits above the garden wall. I flipped the switch and contemplated my breakfast options.

In the office I found Mabel where I last had seen her, wedged between the counter and the wall. She was fast asleep, though her forehead wrinkled with residual strain. She was lying on her right side facing the shelves beneath the counter, both hands up near her face. The left one held her cell phone tightly. On the shelf within easy reach lay an evil-looking handgun. I decided to let her rest.

* * *

My secretary and I were quite short with each other before she left. She was unaccountably angry that I had dirtied every pan and plate in the kitchen while attempting to sustain myself. She grimaced at the earthy scent of the strong black tea, the pinging and popping (gargling, she called it) of the wakened samovar. I felt justifiably put out that I had been left to fend for myself in such troubled times. We didn't talk about the firearm. I tried to tell her how I wanted to proceed, to hammer out a sensible course to follow, but she stated curtly that on the weekend she did not work for me. She banged around the vestibule, raising an unnecessary racket on her way out. I did notice that she peered carefully up and down the street before launching herself from the doorway.

When I was sure that she was not going to return, I looked behind the counter. She had left the gun. I carried it up to the atelier and hid it behind some books.

* * *

My afternoon work session was interrupted by the furious thumping of some obviously agitated individual at the front door. It took me quite some time to stow away my laptop and other writing accoutrements in the loft, climb down the narrow companionway, navigate the shallow stairs, back hall, and the suddenly menacing closeness of the vestibule, so that by the time I arrived the door was truly in danger of being separated from its frame. Without even looking through the peep-hole (a mistake, I'll own), I threw wide the stout assemblage of good old wood to confront the twisted visage of the police detective who had questioned me in the hospital. He was flanked by two expressionless, muscular young men in starched black uniforms. Without so much as offering a greeting the trio pushed its way inside and closed and locked the door.

"We'll speak in the garden," the detective said, indicating with an open-handed gesture that I should lead the way.

I complied, thinking for the short walk without success of some way to alert Mabel or anyone to my predicament. I had not had time to grab my cane and felt defenseless in its absence.

We took our seats. In the daylight—my habits had me out there mostly in the evening—I could see that the gravel needed raking and weeding. A ropey shrine cat sauntered with its breed's intrinsic curiosity across the roof tiles to get a better view of the extraordinary midday spectacle. We watched its progress for several minutes; finally the creature settled in a self-satisfied pose, crossing its paws over the sluiceway.

"You were spotted in the harbor," opened the detective.

"Your hesitancy ..."

He raised an eyebrow.

"Your hesitancy in English," I said, "has vanished."

"Old trick of the trade. I took my criminology degree at Yale, Mr. Makarov."

"Why not?" I said somewhat brusquely, leaning back and crossing my arms over my chest. The sky was a very light blue, almost like the surface layer of a pail of skim milk.

"You were spotted in the harbor after curfew," he said, gauging my reaction. I strove to maintain a poker face. "This sighting occurred shortly before the launch of an unregistered watercraft, the fate of which I am sure you have been unable to avoid since the subject has been covered relentlessly by the media."

I said nothing.

"The floating world. Have you heard of it?"

"I have. My magazine once did a feature on the ukiyo-e."

"Is that so? This party on the ship … were you invited?"

I nodded. There was no point in denying it now.

"By whom? Do you know?"

I shook my head.

"Very well," the detective said, jotting some notes in his little book with a creased brow. "How are you feeling? Have your injuries healed?"

"I'm fine."

"Funny world we live in, don't you think?" he asked, slipping the notebook into the interior breast pocket of his jacket.

I grunted tentative agreement. He was finished with me, apparently, now just stalling to give his helpers sufficient time to complete their illegal search of my home and office.

"I was rereading Derrida the other day, and—" he began.

I stood and turned my back on him, heading for the walkway door. A man can abide only so much interference in his affairs. He reached me in at most three bounds, the crunch of gravel giving me little time to quicken my pace or glance over my shoulder. His grip was like a vise on my left arm, the sudden attachment whirling me half around. Our faces were very close, his eyebrows flat, an ugly tension pinching his temples.

"Mr. Makarov," he said, struggling mightily to preserve a professional demeanor, "we are not finished here."

The back door opened, and one of the detective's underlings stepped onto the walkway and gave a hand signal. The detective released me roughly and brushed past. I followed at a wary distance. The other black-clad youth was in the vestibule, holding open the front door. The intruders departed without another word, the detective shutting softly behind him the roughened portal.

* * *

Anger fueled me. Not since my teenage years had I felt such white-hot rage at a fresh injustice. I went first to the atelier, went for the gun. It was missing, they had taken it. Suddenly I felt the sweat standing out on my forehead, on the back of my neck. It was very cold. I squatted, forearms on knees, chin on wrists, and contemplated the utility of the pacifism that had defined my adulthood. Against the powers arrayed in opposition I could not triumph through the use of force, probably could not triumph at all. My polarity reversed, I leaned far forward and pressed my brow against the uneven grain of the floorboards.

Twenty-Two

In direct contravention of the protests of my body, I arose early and completed my grooming ritual with unaccustomed dispatch. I had tasks before me, an agenda to discharge prior to the arrival of my irritatingly punctual amanuensis.

First, after fetching and lighting one of the fat white emergency candles with which Mabel had stocked the cabinet nearest the refrigerator in the kitchen, I opened the secret panel in the upstairs bathroom and crawled eagerly to the back of the small cubbyhole behind. It was still there, solid and real. No lights glowed or blinked across the panel that formed its face. I tilted the candle and dripped a small pool of wax onto the floor, righted it and set the base firmly in the flow. I scooted up close to the cylinder, embraced it with my arms and legs. I pressed my right cheek into the cool metal. I held that pose and emptied my mind of all worldly concerns as the candle guttered behind me. I kept, however, in some flickering recess the cursed sense that I am never without, the incurable passage of time. I had another task to complete ahead of breakfast.

I went rapping with my cane all over the house, every wall as high as I could reach, the floorboards systematically. Other than a couple of false positives that I returned to again and again for one last assay, the house was surprisingly solid in its yeoman construction. When Mabel arrived she found me waiting in the kitchen. I had worked up a hunger and read the paper a little grumpily as she prepared our repast. The meal was one of my favorites: a salted soft-boiled duck egg and a small bowl of rosewater and pine nut congee topped with shredded scallions.

Working in the detached ataraxic cocoon of the atelier, I was madly productive all day. The few interactions with my amanuensis were marked by a fresh terseness that in the present circumstances was not wholly unwelcome. In truth I was simply biding time until she departed and had nothing else to hand to fill the interval. I went down to the vestibule to see her off when the time came, and she seemed somewhat chastened by my distance and resolve, gave my shoulder a light squeeze and told me as she quit the premises to call her if I needed anything. Once I was reasonably certain that she was not going to return, I changed into my finery and called for a taxi.

I was on the hunt. The issue after next of *Lit* would feature articles and stories (no poetry!) with a nautical bent, a theme intended to convey dismay at the coarsening politics of all the major countries. The flurry of offshore weapons tests, state-sponsored piracy, and blockades of trade routes represented a disastrous turn toward the blunt, hard end of the power spectrum and set our klaxons calling. For my introduction I had convinced myself that the essays collected in George H. Quester's *Sea Power in the 1970s* would prove indispensable, but no one in Boston seemed able to scare up a copy. I had put Mabel on the case forthwith, and one of her tendrils felt a tug, an intimation that the special collection of the former Royal Maritime Library had not been parceled out at auction to pay the new Chinese government back taxes on the building that housed it as the papers had the story but lay entombed in mechanized stacks in the twisting underhalls. Though deeply skeptical of this rumor, I had agreed to meet its source at a café in the center of the city.

My contact was a very short, very serious chap. I never would have fingered him among the crowd of colorful patrons; I did not have to, of course, as he came straight over as soon as I had taken a table. He introduced himself as Mr. Zhou. The noticeable tic with which he did so made me chary that the name was assumed. He had the appearance of a distracted, disheveled graduate student.

"I can get us inside," he said right off, before even sipping his espresso.

"When?"

"Tonight."

"How?"

"With a keycard. My uncle works security." Convenient. Suspiciously so.

"Can't you just fetch the book for me, Mr. Zhou?" I felt that I was getting a little better at this kind of thing.

"I'm not going downstairs."

"Why not?"

"Fear."

"Of what are you afraid?" This was like pulling teeth.

"Going underground. And before you ask, there's no name for my condition. They've got some impressive sounding words for damn near every possible aversion, but somehow not for the one that actually gives me fits."

"How are we to proceed, then?" I asked curtly, upset at having let my coffee go cold while wasting words on what I had decided was an unpleasant and perhaps untrustworthy co-conspirator.

"Simply enough. We just enter a side-door using the keycard. The place should be deserted in the middle of the night. There is a small guard station inside with monitors for the surveillance system, which is not extensive. I will wait there so I can warn you by phone if anybody comes. You nip down to the basement, get your book, and come back up. What do you think?"

"I think that I've squandered enough of my evening, Mr. Zhou," I said, getting up to leave.

He held the sleeve of my jacket with a weak grip. I shot him a stern look at which he dropped his hand. I went through the door shaking my head. I had had my fill of such foolishness. They were getting awfully desperate to resort to sending a guy like that. And to concoct such a ridiculous fiction, like a scene from some third-rate spy thriller, hoping that it might lure me into isolation so that they could work me over again. Pah!

Having had the foresight to instruct the driver to wait around the corner with his meter running, I was able to dodge straight away into my escape pod. I ordered the man through a series of nonsensical maneuvers, and he was kind enough to humor me without asking questions (I did catch him grinning at me in the rear-view mirror). Reasonably sure that we had performed due diligence in the thwarting potential pursuers department, I had the cabbie nose us toward my next destination: the Italian restaurant at which I had been given the fateful invitation.

Around the corner, meter running, the driver seemed happy to allow me to run the fare as high as I liked. I tugged my shoulder pads into place and clicked down the sidewalk with a dignified gait. In front of the restaurant I checked my step. Yes, this was the right address. No, nothing was here. No awning, no signage, no indication that a functioning commercial interest of any type lay inside. I tried the door and found it locked. Pressing my brow to the glass I saw that the entry was empty save a ladder and a bucket, completely stripped as if the space were undergoing renovation. Somewhat shaken, I hastened back to my taxi, which was not waiting for me around the corner.

* * *

I hobbled about the infernal maze as the evening's darkness relentlessly deepened, too spooked to hail another ride, mental and physical stamina at an ebb. Eventually I stumbled into a convenience store, selected a large plastic bowl of instant noodles—purportedly crab flavored—and prepared it in the large silver microwave oven using sulphur-scented water from the proximate small sink. I let it go too long, forgetting again that these industrial models are higher wattage than the home units to which I am accustomed. I put in the entire seasoning packet and found the broth almost unbearably salty. The cashier looked at me in disgust as he realized that I was going to eat the noodles inside his shop, peering out at the street and dribbling on the short counter between the magazine rack and the photocopier.

I could stomach only a scant half bowl. I put the lid back on and went outside to deposit the plastic porringer in the trash bin at the curb. As I pushed the small metal door of the bin against its springs to make the opening large enough to accept my little bundle of waste, I noticed a woman walking up the sidewalk on the other side of the street, making a left turn at the intersection. Her stature, proportions, and gait reminded me strongly of Mabel.

I hurried to the intersection and leaned around the corner. My able assistant was well swaddled in ridiculous layers of expensive fabric, but I harbored no doubt that it was she. The noir-comic figure stole exaggerated glances up and down the nearly empty street, withdrew a small object from her jacket pocket, quickly licked it, then bent forward and scratched at the lower right corner of the display window of a duck vendor. Stashing the implement, she pivoted rapidly on her heel and walked swiftly up the sidewalk in the opposite direction. I broke cover and proceeded nonchalantly to the window.

The shop was closed, of course, the dim after-hours lighting subtly shading the sinuous roasted birds hanging from hooks slotted into the overhead track. In the lower right-hand corner of the window, some *disturbance* was detectable, an irregular smudge that boggled one's eyes when the observer moved his head rapidly from side to side. I probed the area gently with my right pinkie finger, withdrew the hand to snuffle at the residue, the scent of which was unmistakable. The substance was hand soap, from one of the small pale bars that Mabel kept next to the basin in the kitchen at the office. I bent to the glass and exhaled, the condensation of my breath revealing the Chinese character that she had written there. It was carefully formed, quite distinct. I copied it down in my notebook, then hurried to the next intersection.

I could not perceive my secretary at any remove but for some reason felt certain that she had turned right, heading uphill. Holding to the shadows of the verge I climbed the slope, beginning near its crest to feel my heartbeat in the upper whorls of my ears. The top of the rise had been leveled, and I paused to catch my breath and take my bearings, leaning lightly on the metal-pipe rail, feeling the curling, cracking texture of its thick black paint as a faint tickle in the heart of my hand, a sensation that readily transferred itself to my spinal column and sent an electric jolt of recognition upward, homeward. Ahead of me in the mercifully flat streetscape, a florescent bulb in a three-tube fixture flickered, beckoned at the high head of a bakery window. Gazing through the slightly warped glass, I could just make out the dim interior. The loaves and pastries were arranged around the perimeter on polished wooden racks, which had the functional but shapely mark of an artisan and thus carried the air of permanence—these racks did not migrate about the shop in an effort to spur customers to sample and splurge, no, these racks were part of the shop and could not be ramified or furcated by forces without. A simple table holding the center of the small space fairly glowed with careful pride. There was no doubt that the staples piled there were the specialty of the shop, despite the almost aggressive lack of flash in their packaging and presentation.

I did not *know* Mabel, Eastern Inscrutable, but I had come close enough to recognize that if she had come this way, she had stopped here. Eagerly I scanned the pane for the visual wobble, the tell-tale aberration in the frightening clarity of the glass that would betray the glyph. There! It was in the upper left corner this time. She must have stood on the points of her little shoes on the brick ledge at the base of the window to reach it. Stretching from the pavement, I fogged the area with my unbated breath and copied down the character. The lines were less distinct, showing the strain of her reach. With a snap of satisfaction I closed the notebook and slid it into my sheer pocket.

My spirits spiraled higher than they had in days, buoyed by the prospect of the little puzzle, especially the knowledge that even after I was reasonably sure that I had collected all parts of the message many happy hours at my desk remained—looking up the pronunciations and meanings of the characters, arranging them sensibly, solving any cipher that then might present itself. I strolled along the sidewalk in search of the next likely storefront. I felt like whistling but refrained.

A long black car, running almost silently and with the headlights off, rolled right up next to me and stopped. The tinted glass of the front passenger window descended smoothly to reveal Mabel's scowling countenance. Her hair fell not in its usual silky cascade but stood upon her brow like a thunderhead.

"Get in," she said. The window ascended smoothly.

I hesitated a moment on the curb, perhaps expecting the rear passenger door to swing open of its own accord, like that of a taxi. With a studied air of nonchalance, I breached the hermetic shell and slid gracefully into place, holding my cane fast across my legs just back of the knees.

"Lovely evening for a postprandial perambulation," I began, surveying the dim interior.

The young lout who had bothered me on the bench, who had worn my shirt gripped the leather-laced wheel tightly at two and ten with his white-gloved hands. My secretary stared straight ahead. At the slightest bob of her head, the driver accelerated smoothly.

"Though my yellow cabbie flew the coop, and I've had a devil of a time running another down. Lucky thing you happened along!" I finished weakly. Stony silence reigned.

Through empty streets—and at this point in violation of the curfew, no doubt—our driver skillfully sped, ignoring all traffic signs and signals. In no time at all (I may have dozed) we arrived at the foreign office of *Lit*, at my current home address, how strange it was to think those things in that moment. I expected something then, probably not an explanation but some sort of acknowledgment at least. Nothing was forthcoming, so I let myself out of the sterile confines of the black car and into the deep purple shadows of my rented property's vestibule, where I took off my shoes and hat and slept curled on the floor.

Twenty-Three

I arose before first light the next day, startled sensate by the clanking of a pedlar's cart as it passed my door. When Mabel arrived with breakfast, I was standing in the garden with my hands clasped behind my back watching the temple cat on the roof lick its paws with the practiced languor of its kind. At the kitchen counter I dipped my crullers in warm salted soy milk and savored their sweet snap. I left my tea untouched, and, knowing that we did not have any on hand, asked for coffee instead. Without complaint my secretary walked to the convenience store and returned with a tall black paper cup, fragrant and steaming. I announced coolly that I would be working in the atelier.

The fat Chinese-English dictionary that I had procured from a small expatriate bookshop (where I was the only customer, clearly unexpected; the aged proprietor seemed to be keeping his hours out of sheer cussedness, likely thumbing his nose at the sharks circling the now very valuable patch of real estate, hopefully with a plan in place—a foundation set up to hold the property and turn it into a tiny museum or something—to disappoint the beasts in perpetuity) near the queue for the Peak Tram gave me fits. One apparently was supposed to have been trained in its use by an instructor or another text. I spent most of the morning combing the Web for clues and nearly gave up when a table of radicals jarred my memory. I sensed that I was rapidly approaching the great wall that had first slowed then finally stopped my progress with the language.

Just as I was beginning to despair, enthusiasm for the hunt at an ebb, I discovered a site that allowed one to crudely trace the lines of a character into a quartered box using the mouse. It then happily accessed a very large and accurate dictionary at light speed and even provided example compounds and sentences with pop-up translation. I threw the paper dictionary into the far corner of the loft with greater force than intended, and Mabel came to the bottom of the ladder to check on me. I assured her that everything was fine, pulling up a spreadsheet of *Lit*'s finances just in case she decided to climb on up. Such an intrusion did not seem beyond her character. When

I heard her going back down the stairs, I switched to my browser and contemplated the sign.

鴉

Crow. Of the fire radical, though I was having trouble seeing it. Any obvious meaning proved similarly elusive. I locked my screen, resolved to take up the search again following lunch.

I whistled as I fixed myself a gin fizz at the narrow counter in the kitchen. The light flowing over the stones in the garden through the sparse cloud cover provided a pleasant vista on which I could absently focus my vision until the task had been completed.

As I moved toward the short corridor, glass in hand, Mabel burst onto the scene holding a large, thick envelope. We nearly collided in the doorway, causing me to slosh a bit my overfull cocktail.

"Hey!" she said, as startled as I. Then: "This came for you earlier. I didn't want to interrupt." She passed me the parcel, somewhat reluctantly it seemed.

"Who delivered it?"

"Young guy, very fit," she said with a faraway look. "Bike courier."

"When did he appear? I did not hear the bell ..."

"About eleven, I think," she said, crinkling her nose in an endearing fashion.

"Thanks," I said and pushed past her to the back door.

There was a chill in the air in the shade of the walkway, and I hurried on out into a sunny patch at the far side of the garden, drawing up one of the bamboo chairs.

For a while I sipped my drink, savoring at each draw first the bracing tartness followed by the long mellow slide into deep woodiness. Between deglutitions I set the glass on the wide, level arm of the chair, twisting it slowly to form a ring of condensation as evenly distributed as possible. I felt very old.

With a sigh, a habit that annoys me to no end when I observe it in other people and that I have tried hard—frequently without success, as you have reminded me often enough—to curb in my own behavior, I turned my attention to the heavy brown envelope in my lap. My slightly numb fingers pinched their way across the flap, tearing carefully.

Inside was a hardcover book. It wore no jacket, but the red-orange cloth seemed to be in close to new condition. Maybe it had been issued without a jacket, for the cover bore in large black sans-serif letters the title and attribution: *Sea Power in the Nineteen Seventies*, Edited by George H. Quester. A design element, if one could call it that, appeared in the upper right-hand corner—periscope sighting lines. I turned to the front matter. The binding was tight, the pages clean, bright, not foxed. Copyright nineteen seventy-five by the Dunellen Publishing Company, sponsored by the Cornell University Program on Peace Studies. Presenting papers originally prepared for a Conference on Problems of Naval Armaments held in Ithaca, New York in April of nineteen seventy-two. I closed the book and returned it to its shroud.

* * *

Over a bowl of cold sesame noodles I labored through the afternoon and into evening. The atelier felt close and cramped as the hours wore on, and I found myself wishing for the courage to send Mabel away early, well before whatever mysterious internal signaling system told her naturally it was time to go.

It had not taken long to match through the crude tracing methodology that I had discovered earlier the second character.

Mole, of the rat radical. A good enough stab at early taxonomy, I supposed, but not particularly helpful on its own.

The problem was that no matter where my research into these characters led, the mystery of their relationship became no clearer in my mind. How much of the menagerie was I missing? Had I been able to spot Mabel earlier in the evening or follow her successfully for longer when I did catch sight, would an elephant, badger, and grass snake have joined in, providing the crucial pieces of information to render the message intelligible?

Staring at the screen was not going to solve the puzzle, and my e-mail inbox was filling with messages of escalating urgency, mostly edits awaiting my approval.

Twenty-Four

On Friday Mabel did not show up for work. Because she had hitherto been punctual, I immediately began to worry. Now, you know how I get in such situations. You have given me cause to fret on so many occasions that I have lost count.

You *say* that you will be home from the meeting at the gallery at seven, therefore I leave the office at fifteen until six to have plenty of time to prepare a fresh supper. At nine I am still waiting, sipping wine over a congealing mess on the trestle, no word from you. When you finally arrive at half past ten, my worry and anger catch you by surprise. I: Why didn't you call? Why did you *say* you'd be here at seven if you really had no idea? You could have been in a crumpled heap on the roadway somewhere; I was almost to the point of searching. You: Why didn't you go ahead and eat? Why didn't you just assume that the meeting had run long? If something horrible had happened, surely you would have been notified. What could you have done anyway, I mean, had that been the case?

I was determined not to allow my worrywart tendencies to govern my workday. I made myself strong tea and two pieces of toast with butter and strawberry preserves. Through the long glass above the counter I observed the largest of the shrine cats standing on the gravel of the garden, posterior facing my favorite among the bamboo chairs, tail straight in the air and doing a jittery dance. After marking the furniture as brazenly as could be, the tom sauntered over to the covered walkway, leapt onto the top rail, and settled there with a self-satisfied expression. Today I would not let it bother me. Today I would not.

I ascended to the atelier with an only slightly strained beatific mien.

* * *

After a satisfying lunch of strong tea and goose-liver pâté on toast and just as I was making internal rumblings about returning to the daily grind upstairs, the front bell sounded. As I walked to the door to look through the peephole, the bell-pull abruptly was followed by bellicose knocking. I sidled up to the peephole and spied the cap of an obviously short but stout deliveryman. He knocked again as I mulled over answering this rude summons, and his manner—two-fisted, slow, pleading—was comical, winning, so I opened the door wide and in doing so startled him mightily. With a sheepish grin he pressed an envelope into my hands and held up a form for me to sign. Actually, I was supposed to press my inked name chops into the red rectangle provided, but I simply scrawled some nonsense there using the pen that I luckily (since the deliveryman certainly was not carrying one) had in my pocket. The man dropped a hasty bow and set off down the street at a jog. I closed and locked the door and took the envelope to the front counter.

A quick snick of the letter opener sheared the thin seal. Inside was a list of Web links printed in deep red ink on thick white card stock. I wished that I or Mabel had possessed the foresight to retain the package in which *Sea Power* had arrived. A comparison could have proved edifying but was at this point impossible. I knew at least that a different courier had delivered the earlier package. The middle-aged man of today clearly could not have been the buff young fellow who had prompted Mabel's disconcerting blush. Different days, different hours, different but overlapping routes? Different company? I would have to grill my secretary when she bloody well deigned to put in an appearance or pick up the phone.

Although I was intrigued by the sudden arrival of the clue, prompt, or whatever it turned out to be, I had by now soured on the game. Its phosphor trail had led me perilously close to the abyss of death more than once already, just when I was rediscovering something buoyant, a percolating unexpected zest for life, much like that Russell apparently felt shortly before he died of influenza. I set the envelope on the counter, tucked *Sea Power in the Nineteen Seventies* under my arm, and went to the kitchen to open a bottle of wine.

I carried my overly full glass to the garden and sat in my favorite bamboo chair, only to be whelmed over by the unmistakable and shockingly potent odor of cat piss. I moved to the short bench in the corner. The view was not as immersive, and in the shade of the walls I felt a chill even through my thick cable-knit sweater and notable but not yet paralyzingly embarrassing swaddling of blubber. No cat prowled the premises, but even here one's infernal perfume faintly sullied the air.

And then I missed you. I missed our comfortable and tidy home. I missed difficult, aloof Fabriana. I felt the absence—the loss, I was startled to understand, was how I had come to view it—viscerally; I really thought that something horrible was happening to my body, this shell betraying its captive spirit with gleeful cruelty. The moment of weakness passed, though my grip remained frustratingly unsteady. I wanted to call you right then, but my feeble calculations placed you in bed at rest. Later on, I resolved.

I opened *Sea Power* at random, focused on a paragraph:

> The importance of these missions to the Soviet Navy and the degree to which they impact on Soviet naval planning are contentious points, particularly so for "commerce wars of attrition." Those who believe the Soviets place a high priority on interdiction missions emphasize the importance of secure sea-lanes of communication to the West, particularly in the context of a protracted land war in Europe. Contrapuntally, they stress the large numbers of torpedo attack and cruise missile submarines deployed by the Soviets, particularly those assigned to the Northern Fleet, which is responsible for the Atlantic. This school also notes that Soviet submarines and naval strike aircraft, regardless of their original purpose, would be capable of interdiction missions should major East-West conflict develop.

Self-evident tautological folderol meant to numb the senses while bloody well *begging the question*. If their fleet is large and its purpose is deterrence, then ours must be larger to constitute an even stronger deterrent. If their fleet is large and its purpose is expansion, annihilation, then ours must be larger so that we can expand, annihilate first or at least more successfully. Feed the slavering maw of hideous, unnatural, unsustainable growth. Greed, corporate or military at the extremes of power, is relentless, timeless.

* * *

When at last I did call you, the conversation jumped the rails with alarming rapidity. You were hurt. Was this my (typical!) weaselly way of leaving you? To just disappear without a word and stay out of the picture until things resolved themselves in my absence? I was taken aback by the accusations, the sentiment. I thought that you understood that our bond was stronger than could be sundered by such minor adversity. I thought we were now on the same page regarding this sudden sabbatical. You ambushed me with your pent-up anguish.

"But A, this is the *third* time—only the third!—I have been able to speak to you," you said, in a small voice that I hardly recognized. "It's been months."

It was true that the balance of our communication, and in my mind it had felt substantial, had passed through the medium of my secretaries in Boston and Hong Kong. You were so stern, so sturdy, and as usual so busy with your philanthropy that I incorrectly assumed that anything more than sporadic apprisal at arm's length would annoy, inflame you, would make you dwell on the difference between our old, settled existence and the new, tenuous (but temporarily!) one. In short, I had calculated that greater or more demonstrative communication would produce in you the sort of rare frighteningly out-of-control chemical reaction—I could be unkind and call it feminine hysterics—that I was now witnessing, caused, you asserted, by that very abstinence.

It was in the spirit of the moment, in the manner of a man who has been reading studiously for some hours by candle- or lamplight and glances up to discover that the room around him is ablaze from floor to ceiling, that I cut short our connection. I wanted out of there and could see no needs beyond the immediate. I mumbled some things, petty abbreviations of what I meant to say: that I truly felt that I was doing important work, that my circle would close once I more fully understood the mysterious swirling danger —remember that I was thinking primarily of your safety when I left in such a rush—that I had been successfully outmaneuvered, that in my mind, in my heart, our union was stronger than ever before, that I missed you, that I loved you. I flubbed it entirely. My meaning did not convey. I put down the telephone stung, startled, defeated.

Had I known then that we would never speak again, I would have stayed on the line, would have beaten you verbally back into a state of reason, would then have calmly said just what needed saying.

Twenty-Five

The list of links exhausted my patience. Every one led to a Chinese-language article or posting on a news Web site or political blog. Machine translation had improved a great deal since I had first read about it some years before, but the results of putting these sources through the meat grinder remained unintentionally comical. I could, however, spot the trend. All the pieces were short items of local interest involving business and, perhaps, crime.

I would hire someone to translate the items pointed to by the links. It would not do simply to provide the list of links. No, that might well pique someone's curiosity and bring additional contestants into the game. I would copy the bodies of the articles, removing authorial and editorial attributions (Muses forgive me) to the best of my ability, and print them out. Perhaps divvying the resulting stack among several translators would prove to be a wise precaution as well.

Still I heard nothing from Mabel, not a visit, not an e-mail, not a call. Needing a change of scenery and some mundane task to distract me from my worries, I changed into my finery, which I must say was getting a tad rigid and stale and therefore was in need of a sabbatical at the dry cleaner's, dabbed some after-shave on my neck, took up my stick, and called a cab. I had chosen a promising translator and planned to drop by unannounced to form a snap judgment about his abilities while he was off his game. It occurred to me only after the driver made his first turn that it was extremely unlikely that the man would be in his office—attached to a small print shop, apparently—on the weekend. No matter. I was out of my own office, out of the house, on the town. Other base errands needed running. I could pick up a few staples for the larder, a few consumables for the front desk. A late lunch or early supper, depending on how much time other matters burned and leaving a margin to beat the curfew, at a restaurant chosen through serendip-ity, yes this was the proper course.

* * *

There was no obvious indication that the print shop was open. A light was on inside, but it was well back from the entrance, clearly not the primary illumination. Then again, it was the middle of the afternoon and ample sunshine streamed through the large front window, making it difficult to peer through. No sign, not one that I could read, anyway, told me to return at another hour, on another day. No shadow stirred around the stolid small printing press that took up most of the room facing the street. What gave me some small hope was that the front door was almost imperceptibly ajar. Since the area seemed busy, commercial, a stranding incident seemed a remote possibility, and I had sent my driver away without hesitation. While I was here, and with time to spare, I should try my luck. Plus, you know how excitable I become in the presence of printing technology ancient (more so) or modern (less). In such places the air hums with possibility, with ideas!

The press was a Heidelberg, an offset model from the nineteen seventies that was quite similar, if not identical, to the one Karl and I operated in that dim, filthy basement workshop at the university. I wanted to run my hands over its solid metal, tap gently with my thumb the big buttons of its chunky control panel, close my eyes and live for a while in a bubble of time past, but one does not touch another man's press without permission. Besides, something was odd about the shop. Anyone who has spent much time in such establishments would be able to tell right away that this one was not in service. It was too clean, for one thing. No, not what *you* would consider clean, for a thick layer of dust rested over everything, but clean in a way very foreign to a print shop. No stacks of queued, completed, and in-progress jobs. No inky bootprints scuffed into the slick floor, not even at the corners of the press. No pulpy redolence on the air, no sharp odor of ink, no buttery solvents, no copper-iron tang of machine oil. This little front room was strictly for display and had been for some years.

What I had mistaken for an incandescent bulb turned out to be a small stand mirror on a counter-top, reflecting the sunlight. The rays dropped off quite dramatically at the rear of the shop, the shade of the machinery there so deep as to produce an impression of substance.

"Hello!" I called toward the back of the room, where another door stood slightly open. I moved far-ther into the shop and called again. As my eyes ad-justed to the dimness, I noticed that the doorway ahead was feebly limned.

Unsure whether I should knock, I grasped the handle and slowly pulled the door open, calling again, more quietly, as I did so. The room beyond was deep and narrow, like a widened corridor. The long walls were lined with head-high metal filing cabinets. At the far end, a fair distance from where I stood, was a large desk stacked high with papers.

"Yes, I'm back here. Who are you and what do you want?" The voice was male, if a bit high in pitch, and its owner pushed out the words with a curious, impersonal rapidity. The speaker's accent was pronounced but understandable.

"I'm, well, looking for a Mr. Yip, the translator ..."

"Yes, you have found him. What do you want? Come back here where I can see you." His brusqueness was beginning to rub me the wrong way.

"I need a few articles from local news Web sites translated into English." I walked toward the rear of the long room, holding the envelope of sanitized printouts before me. I still could not see the proprietor behind the stacks of folders and paper on his ample work surface. The faint light was coming from a single desk lamp with a green glass shade, the sort that one used to see in banks or libraries.

"I don't do that. Translate books mostly. Big works, important works." I could see the top of his head, a spectacularly unsuccessful comb-over.

"Yes, well, is there any chance that you could make an exception? Or perhaps recommend someone? I can pay. I can double the market rate for a quick, thorough job." A small man, I could now see. He was hunched over a spread of paper in the center of the desk (standing, not sitting; he was that diminutive) ticking away with a mechanical pencil.

"Double you say? And what is the market rate, Mr.—" He did not stop his work as he addressed me.

"I must confess that I do not know, Mr. Yip. I haven't had to deal with that end of things in many years." I declined to supply my name just yet. Why disclose it if he was not going to help me? Recent events had made me more aware, if only temporarily, that danger wore many disguises. I could make out some of the printed document from which he was working but very little of the light scratches he was making in columns on the vertically lined paper. He seemed to be going from Portuguese to Chinese.

"The truth is that translators are generally poorly paid. I have not worked at market rate or any small multiple thereof since my days as a graduate student. Look online for business translators. They work quickly and cheaply, fine for journalism. I am a literary translator." Still he kept up the astonishing pace of his work, tired eyes downcast behind thick glasses.

"Yip …" Something was belting around in my memory like a fat moth at a gallery window. "Not *Dr. Kai Yip*? Surely—" The scratching stopped. The translator set down his mechanical pencil with a pre-cise click, rested his hands to either side of his workspace, and for the first time raised his head and fixed me with the full and unsettling power of his my-opic gaze.

"Do we know one another?"

"No, but I think that my magazine did publish some of your work a few years ago. In a special South American issue we excerpted Paulo Roberto Silva's novel, the one about the boat. I seem to recall that a Dr. Kai Yip was credited with the—very good, we thought—translation. Unless there is another ..."

* * *

Dr. Yip took me to his favorite seafood restaurant and ordered enough to satiate four embarrassingly athletic men of metabolic needs far greater than those of the two (dare I say one and a half? No, that would be uncharitable and would leave me open to the observation that my own padding could perhaps fill out the fraction) diners now provoking "look but don't *look*" whispers from nearby tables.

These flickering-finger-shushing frumps were right that we presented a bit of a spectacle, were something of an odd couple, but so what. Here's what the doctor ordered: two small lobsters split down the middle with a single cleaver strike, tossed still twitching into a glowing hot wok with a little sesame oil and subtle spice, flipped once, twice, thrice, until the brutally burst surface proteins gathered a hazy light char, "smoked," they called it; six fierce great livid prawns with the heads on, crowning creepily a small salad;

succulent soft crab minced in an egg cup and topped with flying fish roe and a single quivering quail yolk, the whole shortly steamed; peeled vinegared radish and taro fashioned into a fish head—comic relief?; big black mussels boiled with ginger and garlic; a cold squid-and-ink pasta flecked with gold; soft sweet uni rhomboids on friable wheaten toast; perfectly pellucid scallop broth bobbing bits of bamboo and green onion. The courses came with white wine from Europe and white spirits—bai jiu—from sundry provinces. We were well drunk by the denouement.

Yip wanted something from me, obviously. His demands were strikingly unambitious. He recently had worked with a young Estonian poet, sought wider exposure, any exposure at all, for her quirky historical set pieces. He showed me a few. They seemed harmless, utterly harmless. I made a promise, portentous but vague, that *Lit* would do the right thing, make room for as many as two entries in an upcoming issue. He was all about the art, *really*. And my Web clippings?

"Oh, sure. Translate no problem. One week from now, very busy, please understand. Make it the Monday, not really open on the weekend, forgot to lock the door today."

"Forgot even to close it, somehow," I muttered, smiling into the middle distance.

The translator heard what I said clearly, it was apparent, but he looked at me as if he could not understand a single word.

* * *

Following a precarious ascent I knocked around in the atelier. I had not been too intoxicated to sleep for nigh on a decade, but there I was sour and sore. To avoid dwelling on my predicament, I booted up the laptop and read some e-mail from the office in Boston. Nothing really needed my attention, but I liked to send at least a perfunctory reply just to remind everyone that I was watching, that I was still in charge.

Something was knocking gently against the window. Because my table lamp was rather bright, a requirement for my hard-used eyes, I saw only my self and desk reflected in the glass but was reminded of that awful simile about the moth that I had allowed to take hold earlier. I mean that I thought it, the thing about the moth, at the time. Given the circumstances and the speed with which I am composing this account, I could forgive myself easily the slip. At the time I "allowed the moth in," I was under duress to be sure, but no strain that should have caused me so to break. A fierce tapping, conjuring for me a rook cracking snails against some lonely sea-sprayed crag, came at the large round window.

I scooted back my chair, stepped carefully around the right side of the desk—the space to the left I had crammed with unsorted stacks of books and a small waste bin—and approached the aperture obliquely, stooping beneath the hard lines of the close rafters. Away from the harsh gleam of the lamp, my eyes began to adjust to the dimness of the window alcove. Something was there, some shape like that of a giant bat spanned the frame. Within peering distance I saw at first my own reflection, then, shockingly, Mabel's face pressed close against the thick glass. She mouthed some words, but it was hard for me to read her lips because she was hanging upside-down, guyed —from what? the roof?—by unseen means. She looked weary and afraid. She spoke again, faint frustration or annoyance creasing the corners of her dry mouth. *Let me in.*

I felt around the hexagonal frame for a catch. I had never opened the window, had never before been struck with the possibility that it *could* be opened, so it took me excruciating minutes of fumbling to free the latch and swing it wide. Mabel tumbled nimbly, fluidly through into my arms, pushed me roughly away so she could loose the braided cable from the harness hidden beneath her clothes. And those clothes! They were what had given me the chiropteran impression, the subtle silken layers of her tai chi outfit, which I had not seen her wear since the day we met. She closed and locked the window, waving for me to get the light.

I crept back to the alcove, feeling my way along the floorboards. She sat slumped against the wall to the left of the window, trying to get her breathing under control. I could hear the thudding of her heart as I settled cross-legged in the near corner. She leaned against the wall, head back, eyes closed, for a long time. Her heart rate and breathing slowed, eventually I thought that she had fallen asleep. Her head popped up straight and her eyes opened wide with such rapidity that I started. She bent forward intently, and I assumed that she was going to speak; instead she pushed herself up with a long sigh, walked to the ladder, and climbed down.

I found her in the dark kitchen making tea. At the limit of my patience, I pressed her for an explanation, but she indicated through signs that we should not speak. It was hard to tell for sure in the near darkness, but I thought that she blushed furiously, a remarkably schoolgirlish expression catching for an instant upon her face as she inhaled the steam. She finished brewing the tea, which smelled pleasantly of timothy hay, and gestured toward the hall. She took the lead with the full tea tray held in front of her, and I followed haltingly back up the stairs.

She set the tray on my night table and motioned for me to be seated on the bed. With a curiously formal attitude she passed me my cup. Caught off guard, I bowed my head slightly as I took it. She knelt before me and raised her cup. I returned the gesture, and we very slowly, solemnly drank the pale tea. When we had finished, she collected my cup and put it with hers on the tray. She paced back and forth between the night table and the doorway, as if she might leave without saying anything, or maybe take the tea leavings down to the kitchen to stall for time. Seeming to have reached some point of decision, she marched back to the bed and resumed her kneeling posture. Looking at the floor between us, she began to speak.

"I can serve as your amanuensis no longer. In the morning I am leaving Hong Kong. You must do the same. Do it quickly, do not tarry. There is a difference in the city. Two days ago I was walking along Wong Nai Chung Road. It was a lonely stretch of sidewalk. Cars drove by at intervals, but the feeling was very much one of isolation. I like that when I can achieve it in the city, so I walked quite slowly, swinging my arms and humming. Suddenly I became aware of a sound. I could not place it at first, but then it came to me clearly: a dry leaf blown by a low but steady wind, scraping over rough concrete. I stopped and hugged myself around the shoulders. A chill had gripped me out of nowhere. The sound persisted, amplified as if it drew closer to my position. The trees were stock still. There was no wind, not a hint. I turned, looked up and down the sidewalk. I did not see the leaf, but still I heard it. As the sound drew alongside me, I felt the dry rasp of a late-autumn leaf move slowly across my cheek." She stopped and looked up at me for the first time, left hand pressed to the same side of her face. "I whirled around and around but could not find this leaf. It did not exist. But the fact of it remains. I have been touched by it, the sensation was unmistakable. Something is closing in on us here. It is not safe."

I did not know what to say. Plainly something, something of import, had happened. Strong bluff Mabel was shaking uncontrollably at my feet. I helped her up, moved her gently to the bed and had her sit at the foot. She lay back immediately, turned away from me and drew her knees up to her chest.

"May I stay here tonight," she asked softly. Taking up the tea tray, I gave my monosyllabic assent and left for the kitchen.

I know what you are thinking, but forget about it. I did not have sex with my secretary that night or any other. When I went back upstairs, she was snoring softly in the same position. I took my pajamas to the bathroom, changed into them, brushed my teeth, and splashed some water on my face. I wavered in the hallway, propriety tugging at me to arrange for myself a pallet in the office or atelier. I could not face the prospect of the hard floor. I was bushed and unhappy at the coming change if I could do nothing the following day to prevent it.

I slid furtively onto the bed, settled on top of the covers facing the door, a good two feet between my back and Mabel's. Later, when I was almost asleep, I heard her stir. She rolled over and scooted close to my back. I could feel a breast pressing softly just above my sacrospinalis. Even through the hidden harness, the layered silk of Mabel's tai chi outfit, and the thick cotton of my pajama top, I could feel that it was the *good* one.

Twenty-Six

She was gone when I awoke. It's not like I really expected to have a shot at changing her mind. No, at work was the simple, predictable coping mechanism of a man too old to accept the depth and pace of change brought by the past year. And now the prospect of some even greater, horrifically sudden, and utterly inevitable change caused his increasingly rigid network of synapses to seize up, to balk instinctively, absolutely.

But I was resigned. Though I had treated Mabel's superstitious, slightly crazed methodology with distant, wry mirth, I always had seen the wisdom in her conclusions. Whether the hocus-pocus was some sort of smoke screen or something she really believed did not much matter when the situational awareness, the quick intuition, the analytical capacity of the mind at work proved so keen. I would close up shop and move on, and shortly, waiting only for Yip's translations.

Packing put me in a foul temper. Backing down, running away, admitting defeat or even compromising at all, perhaps, is anathema. To depart just as I felt something successfully was being built made me feel like a fool of the worst kind: an old, damned one. And what would I take with me? My rolling luggage stuffed with my meager wardrobe, the ancient laptop and its bulky power supply—I would need a shoulder bag for those—toiletries, a few books. Distilled through strict tangibility, my estranged life seemed pitiable.

By the second evening I did not know what to do with myself, so I took to the streets. I set off walking not in the usual direction, but easterly into the heart of the menacing warehouse district. This was the monster that would swallow, quite soon I had no doubt, my little piece of the city, and I had never confronted it head-on. The transition was in no way subtle. Immediately, brutally the fantasy of the urban village fell away into the shadow of the hulking, marching corrugated rectangles of commerce's lowest tier. Everything was dingy—unwashed metal siding, pothole-pocked side roads and lots, small, utilitarian signage unlighted and unloved, overflowing rubbish containers, rusty pipes seeping effluent—in the aggressively down and dirty way common to business-to-business facilities the world over. Here fell the façade of civilization, the political right's pretty small concessions to human decency. Watch greedily the bloated corpse of late-stage capitalism perform its twitchy jig with unabashed infernal delight.

In the muddy side yard of one of these warehouses, I paused to take stock. I recognized the name on the chain-link fence, a brash American name among the mute Chinese squiggles. Laton Industries, if I recalled correctly, was captained by a criminal whose theater of world travel and trade had been significantly restricted to avoid extradition to the United States, who had borne without flinching brief scrutiny following the death of his mentor in a freakish yachting accident during a gentlemen's race to benefit a center for former child laborers in Vietnam. Yes, I was almost certain that it was the same guy.

A security light was on next to the left-most bay of the long loading dock. A reinforced door with a complicated-looking lock stood stolidly nearby at the top of a short concrete ramp. An annoying electric hum waxed and waned steadily. There was nothing here that I did not already know far too much about, only base truths that my sensitive mind frankly was better off not confronting directly. As I turned to go, someone grabbed me roughly from behind and thrust a tightly woven sack over my head.

* * *

One of my assailants forced me to kneel and whipped the bag off my head. I breathed deeply, glad (grateful, absurdly) to be free of the stifling fabric. We were in one of the warehouses. I had no idea which one because I had been ushered into the back of a van and driven around haphazardly. The concrete floor hurt my knees. I looked around the dim interior—casually, so as not to appear too interested—for some identifying mark or feature. At least two men were behind me. I faced a row of small utility vehicles parked in neat little bays against a long wall. I looked up and caught a glimpse of the ceiling far above, of a crane and catwalks suspended there, before someone cuffed me on the back of my head.

We stayed there for a long time. No one spoke, the three of us eventually synchronizing our breathing (one man, I thought, was a smoker). An occasional, organic-seeming sound somewhere far behind us led me to believe that another man lurked there in the gloom. I experienced a lapse, a loss of time. Mayhap despite the tense and dangerous situation exhaustion overtook me for a while and I dozed. My senses finally were sharpened by the screeching complaint of a large door rolling up or sliding aside on its worn tracks.

I heard voices, could not tell whether they were speaking Mandarin or Cantonese. The timbre and cadence made the mood of the speakers seem relaxed, jovial. After a short exchange with my minders, a half-Chinese, half-Caucasian man stepped into my field of view.

"Do you know who I am?" he said, a touch of amusement pulling his facial muscles lightly from their resting position. The murk of the warehouse exaggerated this effect, sending a shiver down my back like an icy droplet that has slipped past one's collar.

"No," I answered truthfully.

"Good," he said, stepping back around me to rejoin the other men.

They talked for a while, walking away from me it seemed from the shift in volume and tone. Eventually I heard the door roll back into place, finishing its travel with a reverberating bang. I held my breath and listened carefully for movement, muffled speech, coughs or snuffles, anything beyond the dull thumping of my pulse and the dark viatical hum of electricity. I am not sure how long I waited. I may have dozed again, unlikely as that would appear to one who has never been in such circumstances. Finally I could take the physical pain of maintaining position, the mental strain of upholding my impotent vigil no longer and sat back on my derrière, stretched my burning legs out in front of me and rubbed the numbness from knees and calves with awkward sausage fingers. I swiveled my head around to survey the area quickly, to note any avenue of escape.

A man in a purple suit was standing behind me and to my right. I started when my gaze slid across him, and he gave a little exhalation that could have been half of a laugh. He gestured for me to resume my kneeling position, and I complied right away because he had gestured with his handgun, which was fitted with a long and effective-looking suppressor. We maintained our stations for a long stretch, my breathing ragged, his nigh on inaudible.

His watch was relieved, and the new guard stood much nearer, so much so that I was taken aback when he broke wind with a sound like ripping sailcloth and the foul sulphur brume rolled over me. Some minutes later he did it again, muttering something—an embarrassed apology, I thought—and shifting his weight from one foot to the other in a strange, agitated rhythm. These outbursts continued, the blessed span between eroding alarmingly, until, following closely the last wave of the epic olfactory assault, I heard a strangled *ugh* and the hasty placing of some metallic object on the concrete floor (his gun! his gun! now is my chance!) and a brief fumbling, a hurried zipper whip, a shush and squat. All hell broke loose, and amid the disconsolate spluttering I made my move. Thick with stiffness from my lingering injuries and the hours spent kowtowing, I nevertheless managed to rise to a crouch, turn quickly on the balls of my feet, and grab the man's handphone from the floor behind me. The gun was in the right pocket of his red and white track jacket, and he reached for it with some distress, his ordure still spreading beneath him. The other men chose this moment and no other to return.

Vociferation erupted. A shot was fired in the air, not over my head but that of my guard, who fell back with a satisfyingly wet smack. A metallic ringing like the otherworldly tone of a Chinese song bowl lingered from whatever part of the structure had been hit in the shadow far above us. Everyone forgot me for a moment. I edged back toward the line of utility vehicles, wildly hoping that I could hop into one and putter away to safety. The intramural contretemps abated rapidly, however, and I was once more under guard. The boss glared daggers all around.

A sack once again went over my head, very roughly this time, and I was escorted to one of the utility vehicles. It must have been electric, for we were underway with scarce noise and no shuddering or hesitation. Shuffling, thumping, and whirring on multiple fronts told me that the other gangsters were sliding into more of the electric carts and falling in behind us in grim procession. The front of our cart tilted rather suddenly, and I felt my stomach drop. At the bottom of the ramp I heard the squealing of a segmented metal door being winched aloft, triggered by either a sensor or a remote control. The sound changed—we were in a close corridor, whether an enclosed route linking warehouses in the vast yard or a tunnel I could not be sure, but the length of our descent led me to suspect the latter—making my ears itch, though I dared not relieve the discomfort for fear that the motion would be misconstrued as an attempt to remove the sack. My innards lurched out from under me again, and a steep knobbled ramp carried us down, down, down.

* * *

I knelt in near darkness. It was very quiet. After forcing me to the cold concrete floor, my captors had backed away into the space behind me. I half expected a pack of starvation-frenzied Molossers to baying burst the silence neat and in bacchanal fury rend well my creamy cloistered bourgeois flesh. But nothing happened. I could no longer feel the pain in my knees, but knots in my ankles and the backs of my upper thighs burned like overtwined halyard. Attempting to ease the strain on these muscles, I relaxed my posture and immediately felt the sharp toe of a dress shoe in the small of my back. I straightened myself and endured. It felt as though hours passed.

Thunk. Thunk. Thunk. In succession three banks of bright lights burst the darkness. Even through the cloth covering my face, the sudden change made my eyeballs feel as if small nails had been driven into them. When the sack was removed moments later, tears streamed down my cheeks. The five thugs in front of me—at least one remained behind—wore very dark sunglasses with thick black frames. A tall metal cylinder stood next to them, along with a wheelbarrow with a shovel in it. Three sacks of cement and a bucket were on the periphery. In front of me, a few inches from my scuffed knees, a hole perhaps two feet across gaped. The sides of the shaft bore a whorled pattern as if it had been drilled by some gargantuan machine not currently in evidence. All around me small tubes, like reeds in a pond, protruded from the concrete floor.

The boss was sitting casually on the passenger side of one of the small electric vehicles, one leg propped on the dash. He was facing forward, not looking at me. Someone was seated on the other side of him, but I could not see the figure clearly. At a wave of the boss's hand, one of the lackeys retrieved a large jar, two gallons at a guess, from the bed of the little truck and carried it over to me. The inside of the jar was alive with fury. A strange red, orange, and black pattern writhed and swirled. It took me a moment to realize that I was looking at a seething mass of fire ants. I felt very ill. The lackey set the jar down beside me and went back to the utility vehicle to retrieve a length of plastic tubing. When he returned, with a single deft stabbing motion he displaced the wad of cotton from the hole in the lid of the jar, sending it down into the ball of ants. It disappeared quickly, subsumed, devoured. In its place the tip of the tubing filled the hole in the lid, but ants surged up the new pathway until they encountered the opposite tip, pinched closed by the thug's thumb and forefinger. This threatening aperture he held right up to my left nostril for several minutes.

When he whisked the end of the tube away, the gangster carefully wrapped an arm around the jar and scooted it over to one of the reed-like tubes sticking out of the rough concrete of the floor. I inhaled jagged breaths of stale air and felt my pulse in my temple. The man with the ants stuffed the end of the plastic tube into the metal one rising from the floor; the fit was precise. A stream of ants rushed through the clear plastic in pulses like those I felt within my own circulatory system. The seething ball in the jar became more orderly as it diminished, the result of some chemical signal spreading its message through the ant-network. A wail, pained and terrible to hear, rose from the earth. It increased, fell away, came again, more ragged and raw, the forlorn and vile parched sound of rasping mortality, of true and truly cruel torture. I toppled onto my side, pushed myself back from the flat black fact of the bore-hole yawning before me.

Two of the men moved behind me, each pinning an arm against my back, halted my meager propulsion and hoisted me back onto my knees. I shouted something—I could not hear myself over the screaming from the buried cylinder—that may have been entirely incoherent.

Following a motion from the boss, who looked annoyed and disappointed at my loss of composure, the man seated next to him stood and retrieved a satchel from the bed of the utility vehicle. He walked into the light, and the sudden glow reflected from his oily skin was like a small detonation in my struggling consciousness. I recognized the man. I had seen him up close and at length, at the beginning, after my unfortunate introduction to the territory. Dr. Sun set his case on the concrete, squatted and flicked open the latches. He brought forth a vial of clear fluid, set a thin needle atop a short syringe, drew a dose. His every movement was balletic, assured, but when he turned to administer the drug I caught something pleading in his eye, just for a moment. The screaming from the living entombed continued, though the sobbing pauses were lengthening in a most telling manner. I opened my mouth to say something to the doctor, one last attempt to set the world back in order, restore reason. The jab of the needle was not professional, shocked me with its violence. The plunger descended. I thought I saw swinging, flitting among the rigging from which the heavy lights depended a familiar form, that of my fellow Hong Kong dandy, who before had shown me some kindness, or was it my erstwhile amanuensis dressing the part? A flash of light! The glint of the translator's spectacles? I saw many other things, everything I had ever witnessed it seemed. I saw your face, Tanya, bittersweet and fair as on the night we first made love.

Twenty-Seven

An expanding universe of heat and light along its vast frontiers pushes ripples of treacherous time. In these cosmic water-margins billions of possibilities burgeon and wither, subatomic spin encompassing everything and nothing, Ogden Nash was a terrible poet. Clinical white command center surfs the roiling purple abyss. Unseen speakers pour celestial sound; Sagan co-opted pipe organ to prove his point. That crazy bitch who shot all those people who had denied her tenure once in a dream of righteous retribution crafted a potent pipe bomb. Earlier, even. Boom, brother, boom! Left to it so long because of her sex. Motley moted light streams, stretches, becomes fixed in place, everything traveling in all directions at once, all at the same sharp speed. A brief rise, above the turbulence a white light shines. Silhouettes at the limit of vision, rapidly approaching. Giant heads, like the statues on Easter

Island. Three of them loom. They are speaking, but the words are muffled, indistinct. They are facing the opposite direction, if such a conception can have any meaning here. Slowly they turn. Dostoevsky, Tolstoy, Turgenev. An ominous rumbling, the fading power of their previous word-weaving, lingers as a dark vibration. Stern stone beards frame their stentorian mouths, hide the bassoon-deep wells from which emanate such utterances of law, of creation. From left to right the lips part slightly, the cue taken at intervals. They are going to speak again, and their words will eradicate everything. An electric hum fills the void, the universe draws in as if a great breath has been taken. One moment of perfect balance. Their flashing eyes, their floating hair! They speak. Every star snuffed out, so many candles on a sawdust cake. The stark white command center cannot maintain its position. Vertiginous descent, black clouds, baked beans burned. Molasses smell. Frosted earth. The sound of surf. Gulls wheel.

I came to my senses on springy pale turf. I lay on my back, and suddenly there was pain. The gray sky slipped down and to the right, over my tingling bare toes resetting itself for another swoop, as if I had drunk too much champagne at a garden party. My mouth felt stuffed with cotton. On the horizon the sun—was it rising or setting?—seemed an unreal and bloodied orb filtering through the shifting sea-fog. I attempted a maneuver and soon sat more or less upright. A beige expanse that had hovered worryingly in my lower vision like the sort of anomaly that can signal a stroke proved to be a large, tacky building. I recognized the place. This was the hillside on which Mabel and I had taken our picnic, and the building was the casino at its foot. I remembered my former secretary's words, that she had a sister who worked there. Knowing the landmark helped me get my bearings; the sun was rising. If Mabel's sister was on the cleaning or perhaps even kitchen staff, there was a chance that she would soon arrive on the early ferry. If she worked the floor, then I had quite a wait ahead of me. Regardless, I was going to have to find myself some clothing, as not many women of any culture relish the idea of striking up a conversation with a strange man in his perfectly natural state.

Cautiously I hoisted myself. Expecting some lingering dizziness, some weakness of the limbs, I was pleasantly surprised by steadiness and a general feeling of hale constitution. Bending low, I made my way monkey-wise down the slope. The crackled beige stucco of the rear wall of the casino struck me as uncanny in the same manner the rising sun had when I first glimpsed it. I wanted to flake some of it off and carry it around with me. My body radiated, my retreating testicles providing the only clue in my personal sphere to how late the year had grown, how cold it had become. Several metal doors perforated the hilariously crackle-grabble wall (I *did* pinch off a bit, but realizing that I did not really want to carry it around after all and having nowhere decent to store the flake let it drop among my hairy toe-knuckles; I watched it there for a while, motionless, flotsam-looking, imagined it as a watercolor in the MFA—*Detritus on Toe-Fur*, solitary corner presentation, subtly angled "natural" lighting—became incensed at the image, attempted to riffle the fated flake o'er my funny flap-flaps like a brilliantly buffed coin across a stage magician's taut limned knuckles, succeeding only in breaking it apart). One was ajar, and through it I entered a kitchen storeroom.

Boxes of MSG and dehydrated staples such as seaweed, squid, and wood-ear mushrooms were stacked as high as my head. A utilitarian corner cabinet held promise. After opening its flimsy doors, I hesitated between two terribly appealing options: bright orange janitorial coveralls complete with a name patch or a chef's smock and toque. Potentially problematic, either attire was. Furthermore, close inspection revealed that both were intended for a man significantly shorter and slimmer than the one now standing naked before them, hands on his well padded hips. Thinking of the ferry crossing if I could somehow swing it and the trek that would follow, as I had no cash or credit cards, I went with the workman's uniform, squeezing into it with some effort and trepidation, holding fast with one hand my genitals until the cruel zipper had zizzered clear. Looking at myself in the small grimy mirror that was taped to the inside of one of the cabinet's doors, I was reminded of one of my father's crude sayings from his years in the Oklahoma oil fields, "Now *that's* fifty pounds of manure in a twenty-five-pound sack."

It was with that very earnest self-criticism hanging sharply in the air that my intrusion was discovered. Two maintenance workers in orange coveralls identical to but markedly dingier than my own stopped short their breezy banter and exchanged arch glances that were half disconcerted, half amused. The older of the pair held up a hand to the younger, who crossed his arms and stood vigil, then walked calmly to a beige telephone hanging on the tiled wall and lifted the receiver. It must have been a direct line, because without dialing and after only a brief pause he began speaking. I was not sure what language served as the medium for the message, but I was impressed by his casual delivery. One hand holding the receiver to his left ear, the other adjusting his dark blue cap via its bill, he stated succinctly the facts as he understood them. He repeated himself with the same unconcerned aura and slowly replaced the receiver on its hook. I knew from the quiet way the two men awaited whatever authority they had summoned that flight was futile. They, together or separately—even the older of the pair, the stoic phone-wielder, who by my estimation was a minimum of ten years my senior, one never can tell with these Asian blokes—could have easily outpaced me, and though they certainly would have carried out my capture and restraint efficiently and with an infuriatingly quiet dignity such a perturbation lay decidedly outside their prescribed duties and represented a foreign bother that they could well have done without.

Presently a diminutive man in a deeply black, impeccably lint-free tuxedo arrived with two cleaver-carrying line cooks in tow. His manner was quite refined, but the threat at every moment remained clear as he questioned me. I found myself liking him immensely and responded to his inquiries as honestly as my situation allowed. He was unflappable and betrayed no surprise or even judgment at my unwholesome predicament and the somewhat hazy but clearly dire events that preceded it. He explained that ferries packed with gamblers would soon be arriving (giving the lie to my earlier impression that I was facing a rising sun; once again my sense of direction had failed me) and that it was imperative that I be presentably attired and demeanored for my trip back to Hong Kong on the first of these. He arranged with expeditious orders and short soft claps for an outfit to be assembled: a serviceable jacket from a store kept for those embarrassing occasions on which some wealthy but low-born mainlander arrived improperly attired, a spare pair of trousers from the dealers' stock, an only slightly ruffled waiter's shirt, socks and shoes from who knows where. Underwear remained a problem, and it seemed that I would go commando for some time yet. He pressed into my palm Hong Kong dollars, money for the ferry and, generously, a taxi ride at sea-jorn's end. He had an assistant take a high-resolution digital photograph of my startled mug and explained entirely without malice that I was now on a secret list and would not be welcome in any of the company's properties anywhere in the world; he assured me that their facial recognition software was very accurate.

In the half-hour that remained to me, I asked half-heartedly the hospitality staff—the floor staff was almost completely male—whether anyone was related to Mabel, had heard of someone named Mabel, was sister to Mabel. No one, and no fleeting flickers of recognition either. Though I could and would have managed things well enough myself, I was escorted down to the pier and onto the freshly emptied ferry. The little man who had so adeptly managed my expulsion stood on the boards at the end of the bay with a satisfied expression, lingering there until we were out into deep water and churning up foam.

Twenty-Eight

Everything happened quickly then.

I had the taxi driver drop me off a couple of blocks down the street from my office. Using the available cover, I made my way home as carefully as I could. I was feeling tired, sore, and, mentally, cored by that juncture. As I approached, I saw a man loitering in front of the big window. He saw me as well, and I froze for a moment in a rather ridiculous half-crouch. He straightened his posture and patiently waited for me to regain my dignity. Weary of all the Kafkaesque bullshit, I resolved to do my best to brush past him without exchanging looks or words; if he bum-rushed me, then he did. When I passed him on the sidewalk (my vision at range is not what it used to be), I felt a pang of familiarity followed quickly by full recognition. He was the detective who had questioned me at the hospital in Kowloon, who earlier had invaded my home and office. He said nothing as I fumbled with the door. In my distracted condition, I had forgotten that of course my key had been taken with my other belongings. I felt pressure on my right arm. The detective had the back of his hand against my ill-fitting jacket, pushing me aside. I allowed myself to be moved. He withdrew a key and turned it in the lock, opened the door halfway, and with his palm up indicated that I should enter. Again I complied.

"Shower, shave, dress yourself properly," he said, eyeing my ensemble with undisguised contempt. "Gather your belongings—one suitcase only. I will wait for you outside in my car. Choose carefully but quickly, Mr. Makarov. You will not return here."

Hearing the door close in the vestibule, I exhaled and surveyed with deep, defeated melancholy the interior that had in many subtle ways come to reflect my own. My dandy's dress of which I lately had been stripped was laid out on the counter. It had been cleaned and pressed, and my wallet, passport, and pocket effects were arrayed alongside. Anger welled up, and my shoulders began to shake in a way that I could not control, in a way that frightened me. I was utterly impotent, utterly alone. I trudged up the stairs by dint of memory, vision blurred by unshed tears. I shucked my casino-modern mummer's motley, turned on the shower, stood for a while watching the cascading water, the rising steam. Entering the naked sacred space through that hotly wafting vaporous curtain was so symbolic that I nearly suffered an aneurysm.

Scoured and scraped even cloaca-lly clean, boisterously buffed and burnished I carefully clad myself with shattering sensibility for extended travel. I retrieved and packed my rolling luggage mechanically, a strange calm pervading my thoughts and movements. At the head of the stairs I hesitated, turned around and rolled my luggage into the bathroom, popped the panel concealing the cubby, got on my hands and knees and crawled quickly inside. I sat in the grand old way gracious before the bomb, freed my spirit to cross-legged commune, but the old feeling would not come. I embraced the cylinder, pressed my smooth, sensitive cheek into its cool surface. A small thrill, a hum, some kind of resonance was detectable at the very limits of consciousness, a sly sort of sensation, barely there at all, almost playful in its paltry manifestation. Maintaining my close grip, I tipped the bomb gently into my lap, scooted back toward the bathroom by rocking my body and gripping with my buttocks. The far end of the cylinder scraped softly along the sighing floorboards. The passage seemed interminable, but I by sudden synecdoche separated surely from myself, some shell shuttling a-somatic through the terrible teeth of the tyre-trap of time, a muddled American mind forever voyaging. Ecstasy! Bliss!

Again at the hushed head of the stairs I hemor-rhagic-ally hesitated. I longingly left the luggage and languidly ascended the stranded ship's ladder to the amaurotic atelier whilst gleefully imagining a particularly and purposely roughly sketched storyboard daringly depicting the lowly labanotation of my increasingly, alarmingly pathetic limbs as I hauled my choate creaking carcass one last time. The irrefragable impulse had been to take final stock, to fix firmly in mutinous memory—all we mere mortals have, really—these scant dozen precious bifurcated months of perilously perfervid progress (authorial, dolichocephalic, editorial, minatory, uxorial you must believe, always believe) as if identity itself were solemnly at stake. I did disheveled descend to the merchant-builder's accidentally ascetic greenwood-gapped floor. It could have been caused by the sudden exertion or the inhuman stress of the situation; *it could have*. To my credit I rose with alacrity, gathered what I knew I needed—the gosling-gray laptop and its outmoded accessories, including its outsized carrying case, sharply, egoistically in damned defiance of the authority impatiently awaiting downstairs—and bade the one-time sanctuary abrupt adieu. I hope that this passage has sufficiently conveyed the Bernhardian tori along which my thoughts sluiced during those days; clearly I should have been getting out more, but now it was too late.

* * *

"Where are we going?" I asked the detective.

"To the train station," came the curt reply. The driver was one of those infinitely exchangeable hirelings.

"Not the airport?" I offered.

"Politically problematic," said he. Note now that I am being relatively lenient in my cold-insensate transcription of R's and L's.

Silence in the curiously ataractic, antagonistic taxi-space reigned. Along the way and especially in the gloaming of the tunnel I imagined some understanding exchange, some cinematic worlds-colliding acknowledgment of our necessarily, eternally separate-but-equal spheres. Instead I was dumped without ceremony at the farthest curb bordering the dingy thronged station. Tickets had been pressed harshly into my sweating pale hands, an entire itinerary out of my control. Minders pushing from behind, past as prologue, what have you, alongside as well with little room for Western doubt. Security was very tight, and all of those wending through the pass-gates were subjected to detailed questioning. When my turn came, I was prepared to acquit myself with honor but instead faced an abbreviated screening as the security workers exchanged nods with the undercover agent behind me. I waited with the masses (with police agents all around, leering openly, making a display of their status rather than trying to conceal it) for the somewhat late Through Train; it was quite distressing or terribly impressive to me that these were running at all in the present situation. I vacillated between these thoughts, as you claim I do in all things, through the remainder of the process for gaining the station proper and its utilitarian platforms. When the train arrived, I percolated up the more-or-less orderly queue, boarded, found—blessedly, as explaining why the bag was too heavy for me to lift more than a few inches would have required an effort I was in no shape to expend—a floor-level rack for my rolling luggage, maneuvered through the press of settling riders to my assigned seat, all with a hand on my elbow. I was wedged in the center seat between a tired-looking man of middle age with an agricultural air about him at the window and a corpulent young man with thick glasses at the aisle. The former pulled down his dark blue baseball cap and leaned his head against the window, while the latter withdrew from his handbag (very like a woman's purse, but I had come to expect that) a comically tiny laptop computer, unfolded it with a snap, balanced it on his considerable paunch, gazed down his nose and through his bottle-ends at the oddly proportioned screen, and proceeded to tap away at the flat faces of the little keys using only his pinkie fingers.

Mr. Hand had lowered himself magisterially into the aisle seat of the row behind mine, but my attempt to get a better look at him had been thwarted by the arrival of my young neighbor's eclipsing bole. It took a long time for the train to get under way. I fought back the feeling I often get in such circumstances, the sensation that there is not enough oxygen to go around.

* * *

We were well up the coast, and night was falling. Taking a cue from my portly neighbor, I had spent a few distracted hours tapping words into my computer. It felt good to thus flex my fingers. Because the laptop's ancient battery was good for nothing, I had to run a power cable under the sleeping farmer's legs to the electrical socket with which long-distance trains thankfully were equipped. The big guy with the little computer had expressed mild alarm when I withdrew the chunky, hopelessly outdated system. He and several others seemed also to find annoying the light clicking of the keys. This is the sound of creation, you philistines! You should have heard the thrilling chaotic clamor of the newsrooms of old, or even the persistent saturnine rat-a-tat of the solitary writer in the dusty birdcage of his walk-up city apartment. I turned the screen down low and typed the present straight out of my mind. Even with my history, my *literary* history I mean, it took me some time to realize just how I was going about it.

Letters. E-mail, really, addressed and saved for later sending, if where I was going one could hold out the faintest hope that a network connection might materialize. But these letters were outrageous, filled with all manner of things that I would never say to the addressees, certainly not to their faces, nor even at such a remove (well, if I were terminally ill or something, I suppose I might let 'er rip; probably not on second thought, considering the admirable restraint that I demonstrate under present conditions). I would never send these messages. I began moving them from the outbox to a newly created dead letter folder. Storing the new ones there directly exacerbated the brashness of my endeavor, and I truly became lost in time, tapping out messages to figures long dead, to figures B.E.—before e-mail, before *electricity*. Somewhere in the middle of my missive to Caesar on the Gallic front, which for some further wildly sentimental, grossly ahistorical reason I composed in the manner of a series of telegrams, came my minor epiphany: I was aping Moses Herzog. This little speed bump of base rationality did not halt my progress, but it did alter the course of my manic episode (I, quite sensibly, averring as if by solemn self-oath that the ocean of history is of unconquerable depth and that as we dive

even a short distance, all while thinking we have penetrated quite far, the pressure quickly mounts to crushing strength). I began working, after finishing a few
final clever admonitions as to the folly of imperial ambition, my way back toward the wan light of our
cursed age.

Twenty-Nine

As we approached a drab commercial city, the engineer had to stop short of a switching station to let another train pass, and the sudden cessation of my stifling, shabby car's gentle rocking motion woke me. An azuki bun that I had purchased from the refreshment trolley and had been absently nibbling from its paper bag had tumbled down my chest during my unintended snooze, leaving a trail of crumbs and several sticky splotches on my shirt and keyboard. I was grateful that the weighty computer itself somehow had stayed firmly in my lap, but I had mild difficulty locating the bulk of the wasted snack on the thin gritty carpet that ran beneath the basely squelching faux-leather seats. It was under the seat in front of mine, wedged between the soft lustrous side and wide buckled matte strap of a lady's enormous handbag. Bending awkwardly around the bezel of my laptop's screen,

I stretched my hand downward and came up far short of my goal, even with my stomach scrunched painfully and my face pressed hard into the whitish cloth swaddling the seat back (these covers feature snap locks that click onto small posts at the top and bottom of the seat, providing the illusion—rather enfeebled by the well layered presence of oil and grime—that they are regularly removed and cleaned). The already temperamental hinge at the base of my computer's screen groaned alarmingly, so I aborted my bumbler's effort at bun retrieval. As I straightened myself and drew about my shoulders through quite a performance of collar tugging, lint picking, and seam smoothing the invaluable invisible cloak of human dignity, I was jostled by my portly row mate. Treating the incident at first as no more than an unfortunate side effect of the man's corporeal condition, some sudden shifting of one roll over the top of or out from under another, some personal tectonic event no doubt terribly embarrassing to the individual in question, I took no offense and turned my eyes and fingers back to my electronic folly. In short order the assault was repeated, accompanied by a low but clear harrumph. This time I pointedly, dramatically withdrew my left elbow from the sea of warm nauseating gelatin that had on the arm rest overlapped it handily, whipped around in my seat with venom on my tongue. The man was doing something funny with his face. I thought for a moment that he was suffering an infarction, felt terrible about what I almost had said, almost had shouted. But this was no mere involuntary reaction to pain or fear. The contortions passing along the deeply buried facial muscles spoke tremendously of will: their singular purpose through a minor feat of detection I realized was the slight dipping of an oily black eyebrow. I followed with some composure the bafflingly inept cue, and my gaze fell upon the tiny screen of the man's ridiculous flab-top computer, on which were written the purpled words, "Be Ready."

I felt a low judder perturb the train's rhythmic rocking as the engineer began the stages of braking. The man seated next to me put away his things with surprising focus and efficiency, and grim lines settled around his mouth and eyes as he shifted his considerable weight to the front edge of the cushion. He held in that expectant position a certain human dignity, an unaccustomed lightness that lifted his latent sapience momentarily free of its unfortunate faineant shell. I almost admired him then, eagerly awaited the unfolding of whatever plan of action he had on short notice concocted regarding my freedom.

The fat man's timing was impeccable. As other passengers stood and began rummaging in the overhead bins in anticipation of our arrival at the station (and in contravention of the multilingual announcement now into its third repetition), he sprang from the seat edge, pulling sharply on the head rest of the man in front of him, who was still seated and became annoyed at the thoughtless jostling. At the same time, and just as the car lurched to the left—clearly my savior was familiar with the route and had expected it —he pivoted to waggle through into the aisle his ungainly trunk, became unbalanced and fell in a slightly comical, entirely believable way. My watchers were standing in the aisle, momentarily trapped a couple of field workers and one flailing fat man back from my position. I sat for a little too long, admiring the performance.

"Run, you fool," said my exasperated ally in a desperately loud whisper.

I stood and entered the chaos of the aisle. It came to me quickly that I was not going to be able to retrieve my rolling bag without interference. I hesitated with my hand on the latch of the bin. I turned toward my watchers. My eyes met those of the taller man. He had donned tight leather gloves, the kind that would creak when the wearer flexed his fingers. He held my gaze for a beat, then slowly shook his head. I twisted the release, let go, and watched the oblong door rise with an agonizing lack of urgency. Movement transformed the periphery into a surging blur. I grasped the side handle of my luggage, tugged at it, determined to haul it out into the open, to nudge it into the fat man's wake with my knee, to deal with it somehow. In the event, it crashed onto my left foot with a force that in my customary slight detachment I considered sufficient to splinter bone. In seconds I was held fast. The taller watcher looped his left arm through my right, held that shoulder firmly with his taut glove, which seemed like an entity unto itself. He wore an almost kindly expression. His companion straddled my suitcase and gripped me firmly at the waist; this, I think, prevented me from sinking to the thin, grubby carpet of the train car's floor.

My former row-mate in the meantime had made good his own escape, slipping out the forward door of the next car back. I saw him run lightly along the high chain-link fence at the edge of the platform, glance once over his shoulder to gauge the proximity of any pursuers, and with a gentle kick, or not even that but simply a fillip of his shiny black shoes, lift off the paving stones, and wheeling his arms in front of his torso as would one operating a nearly frictionless crank soar over the razor wire topping the tall fence, over the prominent swell of the hill beyond. Am I getting confused? Could it really have happened like that? Yes, that is how I remember it. Yes, that is a small part of what happened on the train ride to Siberia.

Thirty

They must have drugged me. I can recall only episodes, things out of a childhood fever dream. The strongest of these, and the fondest oddly enough, is of waking in a small state, full of fear and an isolated incomprehensibility of self or other that triggered a vertiginous sensation. A firm hand, in my memory it was gloved, but the gloves were traced with veins, the veins throbbed with life, pulled me in, smothered me against the solidity filling the coarse blue dress shirt of the larger of my minders. This memory is layered, overlapped, deep in a way that makes me think that this scene must have repeated many times during our journey. I was embarrassed by the dark spot spreading across the shirt, over the man's sternum, the prodigious drool pool of my sodden slumber. He did not speak during these intervals, but kept up the reassuring pressure as if to convey the sentiment, "It's all right. It's okay, don't worry about the shirt, don't worry about a thing. I'll watch over you until the end."

Once, I came to my senses in the toilet. The three of us were crammed in there cheek by jowl. The smaller man, who rarely spoke or showed any emotion, was splashing my face with cold water. In the toothpaste-spotted mirror glass I glimpsed my slack facial muscles, the effect bringing to mind the sort of Halloween masks—terrible former presidents, such as Nixon, Reagan, all three bozo Bushes—that I always found to be truly frightening. My minders were trying to indicate that I should drink some water from the tap and then urinate, that I had gone too long without attending to either need. In the moment their concern was deeply touching. My eyes may have become slightly moist. I wanted very much to please them, but the problem was that the signals that my brain was dispatching were being lost somewhere on the way to my extremities. I slumped against the small sink and twitched my arms ineffectually. The taller man wetted a wad of toilet tissue and very gently dabbed it all over my face and neck. This minor ministration felt quite good, and I closed my eyes for a while. The next thing I knew the taller man had me in a sort of half nelson. His companion stood stock still against the flimsy door with a look of mild disgust on his waxy countenance. My supporter had managed to undo my trousers and push down my boxer-briefs, but no amount of shaking and lifting produced the cherubic stream. Finally he sat me down on the toilet, with his gloved hand poked my penis downward as if prodding a venomous snake to see whether it still lived. I sat there happily for a while. The smaller watcher left, saying something that I could not understand as he closed the door. The remaining attendant turned off the lights, and, I thought after becoming accustomed to the near darkness, held his breath. Eventually he turned on the tap, first letting out a trickle, then allowing a cascade of roughly half force. When he heard that this gambit had worked, he opened it fully, let the water gush forth. We giggled like schoolboys.

Too much. Given too much, I had taken it. The train was traveling at impressive speed over an open snowbound landscape, but to me we were in an unfathomable tunnel, a sharp descent. A dark, oppressive atmosphere weighed all around, threatened to crush the cars like a line of aluminum cans tied together with short lengths of string. Bat-wing shadows flitted among the oblivious passengers, sucking the vital essence from their nostrils as they dozed, babbled to one another, or watched the unspeakably awful martial arts movie playing on the tiny swing-down screens, half of which (to the bitter disappointment of the occupants of rows where such duds were distributed—it was a rather odd arrangement, anyway, having two screens for each row of three seats—judging from the wretched wails following the announcement of the showing) were out of order. A high, piercing sound like the call of a kettle grew in intensity as the revenge farce played out on the tiny yellow-tinged displays. Was it some side effect of the functioning of the train? Of course not, no modern caravan such as ours was pulled by a steam engine. It struck me suddenly as the vibration of the life forces of the victims in the crowded car, a resonance, an amplification of the individual distress each would express if only he or she possessed the faculties to comprehend what was happening. I became aware of a contralto drone, lasting well beyond the endurance of a typical set of human lungs, projected through the close air with startling clarity. The swiveled heads of the formerly quiescent passengers and the sudden intimate attention of my watchers led me to the conclusion that my own gaping mouth was its source. The short and the tall man stood, goaded me into rising as well, guided me into the aisle and forward, into the clacking accordion purgatory between our car and its leader. There my cry continued until no air remained, either within or without it seemed to me as I saw shifting constellations suspended in the half-light. Exhausted, I slumped to the stippled steel and felt as one with the bumping, grinding progress of the train, the vibration of each

hard thump penetrating to my marrow, there subsumed, integrated in a more or less sustaining way.

The train had stopped. We remained in the space
between two cars, my minders looking somewhat concerned. I retained enough mental clarity to note that
this probably related to the terms of their contract
rather than any rapport that we had developed in the
course of the rail journey. They hoisted me to my feet
and in a truncated train of our own—Tall in the lead,
Short as rear guard, I in the middle—we progressed to
the car in front of ours and from there through the
open doors onto the platform. We were either stopping for quite a while or transferring to a different
train, as passengers poured out onto the long platform
blinking into the several bright lights that pierced the
night from atop their skinny metal poles. Everything
had a run-down Soviet sort of look. No obvious security apparatus constrained our movements, and Short
and Tall dragged me and my luggage wide of the
dingy station, across a rut road, and into a cleared
pocket conscribed by overgrown ruins.

Moonlight shone on a decayed statue of an angel.
Our breathing clouded the gelid air. Short and Tall
backed off, stepped through gaps in the remnants of
thick masonry walls. I was not sure what they expected of me, so I stood there in the suddenly overwhelming relief of semi-solitude and took in the night.
On further contemplation, the statue struck me as

perfectly realized as it now was. Surely this was the intention of its creator all along, making it instead a statue of a decayed angel. Maybe one of the men planned to creep up behind me and put a bullet in my brain, spattering the statue's pocked raiment with my cranial viscera. I thought then of the fat man's blood pooling on the platform and shuddered. I heard a strange, rhythmic sound coming from beyond the crumbling walls. It seemed to shift as I turned to pinpoint its location, emanating first from one side, then the other. What sort of animal made a noise like that?

Mr. Tall came through a gap in the wall with his shirt untucked and his semi-erect penis protruding from the onion-shaped hole of his undone fly. He seemed very agitated and advanced on me at top walking speed. *Oh, just shoot me*, I thought. He mimed unzipping trousers, taking them down to the knees. *I'll not make it* that *easy for you!* He made some lewd gestures in the region of his genitals. When I did not acknowledge his performance, he grew exasperated and gave his penis a few peremptory strokes, then pointed to my crotch. He turned and hurried back through the gap in the wall. What sort of animal makes a noise like that? The animal that is man, no other.

So they were concerned that I had been neglecting that form of elimination as well. I had no intention of joining the festivities, but as I stood there shivering, with the suggestion hanging in the air, I began to feel a certain pressure deep within. *This may be the last time.* With a shrug I got down to business. They gave me plenty of time; the intermittent sharp breeze let me know that they both were smoking. I had to employ a bit of throat clearing and coughing to alert them that I had finished and was growing uncomfortably numb. Together we left the moonlit ruins. The robe of the decayed angel was not splattered with my brains.

As we boarded the train, I noticed that very few Asian passengers remained. In fact, there were very few passengers at all.

Thirty-One

Once we were underway, I was given another draught. I did not question the necessity of this administration, felt slightly eager to embrace the near-oblivion it brought. The segments of track must have differed in length from those across which we previously had traveled, as the clacking came much more frequently even though our speed had been noticeably reduced. A nimbus of diaphanous blowing silk formed the corona of my suddenly constricted vision. I thought, at least for a moment, that I could feel its seductive slide across my left cheek and down my neck.

* * *

You were stunning, you know. When we were young. Oh no, time has not touched you even today in the way that I have come to expect of your kind. There was then, however, something that now, something that for some time now, is missing, and I am left with a vague sense of guilt, the floating feeling that it is somehow my fault that whatever otherworldly glow surrounding you has been extinguished. A trick, another diabolical deceit.

Your father absolved me. I cannot remember whether I ever told you—probably not—but it happened on the fourth of July, the year that we went to Washington for the fireworks. He had reserved a rooftop, you will recall, quite close to the action. He had contrived an embarrassing theme, the gardens of Babylon. Pudgy homosexuals lolled about in loincloths serving little bites of suspicious origin (most seemed Mexican, Spanish at the outside). The featured libation was some god-awful cross between mead and tequila that his personal chef had assured him was deeply authentic. The centerpiece, a colossal peaches and cream cake, stood stolidly in the form of a ziggurat. American independence!

He was not drunk. *Really.* I had noted through the tortured transition of dusk that he was conspicuously sober. Something was bothering the big man. Uncharacteristic flourishes and feints earlier had alerted me that whatever was the matter had an unfortunate personal import, and in the grim devil-you-know spirit of the born proletariat I pushed things to a point at which leaving them unaddressed would leave everyone feeling terribly silly and carelessly self-shorn. We repaired with earthen mugs of herbal infusion to a quiet cool vine-shadowed corner of the artificially burgeoning terrace. We gazed into the hazy sky overarching the firmly subordinate corridors of American power. The infusion tasted of gym socks, but was, your father's personal chef assured him, the product of a curiously snakeskin-like dried root of some stunted desert shrub, the cultivation of which had in modern times become exceedingly uncommon, with a long and respectable history of occasional use as a medicinal quaff.

He began his obviously well rehearsed, tediously eidetic soliloquy with your birth. You nearly killed your mother, he told me straight off. He never would have forgiven you. Irina's blood pressure plummeted, spiked before the countermeasure should have taken effect, cycled viciously thereafter. Your father stood helpless at the foot of the bed, yanked from one extreme to the other time and again for almost two hours. In the middle of the ordeal, a nurse asked, *Wouldn't you like to see the baby? We're doing everything we can here. Take a short break. No*, he said fiercely, then simply curtly, *I will remain with my wife.* No, he never would have forgiven you. Did you know all of this? He never *did* forgive you, simply for those hours of uncertainty, that afternoon of impotence, with witnesses. Irreparable harm befell his outsized self-image that horrible day, and he never forgot —not for an instant—the shameful feeling, and you certainly, my dear, have no siblings (but benefited, in a way I think, from the most obvious manifestation of this lingering fear: a practically house-bound mother). Anyway, following this casual insult to your very existence, Maxim conceded that our union had worked out "fine." He thought that my company was, in general, good for you, given your quirks of personality. He even had warmed to what he had begun in embarrassment, to avoid the appearance of your having an unemployed spouse—my enterprise, something he, trailing the minor notoriety of the two early awards, suddenly liked the size and shape of, the heady whiff of culture that he could produce like a clove-studded orange to cover up the stink of callous capitalism that clung to his clothing and hair, oozed from his large pores. Yes, this was just before the dark period of *Lit*, the terribly trying year or so during which your father attempted—despite his every promise to the contrary —to assert editorial control. But that has nothing to do with what I was saying. It is just that on that evening, in the rockets' red glare, he absolved me, and even through the period of our cold war he never rescinded that minimal blessing. I hope, for your own sake, Tanya, that you will be able to do the same.

* * *

"End of the line," said Mr. Tall.

"But can't it go on forever?" I drawled. We both were using Russian by then, I think.

Short had ceased to speak, even to his companion. He wore the abstracted air of one who had something—many things—that he would rather be doing. He was prepared to bear up, to perform his remaining duties with blunt efficiency. He led me (quite gently, just a finger on my elbow) through the oddly phased fluorescent light of the deserted station and through a battered metal door at its rear that was held in place by a rod welded to its center just above the loose handle; this rod rested on a large nail driven into the mortar of the thick wall to the left of the door, the arrangement apparently compensating for the deficiency of the uppermost hinge, which was broken and dangled uselessly. We crunched across the smooth, twinkling surface of the snow in the station yard to an impressive special-use vehicle parked behind three large rusted gas tanks and a dangerous-looking stack of oil barrels. The powerful lights of the vehicle shone through the deep dark and down onto the snow pack, cutting a glowing corridor for quite a distance. I momentarily was awed by the sheer size of the tank-like treads as our close approach made clear that they rose to the level of my neck. The engine was running, a rumble that could be felt more than heard, and diesel fumes hung heavily about the solid chassis. A little metal stairway, of a design similar to those used for small aircraft, had been pushed against the body of the machine. We climbed its shallow steps and ducked through the cramped oval doorway into the belly of the beast. The engine noise seemed much louder inside.

The driver greeted my minders with a very serious inclination of his furry-hatted head. No words were exchanged, but the other men took his meaning and strapped me tightly to a thinly padded rear-facing seat bolted to the floor of a small bay in the cargo area. The other bays were filled with fuel canisters; the smell in the close space was overpowering. My knees rose to my chest, and I could tell that I was in for an uncomfortable ride. An oiled canvas curtain separated this area from the cabin, which had windows all around and housed four fixed seats representing comparative luxury. An anorak-enveloped figure occupied the seat next to the driver. It made no move at all during the time I was able to observe it, not the slightest swivel, tilt, bob, list, nor even the faint but ineluctable rhythmic pulse of breathing. I was left with the impression of artificiality, of mannequin, effigy, golem. The curtain was drawn roughly into place, and I was left alone in the dark. It was very cold.

* * *

As a child I marveled at the shocking fluency of the world of dreams. I—with no parental prompting— kept from an early age a ragged unlined journal of nocturnal adventures. I desired, desperately it seems in retrospect, to continue from night to night the heady exploration of some vast uncharted realm, to form into a cohesive and compelling narrative the idle neural flashes of semi-sleep, the self-sifting detritus of an ordinary waking life. It is then no surprise that fiction claimed me quick to its velvet fold. Mine was not the typical child's four-color fun-house, neither awake nor dreaming. I dismissed out of hand a recurring nightmare of being dragged around a colorless land- scape by a lurid cartoon crocodile, thrashed into list- less submission by the whirlwind tour of Connecticut scrub, paralyzed but aware as the fiend began with relish in its clear reptilian eyes to feast on my taut calves and thighs (I suffered from night-cramps in those areas so sensitive to a boy's rapid growth), pre- ferring the more adult asides, those subtle intimations that something *real*, something that had transpired within my ken in the swirl of days gone just before, concealed hidden depths, was ripe to bursting with fulgurous meaning, lived truth there in the palm of my little lined hand if only I could will myself to pay strict attention, to see it properly.

Thirty-Two

Sometime during the day, at least I remember it as the next day or maybe the one after, and there was some natural light at any rate, feeble though it may have been, the vehicle clacked and juddered to a halt. The engine strained toward some upper register for a worrisome moment, then died with a cathartic belch. I heard one or two of the men exit and bang around somewhere on the outside, opening and shutting a hatch or the like. I wondered whether we had broken down, but only briefly as the wobbly sphere of my worldly concern had shrunk to approximately the size and shape of my nearly bursting bladder. Eventually Short came for me. When he loosened my bonds I felt leaden, as if my body had come to rely utterly on their strong support. I had a lot of trouble standing and walking after the long hours in that cramped position. Whatever drug they had administered possibly still was at work in my system as well. Short seemed annoyed at my decrepit state and treated me quite roughly.

Outside a camp had been set up on the leeward flank of the craft. Three yellow tents were staked out around a cylindrical gas stove, and three checkered folding chairs with light aluminum frames faced the fire ring. A heavy black pot already sat atop the stove, flames tickling its soot-stained belly. Short led me well away from all of this so that I could take care of my pressing business, a small kindness for which I was absurdly grateful. Once back at the fire, he pushed me onto a pallet of burlap sacks that he had spread out on the packed snow. Tall was nowhere to be seen, but the driver and his construct companion occupied two of the folding chairs, the latter man— mockingly motionless, utterly unnerving—fairly swaddled in multiple quilted thermal blankets over his already puffy anorak, two tiny patches of waxy flesh peeking out beneath his oversized tinted eyeglasses, looking for all the world like a successful practitioner of sokushinbutsu. Tall emerged from the central tent bum-first and clutching a dun leather case to his chest. He trundled over to the unoccupied chair and settled there, placing the case, which was taller than it was wide, in the snow at his feet. With the sense of a man anticipating some great satisfaction, he with four nimble flicks of his left forefinger disengaged the clasps astride the central slit. With a palm to either side of the unfettered divide, he spread the case open before him, scraping small wings in the crust at his booted feet. He rummaged within, exhibiting behind his magician's screen a variety of movements that in their intimate choreography piqued my addled interest but the mystery of which soon fell to the blunt adze of earned experience: clearly he with reverent care was preparing for imminent consumption some sort of liquor. He stood and took carefully the couple of steps that carried him to the swaddled man's side, holding forth a very full tumbler of some clear but cloudy (or the glass was cloudy, it was hard to be sure) liquid. He held the tumbler up to the area beneath the tinted eyeglasses but did not really tilt it or did so with admirable subtlety. I thought at first that it was a trick of the light or a manifestation of my degrading physical and mental capacities, but no, it certainly was the case that very slowly the level of the liquid in the tumbler began to fall. When the vessel finally was empty, Tall wiped the glass thoroughly and returned it to the case. I hoped that he would next set about preparing drams for the rest of us, but he turned his attention instead to the stew.

Short all this while busied himself beating rabbit-trails in the snow between the tents. He was not really doing anything, just pacing heavily to and fro, tugging at the lines repeatedly to test for tautness.

Eventually he came to stand near me in anticipation of the meal, which Tall presently ladled into hefty two-handled bowls, stamping the already packed snow in a triangular pattern. Tall served the driver first, then placed a steaming bowl in his own chair, then motioned Short over to take his portion and mine. This proved an awkward burden, and the latter bowl was fairly dumped into my lap, an open expression of contempt on the face of its deliverer. I ate the first bites with enthusiasm, digging chunks of potato, cabbage, tomato, and lamb out of the glossy sour red-purple broth with the curiously flat wooden spoon provided, and immediately felt a little sick. I slowed down and watched the other men. Tall and the driver chatted quietly, amiably over their simple fare, leaning toward one another in their folding chairs. The enigmatic bundled man remained aloof, apparently required no further sustenance. The still standing Short continued to fidget, holding the heavy bowl against his chest to allow the use of his spoon. I saw that he, the low man of the assemblage, was meant to share the prisoner's pallet but stubbornly clung to some last ragged scrap of professional dignity vital to his self-image. I returned to my rapidly cooling bowl and persevered, knowing that proper nutrition could well be key in enduring whatever lay ahead on this journey. Even at that late date I clung to foolish hope. After the evidence of our busman's board had been cleared away, Tall again cracked his case. He prepared three tumblers and beckoned Short to join them on the other side of the fire. Short, looking very much like a hound that had been kicked quite a few times but now was being offered a marrow-rich bone, emerged from his sulk in stages and by the end of the round was squatting on his haunches to be on the level of the other men and join in their casual conversation. Tall spared me a glance now and then out of sheer professionalism, but clearly was unconcerned by the prospect of flight. Where would I go? I would tire quickly in the deep snow and bitter cold; they could just let me exhaust my reserves and then follow the trail to retrieve me. At first his eyes held pity, but as the rounds went on this turned to repugnance, probably tweaked by my eager aspect each time he filled the glasses. Eventually my turn came. I did not see Tall at work in his case, as by that time I was nodding in and out of sleep. He pressed the tumbler into my hands and stood back with a fist on his hip, an air of motherly "Now be a good boy and take your medicine" about him. I obliged with a deep gulp. The liquor was anise-flavored, or perhaps it was plain buffalo grass or potato vodka and whatever drug it contained tasted of aniseed. I did not care.

Eructations circled the fire, the familiar Homeric rumble-gurgle of men at their ease. The clear dome of sky exploded in riotous swirling color, and I clapped my hands giddily.

"So vivid!" I exclaimed.

Half-smiles shone around the camp fire; perhaps the others were not seeing what I perceived. It suddenly seemed of utmost importance that I share the wonder with my companions, that I endeavor at the very least to describe as accurately as possible the ultrachromatic display fronting the tenebrous void.

"Time for bed," said Tall.

Short hoisted me to my feet and led me to the closest tent, at the mouth of which I had to return nearly to ground level to enter. He crawled in behind me and zipped shut both the outer flap and inner mesh. He indicated which side of the sleeping mat was to be mine and shackled my right ankle to his left, rolling over so that we were pressed back to back under the thick thermal quilt-sack into which we awkwardly zipped ourselves. Despite the conditions I drifted off at once.

* * *

In the morning I woke sweaty but refreshed, though my mouth felt as if it were packed with cotton. While extricating myself from the kip cocoon—which definitely smelled like it had held two heavily perspiring, flatus-expelling men for eight hours—I roused my companion. He took it well, shook his head a few times, puffed out his cheeks, rubbed his eyes. He sat up and removed the shackles, rubbing his ankle where the cuff had chafed in the night. He unzipped the inner mesh and outer flap and crawled through the opening, leaving the gaping void behind him. Freezing wind ruffled the tent and stung my flushed cheeks. I crawled outside and failed in my first attempt at standing. The waxen man remained in his chair, and the scrim of powder coating his wrappings led me to believe that he had spent the night there. Tall and the driver already were busy dismantling the camp, their brusque words and movements betraying some slight sense of irritation, some tension. Short motioned that I should help him take down the tent, so I worked free the lines and weights (stakes were futile in that environment) on my side to the best of my ability. Short had to come around to finish the job, set me to unthreading and collapsing the segmented poles. The coordination of my gloved fingers in the bracing cold proved inadequate to that task as well, and he pushed me aside in annoyance. Tall and the driver were watching impatiently but with amusement playing around their eyes; the swaddled man and his chair were gone, perhaps carried like cargo to the snow machine, but I would have liked to see him walk.

287

Thirty-Three

It became our mode, the arduous days of travel followed by nights of camping under the lurid lights of clear, dark skies. The miasma in the cargo hold increased markedly as the canisters of fuel were fed into the tank of the insatiable machine. I feared permanent damage to my precious brain from the numberless hours of sucking in such potent fumes. I quickly lost count of the cycles and drifted unmoored on the swift current of time's wide river. We stopped on quite a few occasions to refresh our supplies, some days fetching up in a barren flat space on the edge of a dirty village that looked as if the inhabitants had little more than two sticks to rub together but which nevertheless after interminable rounds of negotiation through some conjurer's trick materialized everything we required, others meeting by serendipity or design a military or commercial convoy moving thwartwise our heading.

At one of these meetings we shed the swaddled man—in the morning he had been there, in the evening he was absent; in between we encountered a military convoy that included (I saw while the soldiers labored at exchanging our drained fuel canisters for brimming ones) many fearsome tanks—and though an empty seat now presented itself I remained strapped in the back.

On what was to be our last night of camping, I could tell that something was amiss from the outset. The other men seemed edgy, distracted. The easy camaraderie of previous evenings evaporated, and our repast was perfunctory, the leavings cleared away with unaccustomed efficiency. The only drink on offer was bitter tea, and over even that small indulgence the atmosphere prompted that we did not linger. Afterward the driver boiled a great kettle of clean snow and draped stiff long cloths over its rim. Short produced an oiled leather case, the exterior of which when unfolded presented a rustic triptych—a hunting scene burned into the hide by a skilled if not imaginative artisan. The interior housed leather loops and pouches containing the multifarious implements of masculine toilet from a more civilized age. The other men set to the task at once, stripping off their boots, socks, trousers, and undergarments, soaping up the cloths and scrubbing with vigor their lower reaches while standing on their shucked coverings and avoiding excessive dripping. This activity, begun with a shocking sense of purpose, ceased for a beat as the men made clear with raucous cries that I was obligated to join them. I stepped up to the kettle, stiff from squatting, and did my best to catch up. Following the sudsing, we scraped our legs with rasps and buffed and burnished sloughed cells and freezing water droplets with hot rough towels from a small stand placed perilously close to the fire. Despite our proximity to those very flames, my testicles conveyed in a ripple that traversed my many nerves to the top of my head the unsettling sensation of rising sharply into my abdomen. The haste with which everyone donned his now shabby-seeming duds demonstrated that I was not alone in this feeling. We crowded closer to the radiating dark surface of the kettle, risking burns. Next came our upper environs. We were able to lean into the steam with greater control and decidedly less urgency during this interval, and the mood lightened somewhat, the scrubbing and scraping seeming more like a bracing spa treatment. Following a thorough drying, each man helping his rightward neighbor with the recesses of his back, we put our undershirts back on and prepared brushes and cups for shaving. Straight razors comprised the inventory, and I had never used one, though I remembered watching my paternal grandfather give it a go in one of his rare appearances on the rolling landscape of my childhood. I nicked myself almost immediately, and Tall took over, guiding the blade over my cheeks and throat with a rapidity that came close to convincing me that my number was up; I emerged unscathed.

In the morning we paid special attention to our armpits and teeth, but otherwise tore down the camp and bundled into the snow machine utilizing the established protocol.

* * *

We stopped well short of dusk, which arrived earlier each day. I was unstrapped and hauled from my berth, leg muscles screaming their strident objection to the rude relief of compaction. Outside I closed my eyes against the white expanse, tears solidifying as they coursed down my numb cheeks. The three men from the front changed into sharp black suits with an air of resigned professionalism. A jacket (a size too large) was provided for me. Tall looked me up and down, then shrugged. We piled back into the vehicle and did not stop again until long after dark, a sort of forced march far more extensive than our usual intervals of travel. Any sociological effect that the jacket was meant to accrue was spoiled by the weakness of my bladder.

* * *

I was led roughly down the steps by an impatient Tall. In the distance gleamed a crystal fantasia. The snow machine was parked well away, though other craft, smaller single and double examples in which the riders traveled in the open air, shared space with sleds and dogs arrayed on a packed heath on the edge of the glow broadcast from the otherworldly structure that seemed to pin everything to itself as the singular point of reference on the bleak plain. Short slammed my suitcase down beside me and climbed back into the cabin. The driver remained behind the wheel. Tall, the leather of his gloves creaking in the silence, pointed toward the light. When I made no move, he grabbed me by the shoulders, turned me around, and shoved me with a force that sent me sprawling. I whirled, clung to his leg, begged for him to reconsider. He shook himself from my grasp with a firm finality, though in his eyes I saw something kind, wistful. He spun on his heel and without the aid of the already withdrawn steps clambered into the snow machine, which shortly roared to life, bearing hard to the right of its former trajectory. I knelt in the snow next to my luggage and watched its running lights dwindle away into blackness. After some time, I rose mechanically and half carried, half dragged my rolling bag toward the shimmering vision on the flat horizon.

Thirty-Four

The structure resolved itself into something that made primitive architectural sense the closer I drew. Thick blocks of ice had been been stacked in sound staggered rows to form a large rectangle adhering to Euclid's golden ratio while seemingly drawing inspiration from Le Corbusier for the minor refinements gracing its "windows" and roof. The walls had accreted snow and a certain amount of runoff from the inevitable melting and refreezing of the surface, thus taking on a frosted, mottled appearance; the ribbon windows running along the front wall at a height just above the apex of the arched entryway (and I assumed, correctly as it turned out on this occasion, Tanya, along the other walls as well) were by contrast strikingly clear, kept this way I would learn by the daily application inside and out of hot water, leaving the "panes" slightly inset. I wanted very much to walk the perimeter, but since I already was numb with cold I headed for the front door. Merriment ceased as I pushed through the overlapping sheets of thick plastic to gain entrance to the ice bar. For a moment all eyes fixed on my traveling salesman-like figure blinking on the threshold, then laughter erupted and conversation resumed. The matron tending the bar hurried over to confiscate my rolling bag, which she stashed for the sake of convenience behind the wide bar, and ushered me into a booth of sorts—partition, bench, and table made from blocks of ice—then lit a dark green candle in an artfully molded ice holder with a wooden match produced from a sagging pocket of her saffron apron and struck against the much-abused enamel of her upper incisors. Sausage fingers absently adjusting the edges of her headscarf, she inquired as to my pleasure. Her northeastern peasant dialect made absolutely no sense to me for an embarrassing interval, toward the end of which, and just ahead of my belated reply, she in the same perfunctory speech uttered, "Right. House special." Laughter again rippled across the candlelit interior.

I first was served buffalo grass vodka, neat in a squarish molded ice vessel, accompanied by a shallow ice-bowl of pickled turnips. Before sampling the fare— I was well beyond concerns of drugged or poisoned provender—I caught the suddenly obvious scent of Tunguska fir. It arose from the candle at the center of the ice block serving as my table. I inhaled deeply and closed my eyes. My apparent satisfaction with the meager offerings prompted further glee. Well, it was true that the vodka was harsh (also that I would not have refused turpentine at that juncture), but it kindled my throat in an appealing manner and paired well with the earthy pickles, which were positively *homely*, reminding me forcefully of the domestic exertions of my paternal grandmother, toward whom I had behaved as a total cad during the few years that she shared with us. My reverie was interrupted by the arrival of a large bowl (made of clay, not ice, and with a thick hot pad beneath to spare the slick surface of the table) of sharply fragrant stew. Mutton, beet, and potato sat heavily in a glistening sauce falling somewhere between awning maroon and hog lagoon brown, that thoroughly rustic hue. The scent prompted my nostrils to prickle and flare. Tentative probing with the provided wide, flat spoon surfaced sections of wilted winter cabbage. A peppercorn bobbed atop a beet raft like a shipwreck survivor on the evening news. I levered the first sustaining spoonful to my weather-torn lips. Memory, cursed-blessed memory, thrilled to the dimly familiar sensations produced by this simple act. In an instant I was transported to a small apartment in Queens that for the few years we occupied it felt not at all like the urban prison that by all rights it should have but very much like *home*, haven, a solidly comforting place of solace for the three of us. Ayelet, never much of a mother or wife, had left by then for her first calamitous tour of Europe, and neither father nor grandmother seemed to miss her, but both were of course quite concerned with any ill effects her absence might have on me, probing tactfully now and again for signs of trouble. I did not miss her either. Why open these old wounds? I put down my knife and fork. The bar matron refilled my tumbler with vodka and lingered at my side.

"Well, what do you think?" she asked loudly.

I explained in halting fashion that I liked everything very much, that her house's fine repast brought me warm memories of my lost childhood. She relayed this information to the bar at large in her rough local speech, and the patrons burst into riotous laughter, grabbing neighbors' shoulders and knees in fits of mirth and passing a possessive round and round. A big bearded man in a checked flannel shirt stood suddenly, sending ice vessels and crockery crashing, swayed uncertainly for a moment with murder in his eyes, then trudged sullenly through the entry arch. Squawking laughter followed on his heels. Somewhere in the cacophony I absorbed the gist: I had been consuming with the gourmand's gusto Beardo's recently expired sled laika, Druzhok. The bar mother stood by, hands pressed together and eyes wide, awaiting some dramatic reaction. I raised my tumbler to the room, downed a gulp of vodka, took up with patrician grace my utensils, and set to finishing my meal.

The matron had returned to her bar and set about pouring water into molds to make more of the tumblers. She soon was joined by a short man with a large belly and a fringe of hair that stood in wild disarray as if he had just risen from a particularly hard slumber. He blinked, scratched his stomach through his thin white undershirt, and scanned the room doubtfully. Just then the plastic flaps covering the front door arch parted violently, and Beardo staggered through carrying a carbide hatchet flashing a wicked gleam along its business edge. He roared incoherently and took purposeful slow steps toward the bar matron. Because of the hour and therefore their sunken state, the men around the ice tables were slow to process this turn of events, but once the gravity of the matter had asserted itself they were—almost as one— on their feet and in motion. Three of them reached Beardo, catching at his shirt and trousers with their slow, meaty fingers. Inertia, the bare blade's arc of inevitability as I suddenly saw it, carried the quartet crashing into the thick frosted slab of the bar top, the hatchet coming down hard at the farthest extent of its wielder's reach, sinews straining to their limit pushed there by pure will, by white hot rage. The blade bit home, carving a deep gash in the matron's upper arm. Her wail drew icicles down my spine and, I had no trouble believing in the moment, the eaves of the cursed structure's inviting exterior, pulled up sharp stalagmites of rime as far as the curdled cry carried across the frozen wasteland in every direction. The torpid man in his sweat-stained undershirt shook as if doused with gelid water from a thin tin pail and sprang at the now prone attacker, tearing at his face with long yellow nails, spitting invective fit to blanch the most experienced of sailors. He too was set upon, two other patrons holding him back with the sort of attention to detail that allowed him to land a few good kicks on the cranium of the half-trussed object of his ire. Beardo and (as I surmised) the matron's hen-pecked husband were dragged to opposite corners by their impromptu entourages. Into the chaos came another woman, seemingly only the second on the premises, an Asian in blue brocade with the air of a former beauty about her. She grabbed a thick gray cloth from behind the bar and approached the wailing victim, whose blood had splashed thickly over the slab and continued to seep between the fingers of her trembling right hand which clasped the vicious wound.

"Don't touch me, you shriveled cunt," the matron spat. "Don't you dare come near me!"

The woman in blue hesitated, set the cloth down on the bar, and retreated to the side room from which she had emerged. No one seemed eager to staunch the seeping red wound, and the matron stood there in stolid shock, panting now with a slightly sagging posture, so I did my best to assist her. She shooed me with curiously gentle tutting noises, finally accepted with a modicum of dignity my relatively clumsy ministration. I soon was replaced by the husband, who had calmed himself and donned a thick leather apron with many pockets and stains. He piled several of the gray cloths on top of the bar and bade his wife to rest her arm on them. He pinched the wound at three spots along its length with an assessing expression. The woman flinched at each contact but did not cry out. The man upended a bottle of rye vodka and allowed it to flow liberally over the gash. His wife bit her lip and looked away. The husband with admirable focus prepared a concoction from ingredients withdrawn from the pockets of his apron, macerating them with more vodka in a mortar from behind the bar. The result, with which he seemed well satisfied, resembled dark mud matted with moss and fescue. This paste he slathered over and into the raw wound. Its palliative effect, whether purely psychological or some combination of cooling and anesthetic properties, immediately was apparent on the matron's face. Her regained composure was lost moments later when her husband withdrew a wicked-looking needle—both long and surprisingly thick—and a wooden spool of a stout black thread that appeared to be both braided and oiled. While soaking a goodly length of the thread in spirits, he held the needle in the flame of one of the candles on the bar using tweezers grasped through a tartan handkerchief, which implements he returned to their proper pockets at the precise moment when they were no longer useful to him. He threaded the needle with ease and bent over the arm, looking at it with a dispassionate eye, as if it were a cut of pork and not something attached to a live, loved human being. I had in my youth noted this uncanny ability of detachment, of obliteration of self for the duration of some delicate and often high-stakes operation, among those who routinely dealt with animal carcasses, the hunters, farmers, butchers, and such who of necessity confronted some rather harrowing aspects of living with brisk self-sufficiency. With the first few pulls of the thread through the angry flesh, the matron did wail her eerie keening sobs, but then she too entered some other zone and stood silently beside herself as her husband worked.

It was toward the end of this unexpectedly tender and affecting spectacle that the woman in blue came for me. She led me into the room from which she earlier had emerged. Not much ice was visible there, and the atmosphere was softened by the thick oriental rugs, billowing silks, fine furs, steady candle-light, carefully placed mirrors, and a gentle perfume of incense that was not cloying in the least. My luggage lay next to a large bed, the ample crimson covers of which had been invitingly turned down on one side. The woman gestured for me to sit in an armchair next to a small kerosene stove. Once I had obliged, she served me a small cup of anise-flavored liquor. Remembering the nights around the camp fire with my erstwhile minders, I asked her what it was. We had some trouble communicating at first, our grasp of Russian proving equally timid. It was her intuition that steered us toward English; I never would have guessed. She spoke it with a native's grace, and I, forgetting my as yet unanswered first question, asked her where she was from.

"Once I was American," she said with downcast eyes. The admission had produced obvious pain, so I let the matter drop.

Flailing about for some politic segue, I came up empty and returned to the curious contents of my cup. She told me that it was Bulgarian mastika and that while she had not developed a taste for it she consumed plenty because it seemed to be a favorite of local women when entertaining. Momentarily confused, I nearly voiced my thoughts about the bar matron and her estimable person being the only women I had seen and the two of them not being on the best of terms. It came to me quickly, while my mouth still hung open, that in the current context "local" probably meant all the scattered villages, trading posts, military installations, and homesteads within two or three hundred miles. Instead of conspicuously clapping my jaw shut, I lifted the delicate cup to my mouth and drained it in a gulp. The taste was quite familiar and not entirely unpleasant. Without hesitation my hostess came to my side to refill the cup from her plainly fashioned silver ewer. She had a cup herself this time. As she took tiny sips with an easy grace, she developed a faraway look that produced in me a vaguely unsettled feeling that I was failing some social test, proving both boor and bore in this intimate environment.

"We haven't been properly introduced ..." I ventured.

"Honey," she said huskily with a hint of amusement. "They call me 'Honey' here."

We looked at one another over our cups for a time, and then she rose and walked slowly over to my chair, an unmistakable swish in the hem of her dress. She knelt next to my right leg and ran her hands up and down my calf, gently squeezing the tired muscles. Looking up at me all the while, she languidly removed my battered shoe and caressed the arch of my foot through my no doubt somewhat unsavory sock. She soon repeated this procedure on the other side, and I felt myself relax in a way that I had not experienced for weeks, possibly months. As she moved up to tug at my zipper, I pushed her away gently and explained in plain language that I was a married man, loyal to a fault. She produced a stun gun from some hidden pocket and hit me full in the chest before I could react. Demonstrating surprising upper body strength, she slung me over her shoulder and carried me to the waiting bed. I was paralyzed completely, stiff top to bottom, and she at her leisure removed my clothing and violated me most hideously with her red-rimmed mouth, leaving lewd lurid streaks of lipstick as a calling card, a reminder of who had held the power in this trashy provincial evening encounter.

Oh, all right Tanya, I consented to the blowjob, there in the chair. I did protest at first, but Honey assured me that any entertainment had been prepaid by the gentlemen who had dropped me off and that she would get in trouble if I refused her company. Out of compassion I yielded, honor intact (but everything I wrote earlier about the maid and Mabel was absolutely true). Afterward we changed into soft but thin ramie hanboks that she produced from a small chryselephantine wardrobe. Looking around, I came to the conclusion that the few such containers arranged tastefully around the room constituted her worldly resources. She was trapped in that isolated ice bar, this one chamber become her demesne through an initial demonstration of will followed by constant vigilance, and if her forged balance were to wobble even that small illusion would rupture like a day-old party balloon. It was an ugly, quiet desperation that I came to know that night, dear heart.

Sometime after Honey had fallen asleep, I slipped out from under her arm and tiptoed to the common room. It really was like the main hall of some late medieval country inn in character, as the men who previously had been seen eating, drinking, talking, and gambling were sleeping or passed out on the floor between the tables, most with rudimentary bedding bunched beneath them. The bearded man slept rough in a corner; he was not tied up and no one kept a watch. Wary of waking any man among the company, I crept up the central aisle toward the bar. I took a long look behind, having stolen only the briefest glimpse before in the general scrum following the hatchet attack. It was appointed as one would expect; I was hoping for a trapdoor under a rug or something, I suppose. I continued into the small kitchen and found few surprises there as well. There seemed to be no refrigeration (naturally) or plumbing (worryingly). A large clay pot stood over a carefully constructed fire pit on an insulated plinth in a central depression. A metal door on the wall to my left bore a small window that confirmed my suspicion that the portal led outside. An arch draped with thick vermilion velvet with a green and gold grosgrain border beckoned from the opposite wall between dull stainless steel appurtenances. As I approached, a soft sound tickled my ear hairs. With subtle movements of the middle and index fingers of my left hand I drew aside a section of the central slit and pressed my eye to the opening. The room beyond was small, significantly smaller than Honey's close chamber. Not on a raised bed but a pallet on the floor lay the matron and her husband. The woman was on her back and from the beatific appearance of her lined face neared sleep. The man was on his right side slightly in the foreground, his body obscuring the lower reaches of hers. I could see from the straps across his shoulders and back that he still wore his apron. He sang softly to his mate, stroking lightly the injured arm. I at once felt like a cretin for intruding on this intimate scene and hastily withdrew to the common room.

"Did you need something?" came a high-pitched but strangely authoritarian voice.

I jumped. Turning in place, I found that the short man in his stained apron was right behind me. He did not seem angry in the least, just sort of matter-of-fact, as if this type of thing were the smallest parcel of his innkeeping duties. In the clutch of consternation, I smiled weakly and somewhat desperately gestured to my groin while mouthing "bathroom" into the air above and well to the left of his disheveled pate. His expression softened almost imperceptibly, and he led me to a large brass urn just inside the entrance. I had noticed the vessel on my way in but had dismissed it as mere decoration. In fact it was filled with hibiscus and urine. What a strange location for the latrine, I found myself thinking once the lid was lifted. The smell was not so bad, really. Lots and lots of hibiscus buds gave a reddish color to the contents and masked fairly well the odor, slight hints of popcorn drifting through the sharp floral screen. The urn was filled to within centimeters of its rim. I worried that it would not hold what I had to give, but the innkeeper encouraged me with a hearty slap on the back while not budging from my side. My need was too great for me to object, so I made my deposit. The line settled comfortably below the rim, well short of sloshing range.

"Is that all?"

I was not sure whether he meant did I have other bodily business or that he was unimpressed with my output given my urgency, so I did not reply.

"And the shitting?"

The former. So frank! I shook my head.

"Good. But we have a tradition here. He who fills the urn must empty it."

"What about the women?" I blurted.

"Only the men," he said curtly. I wanted to probe deeper into the logistics of female elimination in such circumstances, but his manner made it clear that this was not an appropriate topic.

"Where?" I asked.

"Through the metal door, which you have seen, in the kitchen and to the left. Looks like a well. Isn't."

"What about the flowers?"

"Dump as many as you can, we have plenty. Hold the lid tightly as you walk," he added over his shoulder as he returned to his wife.

The urn was very heavy. It probably would have been heavy holding only air. With unaccustomed effort I hoisted it a few inches and waddled around the corner to the edge of the bar. Keeping a hand on the lid was almost impossible for a man of my build, and I abandoned the idea early in my trek, opting instead to cradle the vessel as steadily as possible while making my steps glide smoothly, the faded trauma of high school marching band proving suddenly beneficial. It took three such heats simply to move from one end of the bar to the other. Why must every damn thing be so trying? Bit by bit I progressed, and eventually the tall brass urn rested next to the metal door. I thought I heard a brief chuckle from behind the velvet curtain as I wiped my brow with my sleeve. I went back to Honey's room to put on my jacket, returned to the kitchen, fogged the small window in the metal door with my breath, rubbed a peephole, saw nothing. When I pulled open the door, the icy intake hit me with considerable force. I braced the door with my foot and got both hands under the cursed piss pot. The path that I had to follow was well beaten, but there were some tense moments as I stumbled over a snow mound or simply stepped awkwardly under the burdensome influence of the brazen urn. On these occasions, the lid chirruped little metallic warnings, and I stopped to rest my arms and legs and to inspect myself and the towering cuspidor for signs of leakage. It felt like a hard slog to me, but in reality the sump was quite close to the kitchen door. The ring wall around the hole was made from blocks of ice. I leaned over the edge for a look but could see nothing in there. Setting the lid in the snow by my feet, I eased the urn up and onto the top of the ring wall. With my right arm around the tapered base, I tipped the vessel until I heard splashing a surprising distance below. The urn shifted suddenly as some inflection point was reached, and I nearly lost my grip. Thinking of how *that* conversation would play out brought beads of sweat that sent chills across my scalp and down my back.

It was during this lull that I noticed the odd structure behind and to the right (when coming along the kitchen path) of the wee well. It was shaped like a hangar, but slung very low. The walls appeared to be made of packed snow, but perhaps that layer simply concealed ice or concrete. The roof appeared to be more packed snow over a lath of something that, where it protruded, looked like twisted beef jerky. A panel woven of the same material and daubed with mud, leaves, scraps of cloth, and similar detritus served as a door. One simply shifted the thing aside to reveal the opening. Curious as to the building's purpose, I did just that. Sticking my head through the opening, I was met by darkness and the earthy scent of a barn full of overwintering animals. I could see next to nothing, but my groping around the entrance encountered an oil lamp and long wooden matches. Once the lamp was ablaze, I stepped through the squat arch. Inside I—stooping as the cramped interior required—discovered an expanse of gray sand. Small bales of hay were stacked along the walls, excepting the alcove containing the lamp, the respectful space around which impressed upon the viewer some sense of reverence, the atmosphere of animism, of a small and out of the way shrine in the unspoiled country-side. Lines scraped across the surface of the sand divided the span into an orderly grid. Some cells contained miniature dunes, presenting an inviting alien landscape like those sometimes seen through the peepholes of papercraft shadow boxes. My bemusement soon was remedied: the shitting! It was a human-scale litter box, love. Indeed, leaning against the bales I found something like a sturdy rake with closed tines, looking for all the world like the miniature version with which you conduct your amateur archeology in Fabriana's covered loge. Though I did not have a pressing need, in the excitement of the moment and not knowing what the morrow might bring it seemed prudent to avail myself of the rudimentary facilities. The mounds marched in an orderly fashion from the corner opposite the entry, so selecting the next in sequence was a child's task. I dug out a shallow depression with the toe of my shoe, dropped my trousers, and squatted. Out of the wind and within the confines of the ice blocks and bales, the cold felt less menacing, more bracing. For not having to go I produced an impressive pile. Belatedly I realized that one probably was expected to carry a wad of tissue in one's pocket. I raked the sand, and at this remove it presented itself as not merely gray sand but a mixture of the same and rock salt, over the practice grave and mounded up more to indicate that this square was now occupied. I wondered a great many things about this curiously practical and surprisingly pleasant arrangement. How long did it take to fill the grid? Not long, by my calculations, if this night at the "road house" proved typical. Who was responsible for scooping when the grid had been completed? He who filled the final square? What then was done with unearthed artifacts? And then of course there were the women to consider. Mysteries piled upon mysteries during my mad journey, Tanya, and perhaps that is what I wanted all along.

Back in the ice bar I cleaned myself with a rag and bucket of water that I found in the kitchen and tiptoed through the common room. I stripped to skivvies and shrugged on my robe, slipped back under

Honey's featherweight forelimb to pass what remained of the night.

Thirty-Five

It was to be an early start. Honey shook me gently, led me to the armchair where she had set up a tea service on a low table. While I sipped the strong black tea and ate with little enthusiasm cold sausages and pickled beets (she apologized for the fare), my hostess prepared a bathing station. First she placed a thick rubber pad, about three feet to a side, on the carpet in the sole gap of suitable dimensions, then she laid a terrycloth mat that was slightly smaller. On one corner of this she set a large wooden tub that smelled pleasingly of spruce. Next to it she deposited a long-handled scrub brush, a bar-shaped brush like those used for buffing shoes, and a small stand akin to the type upon which a classical guitarist rests his foot. She departed and stayed away for some time. I helped myself to a second cup of tea. When Honey returned, she bore a dual burden. Under her right arm she carried a low wooden stool, and her left hand grasped with the aid of a thick pot holder the coiled wire handle of a very large kettle. The latter she held well away from her body, and the steam trailing in its wake provided a more than adequate explanation. She eased the stool onto the central portion of the unoccupied half of the terrycloth mat then with obvious strain tilted the humongous kettle to empty its contents into the tub. I was not moved in the least by this display, felt not the slightest urge to act the white knight. Now why was that? Honey departed again to refill the kettle. I set aside my cup and saucer and knitted my hands over my belly. Honey appeared again—minutes had passed, I lost in reverie, long enough to boil water anyway (this came perhaps primarily from melted snow in the present season, I suddenly surmised)—and poured another kettle of steaming water into the tub. She went away a third and final time, returning shortly with the kettle from which she poured a prosaic stream. She summoned me to the rustic approximation of a spa with a flutter of her fingers. With a pronounced business-like set to her jaw, Honey shucked me and started scrubbing. She had perfumed the water with rose hips and sandalwood and these scents surrounded me as she vigorously ran the long-handled brush up and down my arms, around and around in the pits, side to side across my chest and back. I felt as if the stiff bristles (boar?) were epilating me something fierce and had to bite my tongue to keep from moaning. The leg and buttock treatment was just as trying. She did my hair, face, and privates by hand, rubbing through generous amounts of Castile soap suds. I was both relaxed and aroused by the time she finished, and when she bade me sit on the low stool I naturally assumed that a repeat performance was in the offing. She, apparently, felt that her duty in that regard was done and lifted one foot after the other onto the little stand for a truly frightening buffing with the even stiffer bristles of the bar-shaped brush. I would like to meet the man who could maintain his interest through such an assault; or rather, I surely wouldn't, what a stupid saying that is. I had no autonomy in anything that morning, and soon I was dressed and wheeling my luggage out of Honey's room with her hand pressing firmly into my back.

The common room had cleared out in the meantime, and an awkward scene met me. The matron and the bearded man were seated at opposite ends of the bar, steadfastly looking away from one another. The innkeeper stood in the doorway to the kitchen wearing his tatty apron. By stages it came clear that Beardo was my ride and furthermore that the matron was coming with us to consult a doctor in a hamlet along the way. Along the way to where? Silence was the only reply, and a hard set to the three pairs of eyes, as though all knew the answer and were afraid to talk about it. I was beyond caring—were I to get away, where would I go, how long could I last, the situation remained the same—but relished not the thought of further travel, and this time exposed to the elements. Well, nobody asked me what I would prefer, and the matron and I in short order were wrapped in furs and bundled onto Beardo's sled train like sacks of wheat, and his impressive team in concert pulled us toward the taiga.

* * *

The scenery changed little at first. More rills and bumps crisscrossed our path, and I felt every one, but the white expanse under deep gray sky provided such little context that I often had the impression that we had ceased to move altogether. At first I was worried about the health of the matron, as she kept lolling to the side. We sat facing each other, she on the lead board with her back to a covered stack that separated her from the driver, I on the trailing segment and pointing forward, a similar stack of goods or belongings behind me. One of these times she caught my concern and confided across the gap that sled rides always made her sleepy, had since she was a little girl. She seemed lost to memory after that, and I left her alone, eventually becoming a bit drowsy myself.

We did not stop at what I by my best possible estimation determined to be midday. Hunger pangs eventually subsided, and the monotony of the trip became a thing unto itself, a separate pocket of reality that seemed always to have been. The cold seeped into my body so deeply that it felt almost the opposite, like scalding hot water in an improperly run bath. When I felt sorry for myself, I thought of the dogs.

Toward what felt like the end of the day but probably was late afternoon—it was so dim all the time, whether due to atmospheric conditions or simply latitude and I was not sure and had no reference at hand to check—the matron from somewhere produced a snack and ate it slowly with a mien of great satisfaction. Seeing my no doubt pitiful eagerness, she tossed me the plastic bag with its dark scraps remaining in the bottom. I caught it despite the numbness of my extremities by clutching my mitts against my left thigh as the projectile struck it. I had to remove one mitt to get at the strips of jerky, which proved very salty, very gamey. Elk? Reindeer? Bear? It mattered not, and I sucked and gnawed the leathery leavings until they were gone. Thirst asserted itself with shrill haste, but I had nothing with which to quench it. I tried my best to sleep. I never have been able to do so in a seated position without continually jerking awake in the most violent manner, and on the sled I had also the worry of falling off and being sliced by the runners (which were waxed wooden slats with upturned tips like skis and not all that sharp, but the capaciousness of my imagination allowed for real fear) or left behind.

We stopped for the night at a cluster of small cabins that seemed to have been constructed from local lumber for the purpose of temporarily housing travelers along our route. The dwellings were low-ceilinged but impeccably windproofed. All were unoccupied, and we settled into what appeared to be the newest of the quartet. Beardo made a great fuss over the dogs, insisting on making them a comfortable hollow in the lee of the cabin, where he would hear their barking if trouble arose. He fed the team lavishly and gave each dog a thorough rubdown, addressing it by name in a surprisingly gentle voice. The matron and I had offered to help, but stood to the side staring at our shoes as the deep bond between man and beasts presented its full glory. We did not fare so well ourselves, dining on canned beans and huddling around a kerosene heater. The bearded man carefully balanced our stay by leaving as much as we took, though the exchange was not like for like. With the heater's flame turned to a slow burn, we wrapped ourselves in thick furs and tried to get comfortable on our straw pallets. The silence was overwhelming, and one felt powerfully the emptiness of the acreage stretching all around. It affected the others less, their early conditioning having inured them to the realities of such trips, and they fell asleep rather quickly. I found their slow breathing to be comforting, even if I harbored a secret desire to strangle them both, madly entertaining for a heady moment the prospect of surviving for a space on their clean meat and that of the dogs. Eventually I turned my back on the piercing low flame of the heater and succumbed to my weariness.

The next day followed the same dreary pattern, except that we lost a few hours in its fat middle by dropping the matron at the doctor's house in the village that resolved its squalor from the surrounding wilderness with hallucinatory alacrity. Beardo also did a little trading, exchanging a couple of crates of what looked like some kind of fish packed in salt for a can of fuel, a couple of tins of smoked oysters, a tall bottle of beet vodka, and a large bag of meat scraps and fat for the dogs. The bartering was very casual, and all the men seemed to be well acquainted. Beardo stood upright as he called the team to action, bolstered by the simple and humanizing encounter at world's end.

Thirty-Six

Days, though they hardly deserved the name when they produced scant evidence of the sun, passed in fearful isolation as we progressed slowly but inexorably toward a reckoning that had begun to fill me with existential dread. We stopped in villages, which became scarce as the journey continued, and camps, in which we were the only occupants, and all the while Beardo spoke exclusively to his dogs, and even then the curiously tender monologues came at the end of a hard day of travel. The gloaming had become oppressive, obliterating not only the familiar sights of the sun and moon but also the wide distant accompaniment of stars, as if some black beast had swallowed the universe whole, leaving us to labor needlessly through a gray purgatory until the loosening coils of life wound down. I did not begrudge Beardo his silence. In fact, as the days wore on his example proved

319

buttressing in a way that I did not previously know I needed. Now, I had been a captive for quite some time —long enough to question whether I truly had been free even before my movements became constrained— and I knew about the phenomenon called Stockholm Syndrome and its cohort of coping mechanisms, so I am not saying there was no element of *that* in my behavior, just that I was not goaded by that alone, that beneath an oily surface of primordial filth I found the sure footing of bedrock in a surprising place. Thus I endured.

* * *

The outer structures of the compound materialized like glacial floes from a thick sea fog. The cylinders I identified first, large fuel and water tanks in both horizontal and vertical orientations. A communications tower loomed, a red light blinking at its apex. A limpid windsock hung in front of a hangar. Several storehouses held a flank, crenelated loading docks jutting aggressively into view. Opposite them lay a series of garages. The doors were down, so I could not see what they contained, but the bays were large enough to hold even construction vehicles and numerous enough to shelter an impressive fleet. We passed through the wide lanes of a park containing large-scale ice sculptures of bizarre subjects: a mare giving birth to a two-headed foal; a swarm of crows pecking at a vagrant who had, the scattered glimmering popcorn suggested, been trying to share his scavenged lunch but now held an arm to his head to protect his eyes; a giant squid approaching a small deep-sea submersible vehicle in a menacing posture; a cyclops with a fatherly expression baring his phallus to his flock, several ewes lapping at boils along the shaft; there were others, each as disturbing as the last. Behind this menagerie loomed a concrete building, the first structure to in any way resemble a residence. Wide marble steps swept clean of ice and snow ascended to a cavernous portico the ceiling of which sparkled with the refracted light of many slender crystal fixtures made to resemble icicles. We swung wide of this imposing, inviting entry and shushed along the left flank of the house. Out back, some distance from the building, we stopped next to what appeared to be a utility shed. In the steady yellow light of a sodium lamp above the door, Beardo made a great fuss of tending to his team. I stamped and made muffled claps with my mittened hands, which felt like a couple of pork chops as they came together with such little sensation. I walked around the shed a few times, stepping high to stretch and promote circulation. My movements seemed to annoy my companion, who after so many days broke his silence.

"Stand still!"

I complied, more out of shock than submissiveness. When he had finished with the dogs, Beardo grabbed my arm and hauled me over to the door, which slid open with an electric whoosh like something from a syndicated science fiction program.

"In!"

I stepped inside, and he soon joined me holding my suitcase and a small crate.

"Stand in the middle!"

He gave a little wave into the gloom above our heads, and the floor lurched and began to descend. We sank slowly into a large chamber with the appearance of a warehouse. There was no shaft around the lift and no rail around the platform, so I felt a bit giddy the entire ride. I suppressed a powerful urge to push my companion over the edge, and I am sure from the twitching around his lips that he confronted and mastered similar feelings. Our landing was surprisingly subdued, with no shuddering or clanking, and only a slight wobble. Two men met us. They looked like normal workingmen and clapped shoulders with Beardo with casual wariness. They gave him quite a lot of Euros and he relinquished his little crate and jutted his jaw in my direction before going back up on the lift. One of the men took the crate under his arm and motioned for me to follow. The other apparently was to stay at his post.

We passed through the center of the warehouse down its long axis between rack after rack holding towering cylinders of ice sandwiched between thick panes of glass, the void space no doubt filled with some inert gas. Was this, then, a scientific enterprise? The possibility calmed my nerves somewhat. The sorely abused wheels of my luggage did little against the stippled floor, and my arms soon tired from dragging the case along and correcting its course every few steps. I could not keep up, and the man whom I was following laughed when he saw how much trouble I was having. He slackened his pace but did not offer to help. At the far end of the warehouse we entered a well lighted tunnel with a smooth floor, and the going became a bit easier. The man returned to his normal walking speed, but we did not have far to go. At a junction he gestured for me to step into an alcove with a painted saint. He mimed holding one's arms close to one's body and one's possessions with a firm grip. I was in another lift and with the forlorn saint soon began my ascension.

The chamber into which I emerged came as a minor shock. It was *cozy*. After the sprawl in front of the mansion and the cavernous recesses of the warehouse, I was not prepared for such a homely touch. A cheery gas flame flickered in a small, artful fireplace, casting velvet shadows that made the mournful saint look as though his mascara were running. The tiles of the floor were quite large, hard to step across in one go, and had the texture of sandstone. The smaller tiles that covered the walls were arranged in a maddening display. One detected the beginnings of a pattern only to have that perceived regularity slide away in an entropic spray. Stepping out of the niche into which I had risen, I realized that I was in a bathroom. The familiar appointments presented a comfort that I was all too eager to embrace. I checked myself in the ornate mirror before moving cautiously to the doorway. The hall was wide and dark. Many closed doors broke up the swirling finish of the concrete walls. One at the end of the corridor, a large double door to my right after exiting the bathroom, stood open, a soft flickering light playing over the floor flags from the aperture. I wheeled my luggage in that direction, keenly aware that my progress seemed to be generating a good deal of noise in the hushed space.

Inside, a feast of decidedly medieval slant was laid down the length of a long gilded table. The soft light came from candelabra rising at regular intervals among the platters. Aromatic steam—from a trio of suckling pigs, skin crisped to a deep burgundy; a peacock displayed dramatically with its plumage; a spit-roasted kid propped strangely on its bent limbs atop a mound of root vegetables—wafted over me in waves that were alternately inviting and revolting, such was their primitive intensity. Surrounding the meat dishes were crystal tiers of tropical fruit, heartwood trenchers of earthy mushrooms and truffles, soapstone trays of soft and hard cheeses, and sundry towers of nutmeats, brined eggs, caviar, quince paste, other accompaniments and delicacies. Silver pitchers held red wine, its deep fragrance cutting pleasantly through the miasma. Tall glass cylinders with cup-caps contained what I assumed to be aquavit, vodka, or, disappointingly, water. Two high-backed chairs anchored the short ends of the table, the spread stretching ridiculously between.

"Please be seated," said an impeccably dressed butler who had got the drop on me. He stood next to the chair that was closer to the door through which I had entered, pulling it back and swinging it out slightly as I approached. "Leave the suitcase; I will see to it."

When I was alone again, I tilted my head back to look at the richly painted ceiling half lost in shadow at some considerable distance above my seat. The kinetic depiction of the quelling of some sort of peasant rebellion made my head swim, so I reluctantly returned my gaze to the obscene expanse of the laden table. I nearly nodded off watching the dance of the flickering flames. A man—a substantial man, the host I presumed—was being seated at the other end of the table with an excess of ceremony. He wore a white, crisply starched jacket, complementary ivory shirt with subtle vertical piping, rear-tapering trousers generous at top and bottom all carefully tailored to flatter his physique. His hair was lanky and black, shoulder length, and he sported a neatly trimmed, oiled mustache and goatee that deflected attention from his rounded, ruddy cheeks and weak if repeating chin. He wore many large, ornate rings that caught the candlelight in their astonishing settings, leaving any observer seeing overstuffed sausages only as an afterthought.

"Good evening, Anatoly," he said, and I almost choked on my saliva. His voice sounded uncannily like that of Akim Mikhailovich Tamiroff at his hammiest, but of course in a Russian that I found challenging to parse. I additionally bridled at the assertive use of my given name but mastered myself before worsening my position. We both had to shout to cover the distance between us.

"Good evening, Mr. ..."

"Platonov."

An uncomfortable silence descended. Rousing himself as if merely a virgule had interrupted our otherwise pleasurable pre-dinner banter, Mr. Platonov clapped flabbily his meaty manus and with imperious impatience ordered his reedy butler to serve us. My plate arrived with an unseemly heaping of meat and root vegetables, as if a common laborer had selected from the banquet the few things that he at first glance recognized. The butler also filled too full my glasses, the liliaceous as well as the highball. The clear liquid proved to be vodka after all, very fiery with a faint metallic aftertaste. The wine was quite good, a famous and justly lauded Bordeaux château unless I missed my guess. I drew amply from both wellsprings. My host supped loudly, greedily at his advantageous remove. I with some measure of dignity carved and consumed the choicer bits. Whatever the state of his general staff, Platonov kept an actual chef in his kitchen who did his very best with whatever raw material was dumped on his doorstep. My host had polished off his plate while I still picked around the edges of my own. He called for the chef, who arrived momentarily and nervously doffed his toque. His shock of limpid flaxen hair raised my eyebrows, and when he spoke my brain's fuzzy geolocation faculty circled Scandinavia. His coolly deferent demeanor was that of the political prisoner. He was put on the spot, was asked to fill our fresh plates (my mostly full one was whisked away by the butler) with *all the best* of his lavish board. I saw the sweat beading on his shapely brow as he with an increasingly unsteady hand made his selections. Platonov, naturally, was served first. My own plate quickly followed, since the chef hardly could alter the offering under his lord's scrutiny. Even so, my host's patience was tested, and though he waited for my plate to be delivered he did so with upraised fork. The chef had done well, in my not entirely modest estimation. The presentation was clever and enticing but the artfully presented round—a large plate of small plates in essence—carried little risk of offending a conservative palate. After tasting the first precious bite (beginning his exploration unimaginatively at six o'clock), duck confit with lingonberry he let me know by bellowing it like distant thunder down the table, Platonov consulted with his butler, who left the dining room in a hurry and returned a short time later with two wireless intercom units, which he placed at the extreme ends of the table. Soon enough the cone speaker of the off-white unit at my right elbow squealed to life, and my host's voice, rendered even stranger, implored: "You simply must try the spiced beets with young capers."

I looked at my plate and found no such thing. There was, however, what looked very much like red-cooked calf's tongue with flying fish roe. I glanced at the chef and beheld the purest terror I have witnessed. I cut a modest sample of the tongue and with my fork swizzled it lightly in the savory reduction atop which it was served. I closed my eyes and chewed slowly. The morsel was exquisitely tender and full of flavor. It brought some sanity, some sense of worth to the entire ridiculous supper. I pressed the talk button on my intercom and effused: "Delicious! Simply divine!"

The chef, to his great and, I felt, audaciously obvious relief, was dismissed. Platonov settled into his plate and seemed content that I had been suitably impressed by his largesse. Only a few crackled exchanges punctuated the rest of the meal, which ran on to cheese and nuts, fruit and parma ham, and, finally, a decadent torte. I ate some of each so as not to offend my host, even though I by that time was feeling awfully full. Afterward Platonov called for cigars and cognac; I accepted only the latter with mumbled thanks, having never developed a taste for the former. My host seemed to take my decision in stride and chomped at his rich brown cheroot for quite a while before lighting up. When he did start puffing slow curling gouts he did so with great pleasure and, thumb on the talk button, held forth on a surprising range of topics. I learned that while he harbored a nostalgic adoration of the political left he as a hardnosed businessman found most of his fellows on the other side of things. His fleet included all the status symbol passenger cars, utility and construction vehicles, and even several tanks. The tall cylinders of ice in the warehouse through which I had entered were core samples from Lake Baikal taken in February of each year under the auspices of a scientific study. A bothersome tangent (he had the manner of one swatting gnats the entire time) seemed designed to convey his knowledge of the incestuous world of literature in general and *Lit* in particular. With a palpable easing of tension, he moved on to the subject of animal husbandry, placing special emphasis on the most challenging breeds of dogs and horses. I grew very sleepy as this monologue continued and tried foolishly to pass my intermittent dozing off as a series of comradely knowing nods.

"Well, now I've bored you half to death!" Platonov exclaimed, scraping back his chair and rising with a crisp and discomfiting alacrity. "Where are my manners? You, after your long journey in the wind and cold, surely are in need of a hot bath and a soft bed." He seemed much more upset with and disappointed in me than chagrined.

It seemed that something was expected of me, but a dangerous glint in his eyes left me unsure of my words.

"Come on, we'll get you settled. Your things have been sent on ahead."

I followed him into the hallway through the door from which I had entered. We walked briskly past the lavatory with its secret lift. The corridor seemed to stretch into an indefinite space, a gentle and bland infinity that comprised neither promise nor terror. The faint light faltered further as we progressed until we walked through inky shadows, I unsure whether any structure I glimpsed constituted a real and solid body or some erroneous pattern matching triggered by the deprivation of my sense of sight. My host seemed to have no trouble, but he slowed his pace considerably as we moved on and on down the endless hall. Finally I had to consciously match my step to his not to outpace him, where before I had struggled to keep up. The walls and ceiling appeared to be closing in as we made our way deeper into the house, surely some trick of perspective or the dim lighting, which now radiated from some indeterminate source.

Suddenly Platonov stopped. "Go on, it's just ahead. A bit of sleep will do you good, friend. We will speak again in the morning."

I walked slowly forward with my hand held out in front of me, now wary of encountering a turn in the passage or a closed door. My host called out encouraging words, urging me to keep to the center of the way as it narrowed. So, the closing in was not simply my imagination. The light faded perceptibly just then and I nearly lost my balance. I put out both hands, holding one always in front and waving the other to the side. I worried about low beams and the like. My next footfall, trained to confidence by the surprising indoor trek, found nothing where the floor was expected. I pitched forward and came down hard on metal, found myself sliding uncontrollably on a steep incline into the utter darkness below.

Thirty-Seven

I could tell by touch that I had been changed. My
clothing, I mean, and not something more metaphysi-
cal. I was wearing a smock akin to a hospital gown
but thankfully at least marginally less immodest. I lay
on my side on what felt like cold tile, but I could not
find even the hint of a seam so maybe the surface had
been poured or sprayed. The blackness was absolute,
though it took me some time to come to that conclusion. At first I thought that I spied flashes of bright
light or pockets of gloaming far in some imagined corner or distressingly nearby, but that was all just my
brain trying to make sense of the sudden dearth of in-
put. It reminded me of that time we took your niece
to that grotty cave in Pennsylvania. In the course of
his inane patter, the spotty teenager leading the group
shut off all the lights so that his hostages could experience complete darkness, many of them for the first

and last time (barring the hideous envelopment of the womb, of course, but memory is uncharacteristically merciful in that instance). I hated the suffocating feeling on that occasion as well and also was beset by sprite-like visual phenomena. Pish and posh, this shit is *burdensome*, Tanya.

Oh, I crawled around the place eventually. That is what one does, isn't it? No matter how hopeless the situation, how forlornly the ogre's stew of percolating peptides tinges one's perception, the most primitive instinct, the one that pushes the starving mother cheetah to consume her kits, the brash badger with a wedged limb to gnaw it right the fuck off, the ... well, you know, there remains the one true biological imperative: survival. The chamber was approximately fifteen feet by nine. I traversed the perimeter without discovering so much as a crack. It suddenly hit me that the crawling was unnecessary. I was not badly hurt, and since I could see nothing I was not trying to stay in cover. I stood cautiously, hand above my head to avoid being caught out by a low ceiling. I stretched my arms to their limit, jumped a tentative then vigorous bounce. I almost took a step, but my cursed imagination kicked in with accustomed force. Picture momentarily the sick mind of an inveterate, unrepentant sadist. Would such an individual dangle meathooks from the rafters at random intervals, say at eye level? Yes, he would. Of course he would, and that was just the beginning of the depraved torments such a person could concoct in the most casual manner. Even the crawling then was suspect, with further pitfalls, rusty strips of carpet tacks, broken glass and more rearing as frightening possibilities. Soon enough I again was prone, and for a good while I lay there in utter defeat.

Something brought me around. I was present, aware. Had it been a sound? The impression of a clack or a rasp persisted, though when I strained I heard only my own heartbeat. I eased myself into a sitting position. Nothing, nothing. A new and uncomfortable thought asserted itself: an oubliette. This was it for me. There was no returning the way I had come and no going anywhere else. I wept. Not great wracking sobs, no rending of hair or garment, but quiet, honest despair. Then I mastered myself. The kind of individual a profile of whom had been developing in my mind would want to watch, oh yes he would. Night-vision cameras placed high or mounted flush. I would not give the bastard the satisfaction and did my best to emulate my former traveling companion, the waxen man. But there it was again! My resolve held for a moment, yet—almost before I knew what I was doing —I suddenly crawled on my elbows in the direction of the noise. I slowed as I neared the wall, switched to a two-knees-one-hand gait so that I could protect my precious head from the imminent if low-speed collision. Nothing, nothing. More cold black air I eagerly groped. Maybe I had misjudged the distance. I pushed on. I had covered a considerable span. There was an opening where before a solid wall had stood, there had to be. In my excitement, and despite having a hand out in front of me as I crawled, I knocked my head against the wall when I did encounter it. Something was odd about the barrier. It was smooth toward the bottom but transitioned somewhere just above my head (from my crouched position) to a stippled texture. I stood slowly, running my fingers over the surface. The stippled band ended at a point just above my head when I stood fully erect with my arm raised at a sharp angle in front of me as if in salute.

Off to my right something clattered. In a simian hunch I hastened in the direction of the sound. Soon enough I encountered a dead end, the three walls of the box smooth as far as I could reach. My bare big toe nudged something cold, metallic. Bending close, I felt eagerly over the complex surfaces of the new and interesting shapes. It was a cafeteria tray bearing several covered containers of food. Up close I could smell the savory contents. Just as I moved to lift a lid, a harsh siren wailed, causing me to fall back on my haunches. A low terror gripped me, and reverting to instinct I took up the tray and holding it as steadily as I could retreated to the chamber in which I had awoken. There I cowered in a corner, shielding the tray of food from every imagined threat in the most pitiful manner. Finally the screeching ceased, and I was struck by the rapidity with which its shrill echo died. I waited a beat, snapped shut my slack gob. I slid my back securely into the notch of the corner and placed the tray on the floor before me. The curious collection of lidded vessels thereon—generous steaming porringer, chilled low-slung salver, intricately inlaid matlåda, cloying towering scyphus—divulged delights that worked a predictable juju on my suasible self. I set to with alacrity.

Only afterward did the conviction come, the subtle significance of my blind gourmand's repast. I remained in the compound. Some secret sub-level housed my prison, and I was not yet abandoned to a horrific wasting death. And I had an ally of sorts, a fellow prisoner who remembered my earlier kindness and in this instance at least had used his relatively greater freedom to send a deeply sustaining message.

* * *

The remainder of my captive days conformed to a rote cadence. In what I will refer to as the morning (but it could have fallen at any time given the continued deprivation of my sense of sight), I rose to what began as a gentle, undulating thrum that I felt more than heard. This vibration increased in intensity until it shook the walls, the foundations of the place. When it receded, and it did so much more quickly than it had built, the reverberations continued for a cataclysmic-feeling interval, the concrete underfoot and to hand buckling and heaving with the memory of the wave. Sometimes I closed my eyes, clutched a fist to my chest and rode out in ecstasy the phantom oktavist's basso profondo that was so scrambling my subdermal components. With haste I then moved to the corner opposite my sleeping nook. There in the floor was fixed a squat toilet into which I earnestly emptied bladder and bowels, a movement rendered inevitable by the recent aural assault. Thus relieved, I stood and was sprayed clean by a cascade from hidden water jets. The cleanser, scented with balsam and lilac, was mixed in at intervals and was very effective. A soft hissing preceded the water's arrival, and at first this phenomenon alarmed me greatly, leading my thoughts in an ugly direction, straight into Herr Widmann's *delousing* chamber. Well, that fate befell a few in my family, but it did not befall me. After the shower, I invariably wanted a civilized breakfast, fortifying coffee, and a refreshingly brash newspaper; I ever had to go without. From there it was directly into the maze beyond, for that was what it was. I began the day's trail (the configuration was altered fully but quietly, perhaps while I slept)—the stippled band on the wall turned out to be anything but random and rather represented a Braille-like system of information encoding —at a point of shoulder height directly across from the right jamb of my room's doorless portal. The work was exhausting, the hardest I have done. However many hours the puzzle solving took, and I have reason to believe that it was a good many each day indeed, I arrived back at my room utterly spent and slumped into near catatonia until roused by the subtle scrape that signaled the delivery of my extravagant supper, the sole meal of the day. I thought of this period as "evening" but again must stress that I had no evidence at all to suggest that this impression was accurate. It was shortly thereafter that I succumbed to sleep, aided no doubt by the aftereffects of rigorous exertion and the generous portion of alcohol that accompanied my alimentation.

The next day I would do it all again.

* * *

The pattern asserted itself until it did not. Following an initial abortive effort I had lost the very concept of time. What I know is that one day the trail, from its first bold bump, was fundamentally *different*. With an old excitement that my confinement had all but eradicated, I pursued the gossamer thread, which was tricky to follow, much fainter and far more elusive than any I had yet unraveled. After a fevered chase down blind alleys and winding warrens, it led me to an end.

Suddenly there was light!

I threw an arm over my eyes and squeezed my lids tight against the frightful searing, which bored into me like an iron salamander fresh from a torturer's forge-fire. I sank to my knees. When I dared to chance a timid peek, I saw indistinctly through the draped gauze of the right arm of my thin shift an incongruous and discombobulating sight. It could not be, and yet it was. With growing confidence my brain processed visual stimuli. In the alcove in front of my piteously crouched form rose on a garden pedestal a white facsimile machine, utterly anachronistic and strange. It shrieked into unnatural life and began printing with excruciating slowness on curling thermal paper a message. I cupped the delicate scroll in my shaking hands and with growing excitement read each line as it emerged.

00 00 00 00 ff e3 10 c0 00 09 28 3e a8 01 49 00 00 9e f8 28

80 50 28 0c 02 60 98 ac 9d bd 10 02 67 c4 00 80 63 e0 f8 3e

7e 0f 83 ff c1 00 43 ff ff ff ff ff ff f8 04 92 ff e3 10 c0

02 03 64 82 ec cb 82 00 00 49 24 93 c6 20 22 33 b3 a9 de f7

60 4c 5e 38 58 9c 56 83 00 d0 f1 f3 cb 1f b5 e9 49 bd f3 ff

e2 41 52 20 76 a5 c5 96 ff e3 10 c0 1b 09 58 6a bc 01 cc 00

```
00 75 46 d0 78 9c ec bc de df d3 e0 e7 0c d0 62 23 a8 88 48

ba a8 c7 5a e9 e8 22 03 30 48 28 1c 0b 20 78 c3 89 14 4a 42

ff e3 12 c0 1c 09 80 4a c0 00 32 52 24 8c 14 ab 7d b6 ba af

2e f3 e9 79 03 d3 d5 28 89 6c ad b0 80 06 1c af 7a c5 99 5f

1e 43 f9 37 fa 8e 1a fc b8 fc ff ce a9 ff e3 10 c0 1e 06 68

46 d4 00 31 98 24 40 6d 82 be 03 52 f5 ac 77 04 8c f7 ff a8

98 67 ff cc 61 c1 09 9f fe a3 e3 89 ff 3d 0a 10 09 09 b6 a5

00 cc 7f 99 ef ff e3 10 c0 2b 0a 81 42 f3 f8 1b 4e 70 df f7

cb ff e7 ba bd 3b b3 80 8a ff f8 11 9f ff 20 00 53 3f fe a0

8a 52 97 fe 70 4a 52 ff a0 43 27 7c a1 42 40 fc cf ff e3 10

c0 28 09 59 5e f5 94 10 84 94 b0 c3 ff d0 aa e9 af 91 82 af

fd 71 1f ff 40 87 ff c8 52 ff f0 e1 8a df fb 04 7f d4 1a f8

9d 9f 59 af a8 4c fb 48 fd ff e3 12 c0 29 09 79 5a f5 94 51

44 94 cb 3f 4a 50 68 06 9d ff f2 ff fe 28 0b ff fa 09 ff fc

0a 5f fe 80 2b 7d 67 be a3 3f ff 3d f8 64 c2 b8 8e 39 cd 00

80 04 ff e3 10 c0 2b 08 b1 5a e8 ca 39 ca 94 84 95 47 f4 e1

93 4d 37 ff 38 78 93 7c 0c 0d 7d 63 3e b2 df 37 fa c6 00 28

95 88 8c d0 42 18 a8 a7 b7 d6 b2 18 ab 37 ff e3 10 c0 2f 07

c8 ae d8 00 1b 4e 4c 5f 27 fe ce 13 ff d7 ff e5 fa ff 97 34

d1 99 4d 9b 45 00 b0 ef fa 8a 00 6b 7f a1 41 60 4c ff e8 81

1f fa ba 8b 5f d9 ff e3 10 c0 36 06 f8 d2 d4 00 0c 04 70 e9
```

```
46 fd 7f fd 5f 5b 7f 3a 20 37 12 ed 46 10 1d f2 60 2d 40 80

ff e1 c4 b7 fd 87 ff d0 08 df e8 82 8b fe 40 05 6f f4 ff e3

12 c0 41 0b a9 d2 dc 00 39 c4 94 08 60 d7 82 6e f0 45 fe 90

90 34 52 93 ff df e1 52 ff d4 09 ff e5 07 7f e7 8a 03 5f d5

07 00 41 27 fe a3 e0 ec 5b fd 4f ff e3 10 c0 3a 07 39 26 e8

00 10 84 70 51 41 2f cf 7f ff fd 00 c1 0c c4 0f fa bf f4 00

ff 95 79 eb 77 ff 90 0c 9f f0 72 ff c4 ef e5 c3 1e 97 78 ab

bd 3f f8 ff e3 10 c0 44 09 19 52 e0 ca 38 8e 70 b1 df 20 ee

e8 49 24 01 c8 20 f7 bf ff ec 31 3a 41 a3 1e f9 82 28 a8 e2

03 e7 18 bb 20 0e 1f 6e ba 58 f6 5f ea 67 fd ff e3 10 c0 46

08 79 1a fb 84 10 4a 72 46 b4 00 00 1d 5f fe 95 a0 22 1a 55

01 30 58 20 d8 af 46 89 2b 2c 36 6a 5a 92 a2 b3 2a df 91 6f

93 fa ed f6 6f 9b ff ff e3 12 c0 4b 09 89 4a ec 00 29 8e 70

fe 60 48 26 1b e0 e4 54 17 6d b1 33 3d 75 1c 29 f3 a9 b4 31

63 83 41 76 9f 49 b5 26 c0 72 b6 7c be b0 6e 03 26 86 97 19

ff e3 10 c0 4c 09 60 2a eb f8 18 46 01 06 09 43 11 93 42 4c

53 e4 32 52 2a 64 31 1c 05 a3 54 b3 00 c3 9e f7 fe d4 80 71

36 49 1b 3b d5 3e dc 92 a0 41 19 d2 ff e3 10 c0 4d 07 e0 6e

c0 00 62 46 28 e9 41 1e 4d 2b e1 9c a3 e2 f6 68 74 27 1a 78

c6 50 bf bb 28 1a b7 09 7e 80 19 00 50 72 26 09 80 88 1d 3c
```

```
09 8f 68 d3 ff e3 10 c0 54 07 c8 76 c0 00 49 86 48 cc bb d0

1a a4 aa 02 02 42 10 14 44 78 4a 0a 95 01 3f 8a 87 78 32 06

5d 09 52 18 98 1a 24 99 09 1e 61 74 e8 48 69 e2 ff e3 12 c0

5b 09 50 82 b8 00 7a 4c 49 21 23 fc d0 a8 a3 7f 16 17 15 30

cc d3 c0 0b 34 10 40 5b 43 0c 9a a4 99 1a e7 0c 24 00 00 00

00 00 00 00 00 00 00 00 00 ff e3 10 c0 5d 08 f8 6a b4 00 3b

06 28 00 00 00 00 00 00 00 00 00 00 00 00 00 00 00 00 00 00
```

I understood perfectly.

Thirty-Eight

I came out of the labyrinth through a grate in the floor of the warehouse by way of which I originally had entered Platonov's mad world. The core samples stood like a strange but orderly forest in the dim, dust-free artificial cavern. A string of white lights—the sort with which people bedeck their eaves around the winter solstice holidays, this the subtype with plastic sheaths meant to resemble icicles slipped over the tiny bulbs—formed a loose spiral at my feet and stretched into the rows of rimed cylinders and from there through an open door at the far end of the warehouse. I, of course, followed the trail. At first I counted the tiny points of light, noting any break in the sequence (and remembered from my youth with some distaste the truly sequential strands in which a failed node would cut power to everything down the line) caused by poor connections or blown-out bulbs.

Soon I ceased this folly, shaking my head and muttering, *No, this is not part of it.* The chained strings of party lights wound on and on through the close corridors beyond the warehouse door. Carelessly betraying a hint of impatience, I quickened my step. The next bend brought something new. Instead of carrying on through the doorway ahead, on the right side of the opening, always on the right, the lights rose around the low arch, descended its other side, and terminated at a wall socket.

With a raised eyebrow, I passed through into a long gallery. Vertically oriented cases of plain light wood and clear glass stood on matte platforms of light gray. The walls were of slightly darker gallery gray, and the lighting was tasteful, professional. No placards or plates identified the exhibits, but the theme became clear all the same as I walked the length of the room. These were trophies, like those grisly preserved pieces flanking the fire pit in a hunting lodge. I took inventory as I progressed, each step made with greater trepidation than the last. These were the things: a white tuxedo with a very small brownish stain on its high collar, a pair of cowboy boots made from some exotic hide off which one's vision slithered in an entirely disturbing fashion under the carefully placed fill light, a pearl necklace and diamond earrings surrounding some very white teeth, the skin of a human back stretched taut and scraped as thin as vellum bearing bright inkwork of a nautical nature, twin stuffed hounds, a child-sized coffin of birch, what turned out after some contemplation to be twenty nails from fingers and toes arranged into a stylized heart about the pliers that had plucked them, a luridly lighted jar containing a well developed fetus and a rusty speculum, a cigar case holding a fat finger, a set of liar's dice with the pips worn down, and finally against the back wall two new-looking installations. The case on the left enclosed a starched white toque of familiar design and a serving stand in the foreground bearing a trifle dish of aspic in which was set two staring eyeballs with trailing optic nerves. On the right a billowing purple outfit and a support garment of unique, unmistakable manufacture swaddled a copper urn the dull surface of which seemed to adsorb rather than repel the harsh light cast upon it.

Quiet footfalls approached, and I was not surprised soon to find Platonov himself standing beside me.

"Come with me," he said.

My host took me on a proper tour of the facilities. At first I was startled by a curious habit of his, that upon entering a chamber he would flip the light switches on and off several times in rapid succession. I eventually understood that he was trying to impress upon me the solidity of his power grid, that his will and resources could provide a reliable fount of electrons even in this remote and inhospitable location. By the end of it, I was numbed and stumbled along obediently in his wake. We ended up outside, surveying the garages housing his formidable fleet. The weather and light were just the same as when I had entered my subterranean prison. These facts made it seem possible that only a short time had passed, but I had good reason to believe that my captivity had lasted a year and a day.

"And here is the truck that you will drive," Platonov was saying. "You will leave first thing tomorrow morning, after a hearty breakfast of course."

Thirty-Nine

/\
\/

These pages were moved to the front of the manuscript.

/\
\/

Forty

No alarm had sounded when I broke the glass of the display case; it could have been silent, I know.

* * *

A Russian truck driver with no family to speak of takes a series of jobs that lead him into an oligarchic underworld the machinations of which soon have him transporting a cruel weapon of mass destruction concealed beneath a load of samizdat pamphlets from a carefully fabricated people's movement. He misreads the land and becomes stranded on an embankment, there eventually to perish in obscurity and as the hypothermia sets in vividly construct for himself an alternate life, one far removed from the stark reality he has known. But the lovely confusion, at the very end, in the final moments, becomes too much to bear, and his mind lurches to resolve the discrepancy, to reconcile the two lives.

No, even now it does not work. As unlikely as snatches of my narrative seem as I riffle the pamphlets, there is no denying what has happened. If at moments I inexplicably doubted your very existence, know that during the final movement, when it truly counts, my resolve is firm. I have never been a believer, never a follower, not often a dupe. I feel at once the oktavist's terrible splendor. It is agitating my marrow. The universe skips a beat. Facing all-embracing oblivion I hold fast to a single ideal, the coruscating indivisible unit of *us*. In this I must believe!

In a flash of inspiration, I enter numbers from the walls of the maze. I should have tried them first, the very last ones of the sequence that had freed me from confinement, for they smartly popped the latch. The metal box is stuffed with shredded newspaper to provide a gentle cradle for the bomb. I transfer the cold metal cylinder, first laying my chapped cheek along its smooth side and closing my eyes for a while, to my battered luggage. I leave out everything else. I do not need it. I scoop the ashes back into the copper pot as best I can and clutch the vessel to my chest. I am ready now to end it. This is the last I can write, but that also does not matter. Goodbye, Tanya. I will exit the truck, drag the luggage some distance, set the urn beside me, and activate the bomb. Out here it will not hurt anyone. Anyone else, I mean. I will pack these pamphlets into the metal case and set the lock. In my trauma-addled fantasy the bomb will act as a beacon, and some stalwart individual, an incorruptible public servant perhaps, will instigate an investigation of the site. With the mental clarity of a felon under a slate-gray sky taking his first deep breath of midwinter air in the relative freedom of the exercise yard, I no longer actively harbor this delusion but possess instead a single crashing, crushing conviction:

No one will ever read this.

About the Author

G.P. Huffman lives in the Virginia suburbs of Washington, DC.